Montmorency on the rocks :
doctor, aristocrat
D0458221
87256
WITHDRAWN

Montmorency
ON THE ROCKS

doctor

aristocrat

murderer?

ELEANOR UPDALE

ORCHARD BOOKS
AN IMPRINT OF SCHOLASTIC INC.
NEW YORK

Copyright © 2004 Eleanor Updale

First published in Great Britain in 2004 by Scholastic Ltd.

All rights reserved. Published by Orchard Books, an imprint of Scholastic Inc. ORCHARD BOOKS and design are registered trademarks of Watts Publishing Group, Ltd., used under license. SCHOLASTIC and associated logos are trademarks and/or registered trademarks of Scholastic Inc.

No part of this publication may be reproduced, stored in a retrieval system, or transmitted in any form or by any means, electronic, mechanical, photocopying, recording, or otherwise, without written permission of the publisher. For information regarding permission, write to Orchard Books, Scholastic Inc., Permissions Department, 557 Broadway, New York, NY 10012.

LIBRARY OF CONGRESS CATALOGING-IN-PUBLICATION DATA
Updale, Eleanor.
Montmorency on the rocks : doctor, aristocrat, murderer?
/ Eleanor Updale; illustrations by Nick Hardcastle.
—1st Orchard Books ed. p. cm.
Summary: In Victorian London, when Montmorency and his alter ego, Scarper, reunite with Dr. Farcett, the two cooperate to capture a bomber and become involved in solving the mystery of the poisoning of a village of Scottish children.
ISBN 0-439-60676-4 (hardcover)
[1. Robbers and outlaws—Fiction. 2. Identity—Fiction.
3. London (England)—History—1800–1950—Fiction.
4. Great Britain—History—Victoria, 1837–1901—Fiction.]
I. Hardcastle, Nick, ill. II. Title. PZ7.U4447Ml 2005
[Fic]—dc22 2004015368

Printed in the U.S.A. 23
Reinforced Binding for Library Use
First Orchard Books edition, April 2005
The display type was set in Aqualine.
The text type was set in 12.5-point Venetian301 BT.
Illustrations © 2004 by Nick Hardcastle
Book design by Marijka Kostiw

When *Montmorency* was published I was invited back to my old primary school to meet the children and talk about the book. The visit reminded me of my first teachers, whose enthusiasm started me off in the world of history and stories. But the most impressive thing was how, in the face of all the pressures of modern education, the school is still a place that prides itself on encouraging writing for pleasure.

And so Montmorency's second adventure is dedicated to all those young writers at Dog Kennel Hill School —and of course to Jim, Andrew, Catherine, and Flora, who live with Montmorency every day.

Contents

CHAPTER I

SUMMER 1885: THE TURKISH BATH

Doctor Robert Farcett had had a bad day. He had been looking forward to demonstrating his latest operating technique to an audience of medical students and hospital dignitaries. He had been confident that his new method of cutting and stitching around a gallbladder would reduce the time needed for the procedure and improve survival rates. He had been sure that he could break his own speed record from the first incision to the final closure of the wound. He had even permitted himself a slight bow to the gallery as enthusiastic applause greeted his arrival in the operating theater. Within minutes everything started to go wrong. Had he slipped? Or had this patient some anatomical abnormality that made him more likely to hemorrhage? Whatever the reason, the abdominal cavity had flooded with blood, Doctor Farcett's hands had slithered and fumbled in a hopeless attempt to reunite the arteries and veins, and after a struggle which left his clothes and the floor stained with gore, he had looked up from his lifeless victim to the silent crowd: some of them ashen with shock, others incapable of concealing their joy that the rising star of the London medical scene had made a fatal, and public, mistake.

Lying facedown on the marble slab in the Steam Room, Farcett ran through events in his mind, looking for explanations and excuses, but unable to suppress the shameful fact of which his audience had been unaware. The gallbladder had not been diseased at all. The operation had been unnecessary. The patient was one of Farcett's most tiresome regulars, a hypochondriac who constantly imagined himself ill. He had been selected entirely for the purposes of the demonstration: because he was healthy, and more likely to survive. Instead his life had been sacrificed to Doctor Farcett's vanity and ambition, and now Farcett felt he deserved every mighty slap from the towering masseur who was thumping his back and pummeling his sweaty skin in the heat of the Turkish bath. The ceramic tiles on the walls and floor reminded him chillingly of the hospital morgue; and in spite of the heat and the spicy perfume on his skin, Farcett couldn't take his mind off that other body lying cold, lifeless, and incapable of feeling on a similar slab, only a couple of miles away.

He had not wanted to come to the baths, but he

had promised his friend, Lord George Fox-Selwyn, that he would meet him there. For almost a year, Fox-Selwyn, whom Farcett knew to be a spy, had been out of the country on one of his mysterious missions, and the note he had sent on his return implied urgency and concern:

> *Robert,*
> *Safely back, but troubled and exhausted. Meet me at the Xandan Baths at six o'clock. A matter of great importance.*
> *In haste,*
> *George*

As Doctor Farcett endured his massage, Lord George Fox-Selwyn strode from the street through the Xandan's grand swing doors and across the grand entrance hall downstairs.

The population of London regarded the architecture of the Xandan Turkish Baths as exciting, even outrageous. Elaborate stained-glass windows in the walls and the domed roof cast a delicious light onto the shiny tiles, which were painted with scenes of goddesses and slave girls in faraway lands. A fountain tinkled gently in the center of a pool whose azure base made the water glow a deep and peaceful blue. Around its edge was a marble mosaic floor, and luscious potted ferns and palms thrived in the warm, moist air. In the Cooling Room, where customers rested after enduring the steam and the energetic attentions of the shampooers, there was an atmosphere of calm and drowsy luxury. Yet when George Fox-Selwyn arrived at the baths he couldn't help smiling at this sham Eastern exoticism. Only the day before he had returned from his long trip across the Balkans to Turkey and back. In Constantinople he and his companion, Montmorency, had immersed themselves in scents and flavors that made the steamy atmosphere of the Xandan Baths seem like a municipal laundry. The plump and pasty women depicted in flimsy robes on the walls of this new London landmark were celebrated in fashionable circles and condemned by prudes as images of depravity. But they were comical in contrast to the genuine beauties carrying real urns of oil and water who had attended to him in the heat of the Ottoman Empire.

He stripped off his clothes and wrapped a large towel around his ample waist, adjusting it carefully so that the split didn't reveal anything too embarrassing.

Then he sat on the wooden bench to collect his thoughts before seeking out Robert Farcett. For on the journey home from Turkey he had made the difficult and possibly dangerous decision to tell the doctor the truth about Montmorency. Until now he had devoted the five years of his friendship with both men to keeping them apart. The doctor knew nothing of Montmorency's part in Fox-Selwyn's life, and Montmorency was unaware that Doctor Farcett, Fox-Selwyn's personal physician, was the very man who had repaired his own broken body years before.

Montmorency had started life as a small-time crook. Injured in a raid, he had been imprisoned and used by Doctor Farcett as an experimental resource. His body had been rebuilt and exhibited as an example of Farcett's skill. By the time he left prison, nearly six years ago now, Montmorency had been determined not to return to his old life. He had gradually created a new personality for himself as a man about town, funding the transformation with a series of daring robberies carried out in his other guise: as Scarper, a thief who slithered around the capital through the sewers — undetected, underground. Now Montmorency had become rich enough for his money to go to work on its own:

breeding more money through gambling and investments, and on top of that he was occasionally paid by the government for international undercover work.

Fox-Selwyn had met Montmorency when he was already wealthy. He had never told Montmorency that he suspected anything about his past. But he had worked some of it out. By now, Montmorency was confident that he could pass as a natural member of the moneyed classes. For much of the time he convinced even himself. But as Montmorency had put his old identity behind him, Fox-Selwyn had become more and more fascinated by it. He took advantage of Montmorency's reluctance to talk about his background and, comfortable behind a mask of English politeness and reserve, he didn't delve. Yet he constantly watched his friend for signs of a criminal or amoral nature. Sometimes, to his dismay, finding them.

On their way out to the East, Montmorency had been a hero. His ingenuity had gotten them into palaces and parties to pick up information on plots and pacts that threatened British interests abroad. His skill at mimicry and his sheer nerve had helped them mix with soldiers, princes, beggars, and thieves, and even secured them shelter disguised as priests in a distant monastery when enemy agents were close behind.

Fox-Selwyn admired Montmorency, and knew that he probably owed him his life. But he had been appalled to find one of the monks' few treasures hidden in his luggage, and was even more worried by Montmorency's enthusiastic indulgence in the drugs and potions of the Turkish markets. Fox-Selwyn himself had used their brief leisure time to buy carpets, statues, and antiquities for his country houses. While he was arranging for them to be shipped to England, Montmorency had dived into the Ottoman underworld, and come out with substances that changed his behavior, and more than once affected his judgment so badly that their very safety was at risk.

At first Montmorency had seemed to find the drugs immensely enjoyable. He had laughed and joked, and once just lay on his back in their hot hotel giggling with pleasure for two hours. But then the dreams had started, with tears and mumbling, and the occasional shout of a word that sounded like "Freakshow." Fox-Selwyn had tried to ask what was tormenting Montmorency so.

"Don't ask, George. Promise me you won't ask me that," snapped Montmorency, so sternly that Fox-Selwyn didn't force the issue, for fear he might trip his friend over some unseen edge.

Another time, their cover was nearly blown when

Montmorency, almost out of the grip of his latest dose, rose to the provocation of a Turkish official who seemed to be deliberately delaying their departure for home. Montmorency started muttering insults under his breath, but they grew louder as the man ran his finger along each line of the Englishmen's papers, his lips moving silently as he worked his way through every line of the passports and visas they had been given by governments along the way.

"What are you looking for, Ali?" sneered Montmorency. "What do you think we are? Spies or something?" And he slapped Fox-Selwyn on the back. "Do you think he looks like a spy?"

The man was so angry that Fox-Selwyn had had to pay out half his roll of banknotes to get them past the border. He cursed Montmorency for putting him through the indignity of calling on a contact in Bucharest to lend them more money on the way home.

When Montmorency was sober, Fox-Selwyn described to him how deranged and disloyal he had been under the influence of the drugs, and Montmorency had tearfully sworn that he would not take them again. Then a couple of nights later, in a roadside tavern, Fox-Selwyn was awakened in the night as Montmorency shouted and raved. The following week, on a boat up the Danube, it happened once more. Soon there were regular scenes. Sometimes Montmorency was almost paralyzed, staring ahead in a trance. Sometimes he ranted and spat out secrets that his sober self would have taken to the grave. Once he tried to eat his boots. Fox-Selwyn had seen Montmorency drunk a thousand times, but this was something different, something more destructive and even more uncontrollable. He knew that Montmorency no longer enjoyed the drugs, and feared that he had developed a physical and mental dependence on them that he couldn't break, however strong his desire. He had tried to find Montmorency's stock of the stuff, so that he could throw it away, but even though he once found a little in a bag sewn into the lining of a coat, his friend always seemed to have more.

By the time they reached London, Fox-Selwyn knew that Montmorency needed to see a doctor; not just for his own sake but for the preservation of national security. The sensitivity of their work demanded that the doctor should be totally dependable. To Fox-Selwyn's mind Robert Farcett was the ideal man, indeed the only man. He trusted him as a physician and as a friend. But he knew that by bringing Farcett and Montmorency together he could lose the friendship of one or the other, or possibly both.

Nevertheless he had sent a note to Bargles, the gentleman's club where Montmorency lived, asking him to come to the Turkish baths at seven. It was there that he intended to reintroduce him to the doctor who had saved his life: who might not recognize Montmorency by his voice, or the way he now carried himself, but would know him at once from the scars on his body, most of which Doctor Farcett had put there himself. So Fox-Selwyn had an hour to let the doctor in on the plan and to persuade him to help Montmorency again.

He called over to one of the attendants. The man approached him swinging a bucket overflowing with soapy foam.

"Good evening, my lord. It's a pleasure to see you again. Did you have a pleasant holiday, sir?"

"Most agreeable," lied Fox-Selwyn, thinking back to the rigors of the journey home. "I was hoping to meet Doctor Farcett here."

"He's in the next cubicle, sir."

Fox-Selwyn shouted a greeting though the partition as he lay down and the man started soaping up his back. "I'll see you in the Cooling Room, Robert," he called. "We've a lot to catch up on."

Doctor Farcett's muffled voice came back through the thin wooden wall. Fox-Selwyn couldn't make out what he said, but he didn't sound quite himself.

Fox-Selwyn had rehearsed his speech to Farcett several times before he met him in the Cooling Room. They lay on adjacent couches, Farcett lean and fit, Fox-Selwyn monumentally large, overlapping the bed at both ends and both sides. More than once he steeled himself to explain about Montmorency. But he had to change his plan. Farcett needed his help, too. After a few pleasantries about the trip, as Big Ben chimed on the half hour, the doctor suddenly poured out the story of that afternoon's disaster in the operating room.

"I can't carry on, George," said Farcett. "It's made me realize something I never wanted to admit about myself. I've lost my way. I've put my pride before my patients. I went into medicine to help people — not to kill them."

Fox-Selwyn tried to reassure him, growing more anxious as Big Ben rang the news that it was a quarter to seven. He listed Farcett's many medical triumphs, even reminding him of times his own aches and pains had been relieved under the care of his friend.

Farcett took no notice. "It's no good, I'm going to give it all up. I'm not fit to be allowed to practice."

"But nobody knows, do they?" said Fox-Selwyn. "Surely everybody will think today's death was just a terrible accident?"

"But *I* know, George. That's enough. Even if those vultures in the gallery knew the truth, most of them wouldn't think I'd done anything wrong. But I know, and I've decided. I'm giving up medicine for good."

Fox-Selwyn tried to talk him out of it, but Farcett's gloom only grew. All the time Fox-Selwyn dreaded the moment of Montmorency's arrival, panicking inside as he tried to sound calm and reassuring in the face of the doctor's despair. The clock struck seven. But Fox-Selwyn needn't have worried. Montmorency never came.

CHAPTER 2

IN THE SEWER

As the chimes sounded seven o'clock, the air around Montmorency was warm and steamy, but the perfume was quite different from that of the Turkish baths. He swung down from the metal ladder onto the narrow ledge above the river of filth at the base of the sewer. It had been a long time, nearly five years, since his last visit to this underground world, but it had been a place of safety for him when he had been at his most desperate, and it had been home to Scarper — his rough and dangerous self — the rough and dangerous self who had taken the brown granules from the leather pouch hidden under the base of his suitcase and crumbled them into a tumbler of whiskey half an hour before.

Scarper had crept up on Montmorency in his little room at Bargles as he was getting ready to go off to meet Fox-Selwyn at the Xandan Turkish Baths. Montmorency had been doing so well. He had washed and shaved, and dressed in his best evening wear in case they went on to dinner afterward. He needed only to find his second cuff link, which was rolling around somewhere at the bottom of his luggage. Why had his hand strayed to the concealed flap? Why had he given in to the lure of the disgusting concoction? The drug had long since ceased to bring him happiness, and yet he couldn't help himself. He gulped the liquid down. But as he swallowed it he knew that here in London he couldn't risk being seen under the influence of the nauseating potion, and he sensed that the secret stinking darkness of the squalid tunnel was the place to be when the mixture took effect.

Montmorency knew that the initial rush of energy and clearheadedness that gave him the insight to change his clothes and the strength to lift the manhole cover would soon make way for the sickness and oblivion that had so concerned his friend on the way home from Turkey. Sweating and panting, he looped his belt around the bottom of the ladder, so that he couldn't fall into the sewage if he lost consciousness. In the darkness he started to shiver and sway, and images of violence and terror played themselves out in brilliant light on the inside of his eyeballs, which felt as if they were about to burst. His ears rang with the clang of battle and the throb of fear. Just as he could take no more, everything was black again.

>>>

He sensed that hours must have passed when he woke, the sticky wetness of his vomit clinging to his sleeve. Scarper's old survival instincts kicked in, reading the signs of the sewer to determine what the time was. He knew he was near a big hotel, and the flow of waste entering the tunnel was brimming with foam. People must be taking baths. It was probably morning. He had missed his appointment with Fox-Selwyn at the Xandan and he knew his old friend would be worried. He needed to get out, go home, and get cleaned up. He climbed the ladder unsteadily, with none of Scarper's old athletic spring, and nudged open the heavy iron lid of the hole, listening and watching for signs of people in the street. He was lucky, and pulled himself up onto the pavement without being seen. But he had to get back inside Bargles without anyone noticing the state he was in.

Many a time he had returned from a night out much the worse for wear, sometimes smelling of his own or other people's body fluids, but never as bad as this. Scarper's ingenuity came to his rescue again. He would break into the club. He went around the back, climbed a drainpipe, and forced open a tiny window on the same floor as his room. He hitched himself up and squeezed through into the communal bathroom. There, as he ran himself a bath, he heard the shrill noise of a policeman's whistle outside. He had been spotted. Now Scarper's cool nerve came to the fore. He stayed where he was, scrubbing at his body, and washing the evidence of the night before from his hair. When he emerged from the bathroom, wrapped in a thick robe, he found Sam the porter cowering on the landing with a breathless policeman.

"I'm very sorry, sir," said Sam, "but there seems to have been an intrusion."

"I saw him climbing the drainpipe," puffed the policeman. "I ran all the way here across the park. Right from the other side of the lake. I reckon he came in one of the windows on this side."

"Funnily enough, I noticed the window was open when I came in for my bath," said Montmorency, calmly indicating the broken latch. "Do you think he's still in the building?"

"No sign, sir," said Sam. "But we took the liberty of looking in your room. . . ."

"And I'm afraid, sir," added the policeman, "that it seems you have been burgled."

"He must have been lurking in the corridor," said Sam, "and gone into your room when he saw you were having a bath. It's lucky you didn't see him. You might have been attacked!"

Sam pushed open the door and showed the inside of Montmorency's room. It was exactly as it had been the night before when he had fled into the street after swallowing the Turkish drug. His luggage was open and ransacked. A chair he had knocked over in his hurry to leave still lay on its side. The glass that had contained the horrible mixture was smashed on the ground, a dark mark on the wall showing where Montmorency had flung it in his fury at his weakness in yielding to temptation yet again. Montmorency felt a new wave of despair flow though him as he realized the depravity into which he was sinking. Sam, misreading his expression as horror at the apparent crime, tried to comfort him.

"Don't worry, sir. We'll clean this up in no time. You just get yourself dressed. Breakfast will be ready in a little while. I'll get Sam to do you a special kipper, with a poached egg on top, and by the time you're up here again it will be as if nothing ever happened." (At Bargles, for convenience, all the servants were known as Sam.)

"And I'll ask around and see if anyone saw anything," said the constable. "Don't you worry. We'll catch him. Always do!"

No you don't, thank God, thought Montmorency, as he nodded pathetically, accepting the words of comfort and enjoying the role of victim into which he had been cast.

As he ate his kipper he reflected on his luck, and he wondered, not for the first time, how long that good fortune would last. He had Scarper to thank for his survival that morning. Scarper's wits had preserved Montmorency's lifestyle. But Scarper's weaknesses were in danger of undermining that lifestyle, too, and Montmorency promised himself, pouring another cup of coffee and buttering a freshly baked roll, that he would destroy the remainder of the drug as soon as he got upstairs. But he didn't, of course. He wrapped it in several layers of newspaper, and hid it behind the wardrobe, telling himself that he would never, ever, touch it again.

CHAPTER 3

KIDNAPPED

So Fox-Selwyn had two casualties on his hands. Doctor Farcett was ready to give up everything in an orgy of shame, and if allowed to return to the hospital was likely to resign and walk away from a brilliant career. Montmorency must have had a reason for failing to turn up at the Xandan Baths, and Fox-Selwyn, with a despairing heart, knew what that reason was likely to be. He decided to take control of both his friends, and to remove them from London. When he got home from the baths, he wrote to his brother in Banffshire, warning that he would be dropping in at his estate with a couple of companions. Early the next morning, while Montmorency was acting out the pantomime of the "burglary" with Sam and the policeman at Bargles, Fox-Selwyn set off for King's Cross Station, to buy three tickets to the north of Scotland.

He took the first ticket to Robert Farcett's house, where he was greeted by a maid in great distress. She was so pleased to see someone that she launched into a babble of words, remembering after a few seconds to drop into a little curtsy.

"I don't know what's wrong with Doctor Farcett, my lord. I've never known him in such a state. He won't let me into his study."

Fox-Selwyn tapped on the study door. "Go away," said a thin voice from inside.

"Robert. It's George. Please let me in."

"There's nothing you can do. Just leave me alone," said the doctor.

"But what about your patients? Aren't you supposed to be at the hospital today?" asked Fox-Selwyn, hoping to stir Farcett into action by appealing to his sense of duty.

"I'm of no use to them. Leave me in peace."

"It doesn't sound like peace to me, Robert. Look, I know you don't want to go back to the hospital, and perhaps you're right, for now. I've got a plan that can take you away from all this for a while. Let me in, and I'll explain."

There was a silence, then Fox-Selwyn tried the doorknob and it turned. He opened the door quietly. The study was always a bit of a mess, but usually the medicines Doctor Farcett kept at home were scrupulously locked away in a cupboard. Fox-Selwyn noticed that today two dark bottles stood on the edge of the desk. Grooves along the outside of the glass indicated that they contained poison. To his relief, he could see that they were both full, but he sensed that he might have arrived only just in time. Doctor Farcett was sitting, staring at the wall, a half-written letter of self-incrimination lying on the desk before him. His normally trim athletic body was slumped in the chair, his thick brown hair hung limp over his eyes, and his boyish features had sagged, showing lines that were not due to arrive on his face for years yet. There were even signs of dirt under his fingernails. It was a standing joke that the doctor, obsessed with the evil power of germs, was forever washing. He must have been up all night.

Farcett was in a state of such exhaustion and contempt for himself that he was willing to do whatever Fox-Selwyn told him, and Fox-Selwyn took over completely. He helped Farcett compose a dignified letter to the hospital explaining that he would be away for a while, and recommending a junior doctor to take on his duties. Farcett had few personal patients now, and under Fox-Selwyn's guidance he wrote to each one, simply saying he had been called away, and giving them a list of possible substitutes. The maid was sent off to deliver the messages, and Fox-Selwyn considered what to do next. He realized that Farcett was in no condition to be introduced to Montmorency, and that the doctor should not travel to Scotland alone. So he sent home for his own manservant, Chivers, to help Farcett pack and to accompany him on the first available train. Then he returned to King's Cross, bought a fourth ticket, and set off for Bargles to confront Montmorency.

It was almost lunchtime when he reached the club, and the Sam at the door was in a state of uncharacteristic excitement. He rattled off the story of the "burglary" before Fox-Selwyn could even hand in his hat, cape, and cane. For a moment Fox-Selwyn wondered if he had perhaps misjudged his friend. Maybe he had been wrong to assume that he'd been back on the drug. But then he looked down the narrow corridor towards the large bar (known to members as "Drinks Major") where he saw Montmorency surrounded by adoring chums, well into the tale of the break-in. Fox-Selwyn leaned in the doorway and watched. He had seen Montmorency in action many times before. He had heard him talk his way out of trouble all over Europe. He had been there when Montmorency convinced a member of the Bulgarian Secret Police that he was a Benedictine friar. He knew when his friend was lying. As the group dispersed for lunch in "Eats Major" and "Eats Minor" (the big and little dining rooms), Fox-Selwyn caught Montmorency's eye.

"Plotters. Now!" he mouthed, referring to the tiny booth, with room for only two drinkers, where members went for private conversations. A sheepish look came over Montmorency's face. He guessed that Fox-Selwyn had a pretty good idea of what had gone on overnight. They settled side by side on the velvet-covered bench. Montmorency made several attempts to speak, but failed to find the words to tell his story.

"I just couldn't help . . ." he stuttered, only to be interrupted by Fox-Selwyn in a commanding tone.

"You can tell me all about it on the train. We're going to Scotland." He took out his pocket watch from his brightly embroidered waistcoat. "Might as well wait for the sleeper, now. Get Sam to sort out your packing. I'll be by for an early dinner, and we'll get a cab to the station."

Montmorency knew he couldn't refuse, and spent the afternoon preparing for the unexpected trip. It was, at least, a chance for him to indulge in another of his vices: shopping. There was no time for a session with his tailor, but he enjoyed a couple of hours kitting himself out in some of the largest and most expensive shops in London for a stay in what he imagined to be a very cold part of the world. When he returned to Bargles, the Sam who'd been there for the "burglary" chatted away merrily as he gathered Montmorency's things together.

"It will be good for you to get away after a shock like what you had this morning, sir. And you'll get a chance to use your boots at last."

Sam was referring to the long waders that Montmorency kept under his bed. Montmorency had always explained them away as being for a fishing trip, though in fact they were the last souvenirs of Scarper's life in the sewers. For a while, Montmorency had stood one of them up against the wall so that he would have somewhere to flick his ash when he was smoking in bed. He had never really thought they would be used for their original purpose.

"I'll tie them together, sir. It will make them easier to carry onto the train," said Sam, and while he was away getting the string, Montmorency took his forbidden parcel from behind the wardrobe and thrust it down the left boot. His body surged with shame. He knew he should take this opportunity to abandon the drug. He was about to take it out again, to throw it away, when Sam reappeared, and announced urgently, "Lord George Fox-Selwyn is downstairs, sir. He's asked me to tell you that he's already ordered dinner."

And down there in the dining room, Fox-Selwyn was sitting alone, checking the train tickets. He was tired after a day spent organizing the departure of his two troubled friends from London to the peace of the country. He was sure that what they both needed was a period of tranquillity. He wanted them restored to their former selves. He couldn't have known that all three of them were about to embark on adventures that would throw them together in a new way, showing them things about each other that they had never suspected themselves.

CHAPTER 4

THE SLEEPER

Montmorency's luggage filled the cab they took to the station. There was enough room only because Lord George Fox-Selwyn had brought almost nothing: just an overnight bag and a small picnic packed by his cook. As ever, she had tucked in a slab of homemade toffee and Fox-Selwyn's favorite little silver hammer, and the thought of shattering the block and biting into the sticky treat in the middle of the night made the prospect of the journey bearable for him, even a little exciting. Fox-Selwyn explained that he didn't need to take any clothes. His brother would lend him everything he needed, being about the same size. Montmorency marveled at the prospect of meeting another man built on Fox-Selwyn's grand scale, and wondered if this elder brother, even more fabulously wealthy than George, had such tiny feet, too.

Waiting for the train to leave the station, Montmorency sat on the side of the wooden bench that would be his bed for the night. The tiny compartment reminded him of the prison cell that had been his home for three long years. It was where he had planned the campaign of theft that had so successfully transformed his life. Then he had had nothing, for a while not even a firm hold on life itself. Now he was surrounded by possessions, crammed into every corner of the tiny room. He pulled a heavy suitcase towards him, so he could get out his pajamas and settle down to sleep. It caught on the long rubber waders which were sticking out from under the bed. His thoughts turned to the secret parcel inside them. Perhaps just a little of the drug would help him through the night. He reached down the boot and pulled out the bundle of newspaper. As he unwrapped each layer his intentions swung from taking a pinch and hiding the rest to turning the whole lot over to Fox-Selwyn and asking him to throw it away.

In the next compartment, Lord George Fox-Selwyn was having a similar battle with himself. He had already changed into his long stripy nightgown, but was not ready to take up his book. He wondered how Chivers and Doctor Farcett were getting on: They would be well into Scotland by now. He hoped the doctor was feeling better. He feared not. Fox-Selwyn found his hand running across the tray of toffee, working its way under the paper wrapper to feel the glassy surface of the slab. He wasn't hungry, but he itched to get out his little hammer and break it into pieces. But he knew what would happen then: The toffee would be gone before the train was even out of London. He would spend the night longing for more. He knew he should wait, but he could smell the deep, burnt, sickly aroma he had loved since childhood. He delved into his bag for the hammer, and looked at it in his hand with the mixture of guilt and excitement a small boy would feel, holding a pebble and about to smash a window. Ashamed, he pushed the toffee and the hammer aside, and lifted the curtain to look out of the window.

The train was still in the station. On the platform a jolly group was saying loud good-byes to a couple setting off on their honeymoon. The young bride looked embarrassed as her brothers joked with the groom about the night ahead.

"Watch out for the big junction at Crewe! It'll have you jolting!" laughed one.

"Don't take any notice," said an older woman alongside the bride, presumably her mother. "Just remember everything I've told you." And she started to sob, taking out a large handkerchief from her coat pocket and dabbing at her eyes. The bride put an arm around her. Suddenly the older woman's shoulders started to shake.

"Don't cry, Mum," said one of the boys. "You know what they say. You're not losing a daughter, you're gaining a son."

"She's got enough of them already!" said an older man, coughing on a cigarette. "Come on, Molly, cheer up."

The woman raised her head from her hanky. "I'm not crying," she squealed as she pointed towards the train. "Look!"

And Fox-Selwyn realized that she was laughing at him, on display in the window in his nightclothes. He pulled the curtain shut again, picked up the toffee and the hammer, and set off to see Montmorency.

The sudden tap on his door made Montmorency instinctively hide his own package under his pillow. He lay on top, awkwardly, trying to look relaxed. Fox-Selwyn's huge bulk filled the doorway. He had to stoop to get his head through the gap, and turned his whole body slightly sideways to ease his bulging belly into the compartment. Montmorency looked up from the bed, aware that he must have a stupid look of guilt on his face. He was surprised to find it returned by his embarrassed old friend.

"Here," said Fox-Selwyn, thrusting the slab of toffee towards him. "Take it, and don't let me have it back until we are at least past Watford. I just can't trust myself."

Montmorency took the package with an indulgent smile and slid it under the pillow. He knew this would be the ideal moment to pass his own contraband to Fox-Selwyn; now, better than ever, Fox-Selwyn would understand his own struggle to part with the drug. As he felt under the pillow for the leather pouch, a small round face appeared, somewhere around Fox-Selwyn's armpit.

"Tickets please, gentlemen," said the attendant, clearly accustomed to encountering all manner of people in various stages of undress.

Fox-Selwyn started patting himself in the places where his pockets would have been, had he been wearing his suit.

"Ah, I shall have to return to my own compartment," he said while he tried to turn around, wobbling and steadying himself as he got caught up in Montmorency's luggage, his tiny feet dancing their way between the bags and boxes like a ballerina's. Eventually he decided to back out, and the ticket collector, calmly waiting in the corridor, slipped out of the way only just in time to avoid being flattened against the wall.

"One moment please," called Fox-Selwyn, maneuvering himself back into his own room to the accompaniment of crashing, banging, and cursing as he looked for his ticket in the clothes strewn across the floor.

The attendant was in Montmorency's compartment, checking his ticket, when Fox-Selwyn reappeared, triumphant. As they squeezed and stumbled in the confined space to get Fox-Selwyn in and the ticket collector out, the train suddenly lurched on the start of its journey, and the two of them fell in a heap on top of Montmorency. Through the window the wedding party was leaving the platform and Molly's big white hanky waved farewell to the happy couple. It was one of the great joys of traveling with Lord George Fox-Selwyn that he could always be relied upon to see the funny side of things. Sprawled across Montmorency and the attendant, his massive laugh set the other two off, and the tiny compartment shook with merriment as the train trundled off through North London.

Then they all fell silent at once. A loud rumbling *crump* rocked the air, and the car jerked suddenly. It settled back into its normal rhythm in an instant, but all three men knew something was wrong. Only for a moment did they think there might be a problem with the train or the track. Fox-Selwyn recognized that sound. He knew it from his travels in the war-torn Balkans, and he had heard it once before in London. It was an explosion. Maybe an accident, or perhaps someone was making a political point. But the train was gathering speed on its way to Scotland, and until the news reached the papers there, Fox-Selwyn and Montmorency would not know for certain what had happened or why.

CHAPTER 5

NIGHT MOVES

The attendant retrieved his hat, straightened his clothes, and found his way over Fox-Selwyn and into the corridor where several other passengers, some still dressed, others in their nightclothes, one clutching a toothbrush, had emerged to find out what was going on.

"There is no need for alarm," he declaimed in his "official" voice. "I can assure you that there is nothing wrong with the train. If there was, the driver would have stopped. There appears to have been some sort of explosion somewhere in London. Probably a gas leak, I imagine, or maybe there's been a bit of a mishap at that fireworks factory up at Highgate. They work all hours at this time of year, getting ready for Bonfire Night. In any case, we are safely clear of the area now. In fact, you are all very lucky. Probably in the safest place in the world. I shall be coming around to check your tickets, and then I suggest that you all get to sleep. We are due at Edinburgh at six o'clock tomorrow morning, so you have an early start ahead of you!"

The little crowd started to disperse, but not before some snatched conversations about the safety of gas, and a few dramatic anecdotes about friends of friends who had been victims of sloppy maintenance and the penny-pinching of the gas companies growing rich on botched installations while endangering the public. But in a few minutes, the corridor was quiet again. Fox-Selwyn slipped out to his own compartment to get a hip flask of brandy that Cook had put in his hamper. But when he returned, ready for a chat about the threat of violence from Irishmen outraged at the British rule of their homeland, he found Montmorency fast asleep, still in his clothes, exhausted by the events of the past twenty-four hours. Fox-Selwyn closed the door behind him, and went to lie down himself. He was glad the train hadn't stopped. The last thing he wanted was any disruption to his plan to get his two friends away for a peaceful break. And maybe the ticket man was right. Perhaps it was a gas blast. Perhaps he was letting his imagination run away with him after all his foreign travels, conjuring up terrorists when sloppy workmen were the real threat. He closed his eyes, and tried to think of Scotland.

But he couldn't sleep. The wooden car creaked and squeaked, and there was a draft of cold air along the side of the bed, just where the narrow blanket failed to cover his bottom, which curved over the edge. He tried turning over, but only succeeded in untucking the bedclothes on the other side. He tried to remake the bed without getting out of it, but that just pulled the sheet out at the far end, putting his feet in direct contact with the hairy wool cover. He lay still, tired and uncomfortable, and tried to force himself to sleep, but his mind kept settling on the task ahead. How was he to handle the reunion of Doctor Farcett and Montmorency? Was Doctor Farcett all right? He and Chivers would be well on the way to his brother's estate by now. Perhaps they had stayed somewhere in a hotel for the night. Would Chivers be able to cope with the doctor in his disturbed state? Fox-Selwyn wriggled, trying to find a better position. The blanket fell off completely. There was nothing else to do. He would have to go and get that toffee.

It was dark outside now, and there was only the dimmest of lights in the corridor. Montmorency's cabin was quiet. Fox-Selwyn groped his way towards the bed and felt for the pillow. His friend turned and stretched, but didn't wake. Fox-Selwyn flattened his hand and pushed it between the pillowcase and the sheet. There was the toffee, but Montmorency's head was pushing down on it, heavy with sleep. Fox-Selwyn pulled the tray. It wouldn't move. He tugged again, and the hammer fell down onto his foot. He opened his mouth to shout, but stopped himself just in time. As Fox-Selwyn bent to pick up the hammer and tuck it into the breast pocket of his nightshirt Montmorency moved, his face blocking the way to the toffee. Fox-Selwyn reached over the top of him, trying not to breathe. He slid his hand under the pillow again, and grasped triumphantly at what he found. But it wasn't the toffee. It was a leather pouch, and with despair, Fox-Selwyn guessed what it must contain. He probed again, found his toffee, and crept away.

Next door, he opened the unexpected find. He sniffed the dark powder inside, and the cloying smell took him back to the filth of the Turkish market where Montmorency had been lured into his vice. He opened the window, letting in the roar of the train's wheels, the smell of the engine, and a soft drizzle. There was no sign of civilization. All was black. As he hurled the leather pouch out into the darkness, the train let out a piercing whistle, and plunged into a tunnel. Fox-Selwyn slammed the window shut, took out his hammer, and smashed the toffee to smithereens.

CHAPTER 6

»

UPHILL

As Montmorency and Fox-Selwyn were leaving London, Chivers and Doctor Farcett were in Aberdeen, more than four hundred miles to the north. Chivers had not enjoyed his journey. Traveling by day, the line had taken them past some of the finest sights in Britain, including three mighty cathedrals and a glorious sweep of coastline where the water seemed almost to touch the rails. In happier times he had enjoyed his occasional trips north with his master, Lord George Fox-Selwyn. But the sad figure slumped opposite him today drained all the pleasure from the scene. Doctor Farcett was hunched into a private world, hardly speaking, except to turn down offers of food, sleeping a little, and once actually crying softly into the upturned collar of his coat. At Edinburgh they changed trains, and at Aberdeen they were due to change again, but it was late, and Chivers had no trouble persuading his docile companion to spend the night in a hotel. Helping Doctor Farcett to his room, he took the precaution of removing his razor from his bag, just in case he had any desperate thoughts in the night. Then he went downstairs to the chilly bar, too hungry and thirsty to go straight to bed himself.

He entered the smoky room, and two dozen eyes turned towards him, trying to read the signals given off by his clothes and bearing. Each pair of eyes was set in a wide, moonlike face with ruddy cheeks and varying selections of crooked, discolored teeth. Twenty-four chubby hands clasped huge pots of beer in their fat fingers. A dozen bellies bulged over the tops of a dozen pairs of trousers. At an inn so near to the station they must have been used to outsiders, but they managed to make Chivers feel like an explorer in a far-away land. They had him down for an Englishman straightaway, but what was his social standing? He was well dressed, but something about his manner suggested that he was a servant, not a master. They played it safe, ignored him, and went back to talking amongst themselves in a private vocabulary and an incomprehensible accent swallowed right back into the depths of their throats. Despite his hunger, he was on the verge of returning to his room when the landlady arrived, cheerful and welcoming, if a little tricky to understand.

"Fit yu'll b' wantun fair yur tee?"

There was enough there for him to able to guess that she was asking what he wanted for his tea. Where he came from, tea was at four o'clock. It was much, much later now, but he would make allowances. She probably meant supper.

"What do you have?" Even to himself his voice sounded ridiculously English, round, and booming in this company.

Fortunately there was only one thing on offer. He wasn't sure what she'd said it was, but it turned out to be a hefty beef pie, quite delicious alongside the beer that was brought to him without his asking. He was about to leave for his room when one of the men at a small round table in the corner suddenly fell to the ground, coughing, wheezing, and gasping for breath. The others stood around helpless, while the landlady thumped him on the back, and the man's eyes widened and stared out, pleading for help.

"I'll get my master — he's a doctor," called Chivers as he leaped from his stool and rushed up to Farcett's room. The doctor was still sitting, impassive, on the edge of the bed where Chivers had left him. He didn't move as Chivers shouted to him about the emergency downstairs and the need to help.

"I can't help. I can't help anybody now," muttered the doctor.

"But sir, it's urgent. The man can hardly breathe!"

"It's no use. I'm of no use." And Farcett dropped his head into his hands and started rocking backward and forward, his shoulders shaking with his sobs.

Chivers had spent his whole adult life doing as he was told. Never once in his long service with Lord George Fox-Selwyn had he spoken out of turn, or even expressed an opinion unless particularly asked. But now his concern for the choking man in the bar and his rage at the waste of the doctor's talents gave him the confidence to adopt the tone of voice he used with housemaids, or tradesmen who had let his master down.

"Doctor Farcett. You must come. We haven't got time for this self-indulgence! A life is at stake. You are coming downstairs with me now." He grabbed the doctor's bag from his bed, seized Farcett by one arm, and marched him to the staircase. Frantic gasps and a rattling gargling noise could be heard from the bar. The landlady's voice shrieked, "Doctor! Doctor! Hurry. Hurry, please!"

And Chivers hurled Farcett towards her, his face still desperately screaming his reluctance to get involved.

But when Farcett saw the body on the ground, the

contorted face purple with airless panic, compassion overcame his despair. He found his hands moving automatically across the man's body, forcing open his mouth, and with a fearsome set of forceps from his bag he fished out a huge piece of steak that had been blocking the windpipe. The man coughed and wheezed a few times more, then sat up, spluttering his thanks.

Doctor Farcett was genuinely embarrassed by the praise heaped on him by everyone in the bar. He couldn't understand what most of the people were saying, but he caught the drift of it, and insisted time and again that this had been a simple episode of choking that anyone could have dealt with, and that he just wanted to be left alone. He was right. It had been a simple procedure, but something important had happened that night. When he got back upstairs, refusing free drinks and food, he went to the bathroom and washed his hands until they were their usual porcelain selves.

Chivers knocked timidly on his door and entered, looking embarrassed. "Begging your pardon, sir, but I thought I should apologize for my conduct earlier. I should not have spoken to you in that way. It was an emergency, sir."

"Not at all, Chivers," said Doctor Farcett. "I fear it

is I who should apologize to you. I have not been a congenial companion. I have something on my mind."

Chivers interrupted him. "It is not my place to know, sir. I hope you will be feeling better in the morning. I shall wake you at seven, sir. Our train leaves at eight. Will there be anything else tonight, sir?"

"No thank you, Chivers," said the doctor. "Good night."

"Good night, sir," said Chivers and, closing the door behind him, he left to resume his meal, hopeful that Doctor Farcett would be less gloomy in the morning.

The doctor sat for a while on the side of his bed. He had broken his promise to himself never to touch a patient again, but he knew he had had no choice. If he had done nothing, and the man in the bar had died, his despair would have been even deeper. He was grateful to Chivers for forcing him to act. But when he lay down, the image of the dead man in the London morgue returned. For a couple of hours he wrestled with the two images: the man he had saved, and the man he had killed. Eventually he came to some sort of equilibrium. He would never return to his old life of ambitious public display, but perhaps he could acknowledge the skills he possessed, and use them in some way when absolutely necessary. As soon as he had pen and paper he would write a formal letter of resignation to the hospital. Once he had decided that, he could at last get some sleep.

At seven o'clock in the morning, Chivers arrived with his razor and a bowl of hot water. Doctor Farcett managed to eat some of his breakfast, and though he was subdued on the final train journey into Banffshire, by the time he was in the rickety carriage on the way to Glendarvie Castle he was quite presentable. He wasn't quite himself again, but he was fit to be introduced to Lord George Fox-Selwyn's brother as the London surgeon the telegram had warned him to expect.

CHAPTER 7

DOWNHILL

Back in Edinburgh the sleeper pulled in on time at six o'clock. Fox-Selwyn had finally fallen into a deep sleep just as the train passed over the border between England and Scotland. He had trouble waking up, and was still dressing as the other passengers started to leave the train. In the next compartment, Montmorency had hardly stirred in the night, but he, too, was struggling to prepare for the day. His body had started to demand the drug, but no matter how hard he searched his bedclothes there was no sign of the leather pouch. The toffee was gone, too, and he guessed what had happened. He didn't know that Fox-Selwyn had thrown the drug away, or that far behind in an English field lay the corpse of a goat, which had been tempted by the strange, pungent package, and swallowed it almost whole. When Fox-Selwyn appeared in the doorway of his compartment, Montmorency looked up at him with pleading eyes.

"It's gone," said Fox-Selwyn, in a matter-of-fact

tone that stifled any protest. "You're going to have to do without it. I threw it out of the window hours ago."

Montmorency slumped down. Knowing that he had no way of getting artificial help instantly made his symptoms worse. His hands started to shake, and even in the chill of the Edinburgh morning there was sweat above his eyebrows. Fox-Selwyn calmly took over, as he had so often done on the journey back from Turkey. He found a porter, and had their belongings transferred to the Left Luggage Office to await their next train to the north. He helped Montmorency with his new heavy coat, and marched him off for a walk to fill the time before the hotels started serving breakfast.

Climbing the steps out of the gloom of the station, even Montmorency, beginning to enter the savage darkness of his private world of craving, was struck by the beauty of the city. The sun seemed to spread cleanliness all around, picking out the detail of the ancient castle hundreds of feet up on its mysterious volcanic cliff. Deep in the hollow alongside the boulevard of elegant shops, Princes Street Gardens were sparkling with dew. Fox-Selwyn marched purposefully ever upward, and at last laid down the ground rules for their trip.

"You can't go on taking that stuff. You don't see how you act when you're under its influence. In this job, we can't afford to be out of control. Whether you like it or not, you are in possession of secrets and facts that many people — friends and enemies — want to keep hidden. Lives, and not just our lives, could be endangered by one wrong word, and yet more lives might be saved through the bravery and skill you can exercise when you are fully yourself. You have no choice. I don't believe that you will be able to live with yourself if you slip into an abyss of depravity, and I know that others, some of them at the very highest levels of government, will see to it that you are destroyed if you do. I have kept news of your condition from them, and for the sake of our friendship I am prepared to give you a chance."

Montmorency looked up with relief, but Fox-Selwyn had more to say. He took his friend by the shoulders and, forcing him to look into his eyes, issued his ultimatum.

"Conquer this frailty and I will never say a word. But I have to tell you now that if you let me down, and if your weakness should in any way threaten this nation, even I will withdraw my support. It is that important. I want you to survive, and I will do everything in my power to ensure that you do, no matter how rough I have to be with you." He let go of Montmorency's coat, and waited for a response.

Somewhere in his heart Montmorency understood and appreciated his friend's remarks, but his head was thumping, and his tongue felt enormous in his mouth. He tried to speak. He stopped, and reached out to touch his companion's face with a grateful hand. But as he stretched, he felt a rising sickness in his throat. The solid, steady castle on its primeval rock started to spin and lurch, and he fell away, turned by Fox-Selwyn's urgent guiding hand just in time to direct his vomit into a rubbish bin at the side of the path. Fox-Selwyn cleaned up his friend, and discarded his monogrammed linen handkerchief on top of the mess in the bin.

"Look at yourself, man!" he snapped with a mixture of anger and concern. Montmorency slumped and turned his face away. Fox-Selwyn decided that this was the moment to make his first, coded mention of Doctor Farcett.

"I imagine that things are going to get even worse than this," he said. "But I know a man who can help you. A man who I believe can be trusted to cure you in complete privacy. He will be waiting for us at

Glendarvie. However bad things get on the way there, remember that we are traveling in the direction of help and hope. I ask nothing more of you than that you trust me, and do as I say."

Montmorency was too exhausted to argue. But while half his brain gloried in the generosity of his friend, the other half cursed him for throwing away the one substance that might make that morning beautiful again. Up on the Castle Esplanade, alone in the cool summer sunshine, they shared a cigarette. Fox-Selwyn lit it, took a few puffs, and passed it over to his friend. After a couple of drags, Montmorency took it from his vomit-stained lips and offered it back. Fox-Selwyn declined. They were close, but not that close. Nothing more was said until, on the long walk down the hill, they heard a hundred clocks strike seven.

"Right," cried Fox-Selwyn, clapping his hands in his old-matey way. "Time for some food." And he steered Montmorency through the doors of a grand hotel and into the dining room, where he ordered them both a substantial feast. He tucked into his own helping with pleasure, pausing only to straighten Montmorency whenever he seemed likely to topple from his chair.

The rest of the journey saw Montmorency decline, just as Fox-Selwyn had expected. At Aberdeen Station Fox-Selwyn called for a wheelchair to get his friend to a hotel. He hoped a night's sleep would strengthen him enough to face the last leg of their journey. But Montmorency didn't sleep. The very room where Doctor Farcett had spent the previous night echoed with his deranged ranting into the small hours, and only a huge tip and a tall story about a stale sandwich from a station buffet pacified the landlady. Three porters were needed to get Montmorency and his luggage into the tiny train that would rattle his shivering, mumbling, hallucinating form to Banffshire. The porters at Aberdeen Station knew full well who Lord George Fox-Selwyn was. Fox-Selwyn was aware that his strange companion was bound to become the subject of wild gossip after they had gone. He didn't want the truth about Montmorency's identity or condition to get out, even here, so far from London. It was a miracle that in the moment's pause when Fox-Selwyn considered how to answer a porter who asked him the invalid's name, Montmorency sat up, opened one eye, and mumbled, "Scarper."

He was slumped and slobbering again when Harvey, the old coachman from Glendarvie Castle, met them at the station on the edge of the estate. There was still a punishing, uphill journey ahead.

"Good to see you, Harvey," said Fox-Selwyn, relieved that transport was on hand. "So my brother got my telegram. I'm afraid my friend is rather unwell."

"I've been down to meet every train since yesterday, my lord." Harvey looked at Montmorency. "Just as well we've got a doctor staying with us, sir."

"Ah. They've arrived then?"

"He and Mr. Chivers got here last night, my lord. The Marquess asked for the doctor to be put in the North Tower. Will this gentleman be joining him, sir?"

"No, tell Mrs. Grant to make up the spare room next to mine. I don't think I can impose a patient on Doctor Farcett without warning. And take us in the back way. I'd rather arrive quietly."

Harvey understood, and asked no questions. "Very good, my lord," he said calmly, as if this strange arrival was a perfectly normal event.

On their slow way up the narrow road past the castle gates and through the woods, Fox-Selwyn contemplated how to handle the introductions that lay ahead. High up in the North Tower Chivers was sorting out the doctor's clothes: folding shirts, brushing jackets, and polishing shoes. He was listening for his master's arrival, imagining how pleased his lordship would be to see the improvement in Doctor Farcett's spirits since their early-morning departure from London. He had not seen Mr. Montmorency since he and Lord George Fox-Selwyn had left for their expedition to Turkey a year before, and was looking forward to greeting the vibrant young man who was always an invigorating visitor. The first to arrive at a party, and usually the last to leave, Mr. Montmorency was a dependable source of fun, laughter, and generous tips. So Chivers was horrified when, from the window, he saw the shuffling wreck being guided through the servants' entrance with Harvey and Lord George Fox-Selwyn steadying him on either side.

CHAPTER 8

GLENDARVIE CASTLE

Edward Augustus Fox-Selwyn ("Gus" to his family and friends) was getting used to his new name. For most of his life he had been the Earl of Drumillon, but now he was the Marquess of Rosseley, a title he had inherited on the death of his father. His grandfather was still alive, and still the Duke of Monaburn, but he was old and ill, and the signs were that before too long Gus would change his name again, and become the head of the family, the duke. For Gus was the firstborn, and thus, under the British system, heir to everything, even though he was less than an hour older than his twin brother, George. George had gotten the courtesy title Lord George Fox-Selwyn at birth, and he would keep that name for life. The other titles would cascade down through Gus's children, along with the property that went with them. The new Earl of Drumillon was only five years old. His three-year-old brother was saddled with the name Lord Francis Fox-Selwyn. His parents were hoping he would grow out of his lisp.

Becoming Marquess of Rosseley had made Gus the owner of Glendarvie Castle, the family's Scottish seat. It had been a summer home to Gus and George when they were growing up. There had been a grand house on the site for many years, and the Fox-Selwyns were proud (even a little smug) that they had discovered the wonders of Scotland long before Prince Albert had made Balmoral the Queen's summer retreat. Over the past century or so the family had repeatedly altered and extended Glendarvie, most recently in the Grand Baronial style. And now Gus, the new Marquess, was responsible for the castle and the extensive lands around it.

As it happened, this arrangement suited both brothers perfectly. Gus loved his quiet life in Scotland. He had married a Scot: Lady Lorna Gillivrie, now the Marchioness, who was entirely uninterested in London life and was determined to raise their two small sons in the clear air of Banffshire. She didn't like company, and it was lucky that when George and his assorted casualties arrived she and the boys were away visiting her mother near Inverness, a city she regarded as quite exciting enough for anyone. Montmorency's friend George could never have settled with such an existence. He had plenty of money of his own, having inherited, through his mother, a number of English properties. He adored London, and was happy to spend his fortune on gambling, drinking, and horse racing, topping off the fun with his international trips on behalf of the government. Otherwise he and Gus were very similar. Both were tall and broad, but tapered down to tiny feet, so that they were almost egg-shaped. Both were thinning on top, and both favored the bushy beards so beloved by the Prince of Wales.

Once (with Chivers's help) Lord George Fox-Selwyn had gotten Montmorency into the bath and then to bed, he set off to look for his brother. Standing on the steps at the front of the castle, he spotted Gus emerging from the woods, with Doctor Farcett beside him. The doctor was wearing a borrowed overcoat, massively oversized for him. The hem flapped around his ankles, and the sleeves flapped over his hands. Both men were carrying guns, and two small dogs scampered behind them. Over his shoulder the Marquess held something that might one day become part of lunch. They were chatting happily. Lord George Fox-Selwyn was delighted to see that, as he had hoped, his brother was enjoying the doctor's company. Gus waved the dripping birds in the air as he approached the house.

"George! We were beginning to think you'd never get here. I've just been showing Robert a bit of the estate. He's been telling me stories about when he was a doctor."

"He still *is* a doctor, Gus, and a fine one, too. He'll sort out that gout of yours in no time. And I've got a medical project for him, too. I'd like a word with both of you, if you don't mind."

The smile dropped away from Robert Farcett's face, and Fox-Selwyn worried for a moment that the doctor might really have lost his nerve.

Farcett started to stutter something about not wanting to practice medicine anymore. "George," he said, "I'm resigning from the hospital. I don't want to be a doctor. I can't help you."

Fox-Selwyn brushed his objections aside. "Robert. Please. I know you think you've burned your boats in London, but I need you here, now. It's a tough task, and an emergency. You're just the man for it. I'll pay you, too."

Farcett tried to protest, but Fox-Selwyn slapped him down: "Robert, I know you want to punish yourself by making a grand gesture, but what were you planning to live on when you gave up your job?"

"I've got some capital . . ." Farcett replied, though the truth was he hadn't let himself think his future through at all.

"But that won't last forever, Robert. Let me hire you while you find your feet again. Give yourself time to work things out, and let me support you while you do it."

The doctor continued to argue, but he was silenced by effusive instructions from the Marquess, who was uncomfortable with this vulgar talk about money, and insisted they should all go to the library for a drink before dinner. In the cozy, quietly comfortable room, notable for its shortage of books, they settled down on sagging sofas, and Gus got straight to the point.

"Now what's all this about? I'm always pleased to see you, George, but even you usually give more notice than this. Lorna will be livid that she didn't even know you were coming. It's not more of your cloak-and-dagger stuff, I hope."

"Well, in a way I suppose it is," said Fox-Selwyn, rather apologetically.

"Oh, George, George, when will you grow up? Who are you hiding from this time?"

"Well, this time, Gus, it's not just me who's doing the hiding."

"I'm sorry," Doctor Farcett butted in, embarrassed, thinking George was referring to him, "but it really wasn't my idea to come."

"Of course it wasn't," said Fox-Selwyn, trying to put him at ease. "I brought you here for a purpose, Robert, and not just for your own good. I've told you, I need your help. And Gus, I need the security of Glendarvie. I brought another friend with me, and my friend is in serious trouble."

"Oh, not more gambling debts, George!" said Gus, exasperated. "You should let these friends of yours face the music. We can't keep bailing them out."

"No, not money trouble. Far worse. My friend is in danger of losing his life, or at the very least his livelihood and his reputation. And this country can't afford to do without him."

Fox-Selwyn told the story of his exploits with Montmorency, of his friend's many acts of bravery, and of the fatal weakness of his character which had finally brought him so low. The Marquess and the doctor listened, both sensing that something was being left unsaid. George walked over to the fireplace and helped himself to another whisky from the decanter on the mantelpiece. He stood with his back to the fire and appealed to the doctor.

"Robert, I want you to help me save him from this vice. And I have reason to think that when you meet him you will know him, and you will want to save him, too. I know very little of this man's past. I believe I have guessed enough to warn me not to ask too many questions. He is the very man who saved my life the day before I met you, Robert. Do you remember how I called you in to look at my injured foot, and told you about my accident?"

Robert Farcett smiled at the thought of that first meeting, five years before, and how he had been overwhelmed by the enormous personality of the new patient who was to become one of his closest friends.

"Do you remember?" continued Fox-Selwyn. "You bound up my foot, and I left to have lunch with the man who had rescued me. Robert, I have known him for exactly one day longer than I have known you, and he is as close to me as you are."

"Then why have I never met him?" asked the doctor.

Fox-Selwyn looked down into his glass and swirled the whisky around. "Ah, but Robert, I believe you have. I suspect that you know more about this man's life than I do. And when I introduce you to him, I implore you not to judge him by anything you may know about his past, any more than Gus, here, should judge him by the state he is in at present. Trust me, please, both of you, and I beg you: Please. Help my friend."

There was a silence as Doctor Farcett and the Marquess adjusted to the unusual solemnity of Fox-Selwyn's appeal. George had always been, for both of them, the embodiment of frivolity, but he clearly wasn't joking now.

"All right, I'll help," sighed Farcett. It seemed that he wasn't going to be allowed to leave his medical skills unused. "But why all the mystery? Who is this man?"

"I am hoping that you might tell me," said Fox-Selwyn. "If you come upstairs now I'll introduce you."

The three men climbed the wide wooden staircase up to the floor that Gus and George had shared as children. Fox-Selwyn lit a candle and went to the door at the end of the passage, opening it slowly and wincing at every creak. The sound of steady, rhythmic breathing came from inside. Montmorency was lying on his side, deep in an exhausted sleep and undisturbed by their presence. Fox-Selwyn beckoned Farcett over to the bed. The doctor looked down at the face on the pillow. It was handsome, and tanned by the Mediterranean sun, if somewhat drawn and shadowed by the ravages of the drugs and the journey. He vaguely recognized it, but couldn't think of a name. Fox-Selwyn gently pulled back the sheet. The man underneath was naked. His bare back sported a network of old scars. Lines of bumpy white tissue stood out from the smooth skin underneath. In places faint white dots showed where stitches had been, long ago. Farcett knew at once who lay before him. His lips silently spoke the number "493."

Fox-Selwyn was watching the doctor's face. "You know who it is, don't you?" he whispered. "Now come downstairs and tell me all about him."

CHAPTER 9

DINNER FOR THREE

Gus was so rich that he had no need, or inclination, to show off his wealth. Glendarvie Castle was a dramatic building, and no expense had been spared at any stage of its construction, but inside the riches were confined to the few rooms used when grand guests visited. The family preferred a more straightforward life. That life still required the attentions of servants and the finest of traditional food and wine, but with only three for supper that night the Marquess commanded that the meal should be set out in the smallest dining room, on an ancient wooden table, without a cloth. George, Gus, and Doctor Farcett huddled together at one end and, stopping only for privacy as each course was brought in, they discussed the man who slept upstairs. Doctor Farcett described how he had treated Montmorency's injuries in prison. Fox-Selwyn spoke of the brave and accomplished man about town who had lived at the Marimion Hotel. Neither of them could fill in the gap between the two identities.

"Didn't you ever ask him where his money came from?" asked Farcett.

"I just couldn't. At first I didn't have any suspicions, and then when I did, I knew him so well, and liked him so much, and needed him, too, for my work . . ." Gus let out an exasperated sigh, and Farcett nodded knowingly. Fox-Selwyn continued trying to explain: "Gus, I couldn't risk finding out."

"Come off it, George," said Gus. "It's obvious, isn't it? The man's a crook."

"I know that's the only explanation," his brother replied with resignation. "But if you'd seen the nobility of which he is capable, if you'd talked to him about opera or painting, you'd know that there's far more to him than that."

"Probably been swotting up to see what's worth pinching. I'll tell the servants to count the spoons before he leaves here."

"He will behave with absolute dignity, I can assure you. That is, as long as we can get him off this drug. That's where you come in, Robert."

"Well, it sounds as if you've done the most difficult bit yourself, George," said the doctor. "If he really hasn't got any more of that stuff, he's unlikely to find any around here. But if he's genuinely addicted, the next few days aren't going to be pleasant. He'll have to be watched at all times."

George worked out the practicalities. "I could stay with him tonight. Then perhaps Chivers could help."

"And there's a nice new girl working in the kitchen who'd make a good nurse. She's Harvey's niece, just come over from the islands," said Gus.

George was skeptical.

"We'd have to be able to trust her not to spread gossip," he said.

"Don't worry about that. Her voice is so quiet and her accent's so thick no one can understand a word she says. And she's so scared of me that one word about confidentiality should shut her up forever."

As he spoke, there was a creaking noise. The shy figure of the girl in question backed into the room, forcing open the wide oak door with her bottom, while balancing a tray almost as wide as her arms would reach. Three hefty portions of apple pie and custard steamed ahead of her as she made her way to the table and nervously placed them in front of the men. Relieved that she hadn't dropped anything, she bobbed a quick curtsy and hurriedly made off, freezing in terror as Gus boomed: "Young lady!"

"Yes, sir," she whispered, staring at the floor. The Marquess had never spoken to her directly before.

"What is your name?" he boomed.

"Morag, sir," she mumbled, looking scared and much younger than her fifteen years.

"Well, Morag, I want you to come and see me after breakfast tomorrow. And don't look so frightened, I'm not going to give you the sack."

"Thank you, sir," she said, bobbing again, but still not daring to meet his eyes. "Will that be all, sir?"

"That's all for now, Morag. I'll see you in the morning."

Morag left the room quietly, but the moment the door was closed the men heard rapid footsteps as the terrified girl ran back to the kitchen to tell Cook what the Marquess had said.

When she got there, most of the staff were sitting around a long table, tucking into the same meal that the Marquess and his guests were eating upstairs. Two kitchen maids had already started washing up the debris of the early courses, but their heads were turned to listen to Chivers, Fox-Selwyn's manservant from London, who was doing his best to evade questions about the mysterious man asleep in the old nursery. At supper the night before they'd pumped him for information about that day's surprise arrival, Doctor Farcett. Chivers had been quite forthcoming. But Chivers knew his place. He had said nothing about Farcett's great gloom on the train, and had told the story of the choking man at Aberdeen without mentioning his part in forcing the reluctant doctor to act. They had loved the tale of the rescue, and the glamorous Doctor Farcett was already the subject of flirty gossip among the housemaids.

Chivers did not know the full details of Montmorency's problems, but Fox-Selwyn's manner as they had helped him to bed had warned him to be discreet. As so often with his master's affairs, there were things that should not be talked about. But Chivers knew he would have to give out a little information about Montmorency, or his old friends below stairs at Glendarvie would sense that something really interesting was going on.

"So you know him, then?" said Cook.

"Oh yes, indeed," Chivers replied. "He's one of my master's greatest friends. He's full of life and fun."

"He looked half dead when I picked him up from the train," said Harvey.

"What's his name, anyway?" asked Cook.

"Montgomery or something," said Harvey. "I didn't

quite catch what his lordship said when we were carrying him in."

"It's Montmorency," said Chivers. At least he could tell them that without giving too much away.

"So he's a foreigner, then?" asked one of the maids, as she dried the pie dish.

"No, English, but he's just back from the East. He was abroad with my master for about a year."

"Did you go with them?" asked Cook, hoping for stories of exotic worlds.

"No. I was on loan to the Countess of Morbury," said Chivers, raising an eyebrow and hoping that a few tidbits about the goings-on in that household could divert interest from Montmorency. But Cook was not to be distracted.

"Abroad. Is that where he got ill?"

"Urrgh!" said the maid at the sink, plunging her hands into the dishwater. "He might have some terrible foreign disease. We could all catch it!"

"Don't be silly, child," said Cook. "His lordship doesn't seem to have caught anything, and he's been with this Montravency or whatever his name is for months."

"His lordship is perfectly well," said Chivers. "His lordship is his usual self."

"So he'll be eating us out of house and home then!" cried Cook, leaping up from the table to get back to work. "Harvey, I'll have to send you into the village for a few extra things. I'll do a new list for the morning. And you girls had better get up earlier tomorrow. There'll be extra bread to bake, at least three big breakfasts, and an invalid to cook for. It's a mercy the Marchioness isn't here to see all this carrying-on. Let's hope they're all gone before she gets back."

A bell rang from the drawing room. The Marquess and his guests had finished their supper. Chivers volunteered to go and see what they wanted now.

CHAPTER 10

BREAKFAST NEWS

No one staying at Glendarvie Castle was ever likely to die of starvation. The estate included several farms, producing prime beef and pork, oats, barley, poultry, milk, and eggs. Nearer the house, a team of gardeners worked on vegetable plots that kept the castle in fresh produce throughout the year, and with the help of huge greenhouses supplied all sorts of exotic fruit that would not normally grow so far north. Lord George Fox-Selwyn knew he was in for a substantial breakfast, and got up early to raise an appetite for it by walking through the grounds. He had slept well, in the large leather armchair beside Montmorency's bed, undisturbed by his charge who had barely moved in his sleep. He called Chivers and asked him to take over at Montmorency's bedside, then after a quick wash he pulled on his boots, whistled to Gus's two cocker spaniels, Mac and Tessie, and let himself out the back door.

It was a chilly morning. A light mist had settled into all the hollows and dips below the hill where the castle stood. All was quiet, apart from the crunch of

Fox-Selwyn's own footsteps and the snuffling of the dogs as they sniffed the tracks of foxes that had visited in the night. Now and then a shout or a clang rang out from the kitchen, where work had begun, but as he strode away that noise died, to be replaced by sudden rustlings as birds were disturbed in the bracken and, finally, on the flat land at the bottom of the slope, by the rush and bubble of the river where he intended to put in a few hours' fishing before his stay was over. The deer were still asleep, peacefully gathered in small groups amongst the trees, almost invisible at first glance against the vegetation. It wasn't exactly home. That, for Fox-Selwyn, would always be his London house with its modern conveniences and its easy access to all the fun of the city, but he was comfortable with the peace and stability, so long as he only had to enjoy them for a short time. He looked back towards the castle. There was little sign now of the ancient fortification that had been built in wilder times. The huge towers at either end of the building were new, designed to impress and to exploit the magnificent view of the surrounding hills, rather than to keep out enemies. The sprawling spread of rooms between them was made for comfort, not defense, and the wide meandering drive from the gatehouse to the door seemed to say "Welcome," not "Keep Out." Harvey was coming up it now, in the carriage. He had been into the village to collect the post and Cook's extra supplies. Mac and Tessie ran over and followed the cart up the hill and around to the back door. Fox-Selwyn caught up a little later, panting from the unaccustomed exercise. He sat on a low wall watching as Harvey fought off the boisterous dogs, who knew full well that they had no hope of any tidbits but jumped up demanding them anyway. Harvey unloaded his boxes. On top of one was a London newspaper. Gus had it sent up specially, so that he could keep abreast of developments in a world that intrigued him, but of which he had no desire to be a part. The paper took two days to get to Glendarvie, by which time, as Gus was fond of reminding people, most of the important things were unimportant again.

The newspaper Harvey delivered that day had been printed as Fox-Selwyn and Montmorency were traveling north on the sleeper. The journalists had had to work hard to get a late-night development onto the front page of the morning edition. The headline was bigger than usual, reflecting their excitement at the story, and handily reducing the space for the few details they had managed to collect about what had happened. As soon as he saw it, Fox-Selwyn was reminded of that mysterious noise as the train had left the station. It seemed like an age ago. In fact just three nights had passed.

"EXPLOSION AT KING'S CROSS," read the headline. "TWO KILLED, SEVEN INJURED." Then below, in slightly smaller type: "GAS COMPANY BEGINS INQUIRY." The story told of a scene of chaos as firemen had struggled to clear the area. For a while there had been a fear that the big gasworks next to the station might go up, too. Houses and flats on nearby streets had been evacuated in case there was another blast, and the paper's reporter, kept outside the safety barrier with the frightened residents, had spent his time getting their tales of woe. His report was short on detail about the blast itself, but he wrote forcefully of the choking smell of gas, and the bravery of the rescue workers, struggling in the dark, afraid to use lights in case a spark made things worse. The paper said the dead were believed to be a middle-aged woman and a vagrant of no fixed address. Fox-Selwyn thought back to the scene at the station that night. He remembered seeing a filthy tramp sitting at the station entrance, begging money from the passengers arriving for the late train. He was slightly ashamed that he'd ignored him, though money would be of no use to him now. He recalled the party of well-wishers seeing off the honeymoon couple, and how they had laughed at him in his nightshirt. He reckoned they must have been leaving the station, happily exhausted by a day of celebration, just as the bomb went off. That big white handkerchief waving from the platform had been the last thing he'd seen as the train moved away and he had toppled over in Montmorency's compartment. He hoped the jolly family hadn't been caught up in the blast. He feared that they had. His appetite was gone again.

He went into the breakfast room and ignored the groaning display of eggs, meat, bread, porridge, and fruit. He poured himself a cup of coffee, and sat down to read the paper more carefully. Gus, and then Farcett, joined him. Each of them was alarmed by the news, but quickly turned from it to the prospects for the day ahead. As they worked through their breakfasts, Doctor Farcett outlined his plans for Montmorency.

"How was he in the night?" he asked Fox-Selwyn.

"Hardly moved a muscle."

"Good," said the doctor. "I want to be there when he wakes up."

"Is that wise?" asked the Marquess. "He'll get a bit

of a shock if he recognizes you, won't he? After all, he hasn't seen you since he was in jail."

"Exactly," said Farcett. "But what I'm hoping is that he won't be surprised. Think about it. In those few moments after he comes around, seeing my face might actually seem like the most natural thing in the world to him. After all, I was the first person he saw after countless anesthetics. My plan is that we can break the ice while he's still feeling groggy. He can ask questions later when he's accepted that I'm here."

Gus was disappointed. "So you'll be keeping watch today then, Robert? Pity, I was hoping we might get some fishing in. Here, you'd better take him some breakfast." And Gus walked along the sideboard, raising one silver dome after another, loading up a plate with everything from black pudding to cheese. "I'll get them to bring you up some coffee. Off you go."

Doctor Farcett made his way back upstairs, balancing the heavy plate as best he could. For two hours he sat, reading a book and occasionally picking at the food, till only a few congealed scraps remained. He was beginning to wonder whether the mysterious drug had in some way paralyzed Montmorency forever, when his patient suddenly started to stir.

CHAPTER 11

AT THE HEART OF POWER

Down in London, the new Home Secretary was not a happy man. He had enjoyed his time at the Foreign Office, surrounded by clever diplomats and dealing with glamorous foreign dignitaries. He had expected to spend the last few years of his political life there, with the occasional welcome break when his party was out of power. But the Prime Minister was in a pickle. A troublesome but popular Member of Parliament, threatening to challenge him for the party leadership, had indicated that he might find it in his heart to be loyal if he were made Foreign Secretary, and the Cabinet had duly been shuffled. So the man who had delighted in international intrigue was moved sideways to the Home Office, where he was in charge of a ragbag of domestic matters. He could already see that he would be all right as long as everything ran smoothly, but nothing ever did. If there wasn't a problem in the prisons, there was trouble with the police. And now a bomb had gone off in London. The Prime Minister was looking to him for action. He was stuck in the sweltering city while his wife and family frolicked in the country, and he had absolutely no idea what to do.

He'd had one stroke of luck. The blast had split a gas main, and the papers had jumped to the conclusion that gas was to blame. But the gas company was sure that the explosion had caused the leak, not the other way around. Fortunately, the head of the firm had been persuaded to keep quiet "in the interests of national security," and the inspector who had identified the real cause of the blast was assigned urgent work, far away. The new Home Secretary was quite proud that for once he had thought on his feet and done something decisive, but he knew he could only maintain the lie about the gas because it was the summer, and Parliament was on holiday. If he had been asked questions in the Commons, and told them it wasn't a bomb, he'd have risked getting the sack for misleading the House. And even if public panic had been avoided, the fact remained that there was a bomber on the loose, and it was the Home Secretary's job to find out who and where he was.

What had the bomber wanted to achieve? A change in government policy? The release of a particular prisoner? The downfall of the whole political system? He had no way of knowing. No one had admitted setting off the blast. No one had demanded anything. No one had seen anything suspicious on the night in question. A public appeal for information would only stir up the fears and rumors that had washed through London after a series of bomb blasts earlier in the year. At his wife's flower-arranging group there was hysterical talk of anarchist cells simply trying to spread terror so that the people would turn against their leaders. His butler's calm demeanor was occasionally punctured by rants against the Fenians: nationalists who wanted their British rulers out of Ireland. In the office, where a small team was in on the secret of the King's Cross bomb, the new Home Secretary had patiently listened to theories about Indians, Africans, Communists, Nihilists, and assorted nutcases. Who were these people? Where did they live? How did they operate? He had ordered his new officials to produce a briefing, and their fuzzy theories took up page after page of paper, but told him nothing at all.

He had asked to see the most secret reports from the police at Scotland Yard. They had a department that was supposed to specialize in tracking Fenian activists, but it was in demoralized disarray after the comic tragedy of seeing its own office blown up a year before. In retrospect, it had been foolish to set up the headquarters of the unit directly above a public lavatory. It was embarrassing, to say the least, that one of their own men, on duty outside the Gents, had actually nodded a greeting to the bomber on his way in. In the end, the main result of that operation had been the closure of several other public conveniences across London. The new Home Secretary thought the resulting discomfort for the population of the capital was a major victory for the bombers. But he didn't dare say so to his staff.

He had to cope with personal suspicion, too. Officials at the Home Office had long regarded their counterparts in the Foreign Service as featherbedded amateurs. He knew that disrespect extended to himself, and that many of the men employed to do his bidding privately regarded him with contempt. Meanwhile his old secret intelligence machine at the Foreign Office had a new master. They knew more than Scotland Yard about foreign agents at work in Britain, but they had no intention of sharing that information with the Home Office. From another building, the War Office commanded its own set of spies, but like everyone else, they were keeping their precious information to themselves.

It was a mess. Someone would have to sort it out, but as Home Secretary he felt he was the worst person to take on the job. Foiling the bombers was going to mean bending the rules, and the number one priority of the Home Office was to uphold the law. He thought back to how much simpler it had been to track down enemies abroad, and how his old friend Lord George Fox-Selwyn, with his sidekick Montmorency, had done wonders quietly undermining threats to British interests, and without the press on their heels nagging for results. The new Home Secretary knew that some of Fox-Selwyn's tactics were unorthodox. He could never have defended to the House of Commons the sort of bribery, spying, and skulduggery that Fox-Selwyn and Montmorency had sometimes used in foreign lands. It offended the British instinct for fair play and personal privacy. But surely something like that was needed now, here, in Britain itself?

The Home Secretary wanted to talk to Lord George Fox-Selwyn. He told his officials that he needed a quiet walk, took up his hat and his cane, and set off across St. James's Park in the direction of his friend's house. The windows were shuttered. Fox-Selwyn was out of town. The Home Secretary walked on to Bargles, looking for Montmorency. Sam at the door was very solicitous, congratulating the Minister on his new appointment, but unable to enlighten him as to Montmorency's and Fox-Selwyn's whereabouts, beyond saying that they were "in Scotland."

No wonder we can't track down the bombers, thought the Home Secretary, *if it's this difficult to find your friends!*

To make things worse, the doorman went into a grand description of the burglary of Montmorency's room earlier that week. "It's shocking, isn't it, sir, the amount of crime these days? The police just don't seem to be on top of it." He paused, and added, "But that's your department, now, sir, is it not?"

"Yes, Sam," replied the Home Secretary, with a sinking heart. "If in doubt, blame me!" And he walked slowly back to the Home Office wondering why a career in public life had ever held any appeal.

Still, there was one thing to look forward to. He had a ticket for the opera at eight o'clock. He always tried to let go of his troubles there. But somehow that night the scenes of betrayal, depravity, and assassination only reminded him of his own responsibilities and failures. As he walked away from the Opera House towards the Strand, a tall, overly made-up woman, leaning against a wall, pouted at him and called out,

"Cheer up, darling! You look like you need a bit of company!" She didn't sound as if she expected a reply, but she got one.

"Do you know?" he found himself saying to her. "I do believe I do."

Hours later, very much the worse for drink, he thought that perhaps he had told her more than he should about his problems. The next day, as the hangover started to fade, he realized that she had told him something important, too.

CHAPTER 12

WAKING TO A NIGHTMARE

Montmorency knew he was waking up. He was conscious of a cramp in his calf, and the need to stretch out and rub the knot of twisted flesh. He couldn't make himself open his eyes. Strange images were still playing out in his mind, and he was trying to sort them into some kind of coherent shape. Where was he? Why did he feel so ill? His bladder was full, and for a moment he tried to make his muscles pull him from the bed, but his exhaustion and his swimming mind persuaded him that it wasn't worth the effort, and he soon felt a warm wetness soaking into the sheets. He sensed that someone was with him and pried his eyelids apart. It was only Doctor Farcett. He must have had another operation. That would explain it all. He let himself fall back into his dream, this time flooded with images of prison and the hospital, and of his body being on display. But he kept almost surfacing, driven into consciousness by hunger, or was it thirst? He passionately needed to taste that taste: a rancid, sticky bitterness that he could conjure up in his memory, but not put a name to. The pictures in his mind shifted to a Turkish market, and a filthy hand passing him a leather pouch in exchange for cash. The drug. He had to have the drug. He lurched upright in bed, and tore back the sheets. Doctor Farcett grabbed his shoulders and forced him back down. Doctor Farcett. What was he doing in Turkey? But this wasn't Turkey. It wasn't prison either. It wasn't Bargles, or the Marimion Hotel. Montmorency started to struggle and shout, tearing at Farcett's hair and squirming to twist out of his grip. The door flew open, and Fox-Selwyn rushed to help. The two spaniels, Mac and Tessie, ran in, too, hurling themselves onto the bed, and licked at the stranger's slippery skin. This wasn't the gentle awakening Doctor Farcett had hoped for. He seized his bag and poured some chloroform onto a handkerchief, then slammed it over Montmorency's mouth and nose, wrestling him down onto the pillow. After a few seconds Montmorency was quiet, a desperate look of confusion in his eyes as they swept from Farcett to Fox-Selwyn and back again. Then the lids closed, and he sank back into oblivion.

Doctor Farcett sighed, "This is going to be even more difficult than I thought."

"Perhaps I should stay here for a while," said Fox-Selwyn. "You'd better send Morag up to change the sheets."

The doctor turned to go. As he left, Mac and Tessie found the remains of the breakfast on the floor by the chair. They managed to clear the plate before Lord George Fox-Selwyn roughly forced them from the room.

Morag had been given a gentle but stern talking to by the Marquess, who had left her in no doubt that her new tasks required absolute discretion. She was not to engage in tittle-tattle with the other servants about the invalid, and she was to do everything Doctor Farcett asked. To make things easier for her, the Marquess accompanied Morag to the kitchen afterward to explain to Cook why she would be unavailable for some of her usual duties.

He dragged his finger through some cake mixture around the edge of a bowl as he spoke, between licks, of the unfortunate illness that Lord George Fox-Selwyn's friend had contracted abroad. The kitchen maid whose theory of a foreign disease had been dismissed the night before hid a smug smile as she peeled the potatoes. Without actually saying so, Gus implied that the illness might be contagious, hoping fear would make the servants keep their distance; but he spoke hopefully of the prospects of recovery, even though, in his heart, he had his doubts.

Cook said she quite understood (while sliding a block of cheese under a cloth to keep her master's hands off it) and wished the unexpected guest a speedy return to health.

"Will he be needing any special food?" she asked.

"Not at this stage, Cook, though I'm sure Doctor Farcett will let you know if he does."

And as the Marquess reached out towards a very inviting bunch of grapes on the dresser, the doctor arrived on his mission to send Morag to the linen cupboard.

With Chivers's help Morag turned the mattress and at his suggestion she laid an oilcloth under the new sheets in case of further "accidents." Alone, she bathed Montmorency's scarred body as it lay slumped in the armchair, then called Chivers again to help her settle him back into bed. She was intrigued by the scars but, as instructed, said nothing about them when she went downstairs to help serve lunch. Fox-Selwyn sat with Montmorency for the rest of the day. Morag carried him trays of refreshments from time to time, fighting off Mac and Tessie, who leaped up at her on the stairs in the hope of dragging a morsel from the plates. Every time she entered the room, she noticed that Montmorency was more agitated, though not fully conscious. At teatime she helped Fox-Selwyn encourage him to take a sip of water. After a few moments he gulped down the rest of the glass. Five minutes later she was stripping the bed again, this time to clear away the slimy green contents of his belly, which had come up as fast as the water had gone down. When she returned with clean bedding, she stopped outside the door. The two men were shouting at each other.

"Get it for me, George!" pleaded Montmorency. "You know where it is. I know you took it from me on the train."

"I did, and I threw it away."

"But it's mine! You had no right!"

"I had more than a right, I had a duty!"

"But I need it."

"I know, and that's why it's gone."

Montmorency's voice dropped to a pitiful whine. "Get it back, George. Get it back for me."

"I can't, and I wouldn't if I could."

"But I only need a little, George. It doesn't do me any harm."

"It does you nothing but harm. It's killing you. And I'm not going to let you die."

"But it will stop the dreams, George."

"It's giving you the dreams, man! Can't you see? Your whole world is becoming unreal."

Montmorency was sobbing now. "You're right," he said, remembering images that had been running through his head. "I thought I saw Doctor Farcett, sitting in that chair, as clear as you are now. I never told you about Doctor Farcett, did I, George?"

"No, and you don't need to," said Fox-Selwyn, soothingly. He didn't want to explain about the doctor now. Playing for time, he changed the subject. "I wonder where Morag's got to with those sheets."

Morag heard her cue, and tapped gently on the door. She and Fox-Selwyn helped Montmorency into the chair. Then they made the bed, pushing the playful dogs out of the way as they jumped about and got caught in the flapping linens. Morag had not been at Glendarvie long, but she knew her place, and the place of her employers. It was strange to find herself sharing such a menial task with her master's brother. She instinctively knew that she should not mention it downstairs. An odd, conspiratorial bond was growing between her and these anxious men from London.

Montmorency whimpered weakly as they tucked him in. Mac and Tessie snuggled up close to him, offering comfort. This time Fox-Selwyn didn't push them away. He left them on the bed to keep guard while Morag returned to her normal duties, and he went down to ask Gus and Farcett what on earth they should do next.

"It's not really my field," said Doctor Farcett as the men sat down to dine. "I'm a surgeon. There are people who specialize in this sort of thing."

"But you're here, Robert," said Fox-Selwyn with some impatience, "and I can trust you. And you must have talked to some of these specialists over the years. Surely you can come up with some sort of plan."

"Well, all I can say is that we have to get all the poison out of his system."

"He seems to be doing a grand job chucking it out himself!" laughed the Marquess, thinking of the growing mound of washing in the laundry room.

"It's not a joke, Gus." Fox-Selwyn was getting irritated by his brother's attitude.

"No, he's right," said Farcett. "The vomiting is good."

"Pass me the sauce, old boy." Gus was not one to be put off his food by robust anatomical talk.

Fox-Selwyn pushed the jug across the table and continued, "So we clean him out, but then what? His body's still asking for more of that vile drug."

"Well, for every other illness," said Farcett, "I recommend fresh air and exercise."

"Just like school," said Gus. "*Mens sana in corpore sano.*"

"'A healthy mind in a healthy body.' Well, that is what we're trying to achieve here, isn't it?" said George. "More wine, anyone?"

"So it's long walks and a spot of swimming. Should do us all good!" Gus patted his stomach as he reached for the potatoes.

"Always assuming, of course, that he doesn't have any more of the stuff," mused Farcett. "I mean, you say you threw it all away, but how do you know he didn't have any more stashed away somewhere? Mind you, I wouldn't mind seeing a bit. Then I'd have a better idea of what we're dealing with here. . . ."

"Who's with him now?" Gus interrupted, as Morag arrived, backward again, with a tray of extra vegetables.

The three men looked at one another, then ran up the stairs to find Mac and Tessie fast asleep on the pillow and Montmorency sitting on the edge of the bed holding one of his wading boots upside down, shaking it violently, willing it not to be empty.

"I was just looking . . ." he began, as Fox-Selwyn had the presence of mind to push his brother and the doctor out of sight.

"I know what you were looking for!" said Fox-Selwyn, angrily. "Get up, you're sleeping in Chivers's room tonight."

He bundled Montmorency off to the tower, where the long-suffering Chivers accepted the situation without a murmur. Chivers sat through Montmorency's crying and raving all night, while the others ransacked his belongings. They looked in every book, every glove, every shoe. Sometimes they got distracted. Gus was greatly taken with the new fishing rod, and nearly took his brother's eye out pretending to cast a line. Farcett was awestruck at the size of the outfitter's bill folded in among the new clothes. But they found nothing.

"Right then," said the Marquess as they surveyed the devastation around them. "It seems that Montmorency's recovery can begin!"

CHAPTER 13

REUNION

And the next morning it did, but not before the encounter Fox-Selwyn had been dreading, which he knew he could delay no longer. Montmorency had to meet Farcett, and let him back into his life. When the old nursery had been tidied again, Chivers brought Montmorency back down and eased him into the armchair, covered with a blanket. Then, tired after his uncomfortable night, he went to find his master, to report on the patient's calmer mood. Montmorency sat alone, gazing at the room. The shutters had been opened, and for the first time he could make sense of the shapes that had swirled around him in his dark, disordered dreams. The looming monster turned out to be an ancient rocking horse covered over with a sheet. The man with the dagger was a broken hat stand, from which dangled a single, furled umbrella, and the mysterious, mocking laughter was the sound of a bird perched on top of the chimney, its coos and squawks echoing down into the fireplace.

There was a rap on the door, and Fox-Selwyn entered without waiting for permission. In his shame Montmorency turned his head away. Fox-Selwyn tried to sound relaxed.

"Well," he said, rather too brightly. "This is Glendarvie."

"I know," said Montmorency, meekly. "Chivers told me."

Fox-Selwyn walked around the room, distractedly picking up and fiddling with familiar objects from his childhood.

"This was the nursery when Gus and I were boys," he said, as he tried to fix a wheel back on a rusty model train. "We broke just about everything, though. The children have got a new room now, on the other side of the house." George pulled the sheet off the horse, and started rocking it to and fro, patting its neck affectionately. He still couldn't look Montmorency in the eye. "I remember being in here for weeks when I had scarlet fever."

"And me?" said Montmorency. "Have I been here for weeks?"

"No. Two days, that's all. You're looking better," said George, though in fact he was still facing the other way.

"There's nothing wrong with me," said Montmorency, trying to stand up and almost toppling over.

Fox-Selwyn jumped forward to steady his friend, and gently lowered him back into the chair. "Be careful," he said. "It nearly killed you this time, Montmorency. That drug has worked its way into your very soul. You have to get over it. You have to fight back."

"I will, but it's so hard."

"That's why I've got someone to help you."

"But I don't want strangers around me," pleaded Montmorency. "I don't want anyone to know."

"The doctor already knows," said George. "He was here when you were at your worst. And he's not a stranger. Prepare yourself for a surprise, Montmorency. Perhaps even a shock."

Outside the door, Doctor Farcett was listening in. He knew the risk that Fox-Selwyn was taking by engineering this meeting. Fox-Selwyn and Montmorency had depended on each other for five years, and all that time, Fox-Selwyn had kept Farcett a secret from him. Would Montmorency be enraged by the deception? Yet Fox-Selwyn had done it because he suspected Montmorency had secrets of his own. They would have to come out now. Could the friendship survive those revelations? And how would Montmorency react to seeing Farcett again? He had suffered excruciating pain at the doctor's hands, and been displayed, night after night at the Scientific Society as a testament to Farcett's surgical skill. Exposed, almost naked, before an inquisitive crowd, he had been stripped of his dignity as well as his freedom. Farcett had been like the ringmaster in a circus. Would Montmorency be able to forgive him? Should he forgive him? Farcett had his doubts.

Fox-Selwyn went to the door. "All right, Robert," he called. "You can come in now."

Montmorency watched as the doctor entered the room. He knew at once who it was. "Doctor Farcett!" he said, staring up at the man whose hand was reaching out to shake his own. And then, bizarrely, he felt the need to introduce the surgeon to his friend. "George, this is Doctor Farcett. He . . . He . . ." Montmorency struggled to find a way of explaining how he knew the doctor. In an instant, images of the prison, the hospital, and the stage at the Scientific Society took him back to the time when Farcett was rebuilding his body. How could he put all that into words? In the end he simply stuttered, "He saved my life."

"I know," said George, as the doctor shook Montmorency's hand. "Robert and I have been friends for many years. I think the time has come for you to meet again."

Now it was Farcett's turn to grope for words. For all the intimacy of their old relationship, he had never addressed this patient as an equal, or indeed as a fully sentient human being. And yet here was Montmorency, alive and apparently grateful. He felt tears stinging his eyes. All he could say was an embarrassed social greeting. "I'm delighted to meet you again, Mr. Montmorency."

"Or should that be 493?" said Montmorency, referring back to his old prison number.

The doctor smiled. "493, indeed," he said. "I've often wondered what became of you." He thought back to the letter and the money he had left for Montmorency on his release. "Tell me, why did you never contact me? I left my address . . ."

Montmorency remembered the envelope he had been given by the warden on the day he left prison. "So it *was* you who sent that envelope! I never got the chance to open it. One of the guards took it away."

"I was so disappointed that you never came. I was offering to pay you if I could continue to work on your wounds."

Fox-Selwyn interrupted. "That was good of you, Robert."

"No, George," snapped Farcett. "Not good at all. I wasn't doing it for his benefit. I was thinking of my own career. Montmorency here doesn't owe me anything. I owe him the foundation of my success."

Fox-Selwyn sensed that Farcett was in danger of sliding back into professional gloom just when his skills were needed. He appealed to the doctor's heightened guilt. "Well, here's a chance to repay him. If you can bring the real Montmorency back to us, neither of you will owe the other anything."

This time Montmorency jumped in. "You mean we'll each owe the other everything," he said.

It was a debt they both felt they could accept, and doctor and patient spent the morning getting reacquainted on a gentle walk, which marked the beginning of Montmorency's rehabilitation. At lunchtime he was introduced to Gus, to whom he apologized profusely for his behavior and all the trouble he was causing. Over the next couple of weeks, the walks grew more demanding, and Montmorency was to be found taking exercise out and about across the estate, with Mac and Tessie never far away. In time his sudden episodes of shivering or violence decreased, and then disappeared. Now and then there was a little pathetic crying, but nothing like the ravages of despair that had rocked him the first few days. Montmorency gradually revealed more and more about himself to Gus and Robert, and even George found out some things he didn't know. But one question always remained unanswered. No one could coax him to talk in detail about how he financed his transformation from a convict to a gentleman, and any probing brought out his darker side.

Gus tried harder than anyone else to get to the truth, thinking he had picked a good moment in the mellow haze of cigar smoke that followed a particularly good dinner. "Come on, Monty, tell us how you did it. Were you a smash-and-grab man, or a fraudster?"

Montmorency snarled back, "I was a thief, all right. That's all I've got to say," and he slammed the door behind him as he left the room. The others interpreted his reaction as shame. Montmorency, stomping through the garden under the stars, knew it was something else. He couldn't bring himself to reveal the secret underground world of the sewers even to his dearest friends. How close would someone have to be before he could let them share that private world?

⋙⋙⋙

The next day the others let the matter drop. Gus's wife and children were due back from their trip, and none of the men wanted to risk presenting the Marchioness with Montmorency at his worst. As it turned out, she found Montmorency charming and full of wholesome fun. She loved the way he would let the children and dogs accompany him rambling through the countryside or rowing on the lake. She was, as Gus had expected, cross with George for not giving her any warning of his arrival, but she was proud that her staff had obviously coped well in her absence. And though she would never enjoy sharing her home with visitors, if she had to have them, these three congenial men, without any airs or graces, were the sort she preferred.

CHAPTER 14

NEWS FROM NORTH AND SOUTH

Then one morning they were all in the breakfast room, Mac weaving between their feet in the hope of some food falling to the floor, and Tessie in trouble, as usual, for putting her paws on the table and trying to steal sausages from people's plates. She saw a chance when Montmorency pushed a piece of bacon rind to one side. As she lunged for it, Gus shouted his usual harsh, "Tessie — off!" and for once the animal dropped down and ran out of the room, closely followed by her brother.

"Well!" said the Marchioness in amazement. "It seems you've finally gotten control of those dogs, Gus. Well done." But the dogs weren't being obedient after all. They had heard the sound of Harvey's cart plodding up the drive, and had dashed out to greet him, their long, floppy ears flying out almost at right angles as they sped across the grass. The company watched from the window as Harvey stopped to hand an envelope to Morag, then climbed down from the cart and rushed in to give Lord George Fox-Selwyn a telegram. Everyone fell silent as he opened it, pretending not to pry, but all longing to know what it said. The Marchioness cracked first.

"Not bad news, I hope?" she inquired.

"No," said George, folding the paper and tucking it into his waistcoat pocket, "not really. Inconvenient, though. It's from the Home Secretary." Gus let out a loud, exasperated sigh. His wife looked excited as George continued, "I've got to go back to London."

The conversation shifted to train times and packed lunches. Doctor Farcett took Fox-Selwyn to one side and whispered, "You can't take Montmorency. It wouldn't be safe."

"I know," replied Fox-Selwyn, quietly. "You stay here with him. I'll try to get back in a few days."

As he spoke, Harvey reentered the room. When he opened the door a distant high-pitched howling could be heard.

"Ah, Harvey," said the Marchioness, preoccupied with arrangements for George's journey. "We'll need you to take Lord George Fox-Selwyn to the station. . . ." Then even she heard the wailing. "Good heavens," she said. "Whatever is the matter? What is that noise?"

"It's Morag, ma'am," Harvey explained. "She got a letter this morning, and I'm afraid she's had a bit of a shock. Her baby brother has died. Her mother has taken it very hard, ma'am. Her parents want her to leave Glendarvie for good and return to Tarimond. I was wondering if I could take her home, ma'am."

"Oh dear," said the Marchioness, flustered at the possible upset to her household. "That really would be most inconvenient, especially when we have guests staying. It's hundreds of miles, and you'd have to wait for a boat to the island. You'll be away for at least a week, even if it all goes smoothly. I really don't think . . ."

But Doctor Farcett was thinking, and quickly. "It's all right, Lorna. I could take Morag home. I've always wanted to see the islands. And you could come with me, couldn't you, Montmorency?" he added, as if it were an afterthought.

"Oh, would you?" said the Marchioness, unable to disguise her relief at the prospect of disposing of all her guests at once. "I'm sure Morag's family would be grateful, and we could keep Harvey here at home."

"It would be a pleasure," said Montmorency. "A sad pleasure," he corrected himself, remembering Morag's loss and that Harvey, her uncle, was still in the room.

And so, before lunchtime, a carriage was loaded with luggage and refreshments, and all the visitors set off for Glendarvie Station, where they started their long journeys with a slow trundle north. The two parties split at a railway junction famous for having hundreds of empty whisky barrels piled high beside the track. Fox-Selwyn and Chivers boarded the eastbound train to Aberdeen. George had polished off his picnic well before Inverurie. Farcett and Montmorency were more restrained in the company of the grieving Morag. They managed to keep their hands off their hamper, even though they had a long wait for the opposite service, westward to connections with steamboats to the Isles.

CHAPTER 15

CAPITAL CRIMES

Lord George Fox-Selwyn loved London, but it was the summer, it was hot, and most of his friends were out of town. As soon as they were home, Chivers ran him a bath, and took the dust sheets off the furniture, while Fox-Selwyn composed a note to the Home Secretary announcing his return. He wasn't sure why he had been summoned, but the Minister had hinted that it was something to do with the King's Cross explosion. Arriving back on the sleeper, he'd looked for signs of damage at the station, but there was nothing except a bit of new brickwork, and a dab of fresh paint. The explosion had been right outside the ticket counters, at the entrance to the station, and the railway company had been quick to tidy up, afraid that the incident might put people off traveling by train. In the process they had destroyed what little evidence there might have been of the source of the blast. There was almost nothing about the explosion in the paper Fox-Selwyn bought at the station book kiosk. Just a few angry letters railing against shoddy work practices in the gas companies and demanding new regulations to improve standards.

Fox-Selwyn had almost finished dressing when the messenger brought the reply to his note. The Home Secretary wanted to see him, but not at the office. They would meet in St. James's Park, by the pond, at three. Fox-Selwyn got there first, and watched the ducks bobbing happily in the water. He looked up and saw a familiar tall figure walking towards him, but his old school friend was hunched and stared at his feet. He was not his usual confident (and occasionally overconfident) self.

"How's the new job, then?" Fox-Selwyn asked as they shook hands.

"Purgatory, old boy. Purgatory," said the Home Secretary, gloomily. "I don't like it and it doesn't like me. Just when I think I'm on top of one problem, another crops up from a completely different angle."

"But it was like that in the Foreign Office, surely."

"Yes, but there we could always blame Johnny Foreigner, and most people aren't interested in abroad anyway. Everybody thinks they know all about Britain. Everyone's an expert on the bloody Home Office. I've even got my gardener telling me what to do."

"And what's his advice?"

"Lock everybody up. Except him, of course. Sometimes I think he's got a point."

"So how can I help?"

"It's this bomb."

"So it was a bomb, then, not a gas leak?"

"I wish it had been gas," said the Home Secretary. "But yes, it was a bomb — homemade, but effective. Probably left in a rubbish bin or a suitcase. Huge mess on that night. Like a butcher shop apparently. Those poor souls were blown to pieces. They cleaned it all up in the dark, and there was nothing to see by morning. It split a gas pipe, so we can play up the possibility of a leak, and keep down the panic. But it was a bomb. The question is, who planted it?"

"Irish or anarchists, you mean?" said Fox-Selwyn.

"Or anyone else you might care to mention: Russians, Indians, Africans, Afghans, Slavs, Serbs, a single madman. Take your pick. . . ."

"What do your people say?"

"My people, George, say a lot. But they haven't got the slightest idea."

"And that's where I come in?"

"That's where you come in. Treat it like a foreign assignment, George. This is unfamiliar territory. I want you to operate where my people don't usually go.

And I think I might be able to give you a bit of a start. I heard something the other day that set me thinking. When I tell you who I heard it from, and where, you'll understand why I can't pass it on to my people." And the Home Secretary, a man who had kissed hands with the Queen (who would, indeed, in the wholly improbable event of Her Majesty producing another child, be required to be present at the very delivery), told Fox-Selwyn of his night out after the opera, and how a sympathetic working woman had told him of a man who had rented a room in her house on the night of the blast. He had steeled himself many times to tell his Permanent Secretary or the Commissioner of the Metropolitan Police what he knew. Each time he looked into the eyes of those pillars of rectitude he lost his nerve, particularly as he had been too drunk on the night of the opera to remember now either the woman's name or where she lived. He couldn't remember exactly what she had said either, but he could recall a moment of clear insight that had convinced him she held the key, or one of the keys, to the mystery.

"So it's over to you," he said to Fox-Selwyn. "I can't make it official, of course. . . ."

"Of course."

"But I'll back you in whatever you do, and I'll see

that you're all right if you're arrested or anything like that."

"Like you did in Persia?" Fox-Selwyn knew he was being a little unfair, recalling the one occasion when his employer had let him down, and left him languishing in a filthy cell for weeks.

"You know I couldn't admit we were behind that one."

"Exactly, and the same applies now, doesn't it?"

"It might. Unless it works, of course."

"In which case you'll take the credit."

"That's politics, George! Of course, if you're not interested . . ."

"I didn't say that."

"Of course you didn't." The Home Secretary slapped his old friend on the back. "You'll do it, won't you?"

"I'll try, but you'll have to keep me up to date with what your people know."

"That won't take long!" scoffed the Minister, bitterly. Adding, "And get your friend Montmorency in on it. This should be right up his alley."

Fox-Selwyn fell silent as he pondered how the old Montmorency would have relished this task. Was he strong enough to be brought back to work? Could he resist the many temptations of London life? Fox-Selwyn doubted it. The Home Secretary interrupted his thoughts.

"What were you two doing in Scotland, anyway?"

"Oh, just pootling about."

"George, you're not cut out for pootling and you know it. Poor old Montmorency will probably go mad if you keep him up there." (*He'll go mad if I bring him down here*, thought Fox-Selwyn.) "What's up, George? Why do you keep going quiet on me?"

"I don't know," sighed Fox-Selwyn. "Too much country air, I suppose."

"Exactly, you need more excitement. Will you take on the job?"

"I'll do my best for you."

"Not just for me, for the Queen."

"Oh, her, too, of course," said Fox-Selwyn, exasperated by his friend's outburst of pomposity. "But most of all so that a fellow can go to a station without getting blown to bits."

The Home Secretary looked around him. A nursemaid was approaching with a pram and an ugly, bored-looking child who was dragging a stick along the railings by the pond. The two men were in the boy's way, and as he went by he simply beat the stick against their legs so as not to disturb the regular thumping noise he was making.

"Now, now, little chap!" said the Minister, in a tone

that could hardly be described as cruel. "That wasn't a very nice thing to do!"

The nurse grabbed the infant by the arm and tugged him away, tossing her head and eyeing the men with an exaggerated gesture of disdain.

"How many times do I have to tell you not to talk to strangers?" she yelled at the child, shaking him till he cried. "You never know what they might do to you! He might want to steal you and sell you into slavery, or eat you for his supper."

"You see? That's what the public thinks of me!" said the Home Secretary, dripping with gloom. Then, once they were alone again, he drew closer to Fox-Selwyn and dropped his voice even lower.

"I'll take the file home from the office tomorrow night. Dinner at six, shall we say?"

"Yes, and I'll bring my reading glasses."

"Good to see you, old boy."

"Tomorrow at six, I'll be there."

They shook hands again, and walked away from the pond in opposite directions, trying to look like two old schoolmates who'd had a chance encounter in the park on a sultry summer afternoon.

CHAPTER 16

OVER THE SEA

It was a three-day trip from Glendarvie to Tarimond, Morag's island home. The little train led to a bigger train, which led to a port, and a night's stay at an inn. By then Farcett and Montmorency were getting used to the hushed music of Morag's voice, and beginning to take in details about her family and life at their remote farm. From the port, a large boat took them to a big island, where a pony and cart carried them through scenes of almost unbearable beauty to another harbor and a bed for another night. Waking early, Montmorency looked out onto blue water, and rugged hills on other islands far away. In the opposite direction, he could just see the tips of the high mountains they had left the day before. He was hungry, and he realized that this was the first morning he had woken longing for food and not for the Turkish drug. How he hated that drug. But now he was thinking about it, how he would have liked just a sniff, just a taste to remind him why he had once found it so alluring. His thoughts were interrupted by Doctor Farcett knocking on his door.

"Get a move on, Montmorency. I've managed to find a boatman who will take us most of the way. And I've got a map."

Montmorency let the doctor in, and he unfolded the paper, spreading it out across the bed. Harvey had tried to point Tarimond out to them on an atlas back at Glendarvie, but the distances had been artificially contracted to get the whole of the British Isles on one page. Now, for the first time, Montmorency could appreciate how far it was to Tarimond. It was one of the most distant of the smattering of islands that were scattered out into the Atlantic Ocean in a northwesterly spray. Morag joined them, and the doctor told her about the boat.

"But it will only take us as far as this island," he said, pointing to Tarimond's neighbor.

"Oh, that's fine!" said Morag. "I know we can find another boat there. We'll have to row the last crossing ourselves. If we leave now we should be there by nightfall."

It was a long, wet, chilly trip, and only Morag's enthusiasm to see her family again kept the men going. As she got nearer to Tarimond, she relaxed, and they chatted more as fellow travelers, and less as masters and servant. She told them about her home on the island. Life was hard there. Most families kept sheep, but they were nothing like the plump and fluffy animals she had seen at Glendarvie. Like the people, the sheep had to scratch what sustenance they could from the hard, rocky ground, and in an unusually dry year, or a drenchingly wet one, humans and animals suffered together. Contact with the mainland was rare, and in some weather even getting there could be dangerous. The people of Tarimond had to be self-sufficient. They couldn't rely on supplies from elsewhere. Life could be short. It had been all too short for Robbie, who like so many infants on the island had seemed strong at birth, but had shriveled and died before he was two months old. Morag's mother had lost five children. Her aunt had a sickly baby, and other families were worried, too. Doctor Farcett's medical brain seized the problem and pondered it as the small craft crossed from island to island. He asked questions.

"Have there always been so many deaths?"

"Oh no," said Morag. "My granny had eleven children, and nine of them are still alive."

"Have all the deaths been in the same family?"

"No. But of course most of us on Tarimond are related in some way."

Montmorency joined in the conversation. Were the babies nursing properly? When did they get ill? Farcett wanted to know more. What were the symptoms of their final illnesses? What did the local doctors say?

"Doctors!" cried Morag, with the first laugh Farcett had ever heard her utter. "Why, we don't have doctors! You are the first doctor I have ever met!"

"So who looks after the sick?"

"We all do, Doctor Farcett, though some of us are better at it than others. Maggie Goudie is the best of all, they say."

"And you, Morag, what do you know?" asked Montmorency.

Morag snapped back with a quick reply. "More than you think, sir. I'm good for more than changing sheets!" She blushed at her presumption, but in their different ways, Montmorency and Farcett were both embarrassed, too. For all his learning, Farcett knew little of traditional remedies and practices that might put his scientific medicine to shame. And Montmorency had a dim memory of this slight, delicate girl cleansing his body, and making him comfortable when he was at his lowest ebb.

⋙⋙⋙

Both men were keen to get to Tarimond, and to see it for themselves, so although they were tired at the end of a long day, they pulled hard on the oars of the rowboat Morag found, where she expected it, secured to a small jetty.

"Whose boat is this? Whom do we pay?" asked Farcett, uneasy at having untied it from its mooring without permission.

"It belongs to everyone," laughed Morag, amused to see the doctor looking around as if he would find a kiosk and a man in a peaked cap ready to sell him a ticket. "There are three of them. We'll just tie this one up on the other side. When all three end up on our island the men row two of them back."

There was a silence, and the regular rhythm of the oars stopped while Montmorency and the doctor worked out what she meant.

"Oh, I see," said Montmorency, at last. "They take two boats over, so they can leave one and use the other to go home."

"But why don't they have more boats? Then they wouldn't need to come over so often," said the doctor.

"Or someone could be given the job of rowing passengers between the islands," suggested Montmorency.

"Listen to you! Hardly arrived, and you're already trying to improve us!" Morag was growing in confidence as she got farther from the castle and nearer to her home patch. Farcett blushed now, at her jolly teasing, but even so, he came up with one more proposal. "Couldn't they just row over paying passengers?"

"And how would they know someone was coming?" asked Morag. "How often do you think we come and go? It's a rarity for us to have visitors. I should have warned you. You're going to get quite a welcome!"

Both Montmorency and Farcett had imagined a quiet arrival at a tiny isolated cottage. It was true that no one was expecting them, but word got around that a boat had been spotted, and before they reached land they were on their way to becoming celebrities. Everyone wanted to see Morag, and to size up the men who had brought her back from Glendarvie Castle. The islanders were restrained in their greetings, mildly intimidated by the newcomers' accents and clothes. They stood back with stern stares, as if expecting an assault on their private territory. But inside they had a good laugh when Montmorency toppled into the sea as he tried to get out of the boat.

CHAPTER 17

AN ISLAND WELCOME

Morag's parents lived in the heart of the island. They had not heard about the new arrivals and were coming to the end of a normal day of hard work. Her mother was in the garden, fighting against the wind to take down the flying washing from the clothesline before nightfall. Morag rushed to her, and the two of them fell into noisy and tearful grieving for Robbie, her dead brother. Montmorency and Farcett couldn't tell whether they were speaking English or some strange local language. But it didn't matter. The women's tone and movement instantly conveyed raw pain, and the men stood well back, anxious not to intrude. Soon Morag's mother caught sight of them, wiped her tears on the sleeve of her dress, and strode forward to greet them, full of gratitude for her daughter's safe return.

Montmorency and Farcett had underestimated the time it took for letters to get from Tarimond to Glendarvie. The note that had reached them earlier that week had been written almost a month before. It had waited at a relay of cottages and boatyards for travelers willing to take it from one island to another, only speeding up when it reached Oban, on the mainland, and the mail train that carried it to Banffshire overnight. The news in the letter was old news. Doctor Farcett was secretly disappointed that there was no body to examine. Robbie was long dead, and buried in the graveyard of the austere stone church on a windswept headland overlooking the sea. His wasn't even the most recent grave. Morag's aunt and another local family were grieving, too.

Inside the family's tiny cottage, Morag's mother motioned to Farcett and Montmorency, inviting them to sit at the table in the center of the room. She took Morag aside and whispered to her, pointing at Montmorency. She wanted Morag to persuade him to get out of his wet things and put on some of her father's rough working clothes. Montmorency tried to protest, but realized that his modesty might be mistaken for rudeness and gave in, stripping down in a corner as everyone turned their backs. Morag's mother hung the wet garments from a rack above the fire, where a cooking pot was bubbling quietly. She ladled out two bowls of steaming soup. The men waited to be given spoons, then caught sight of Morag miming with cupped hands that they should drink straight from the bowls. Farcett dribbled hot soup down the front of his shirt. Everybody laughed. Morag checked on the bags that had fallen in the sea. Everything inside was damp. She unpacked the clothes, brushes, lotions, trinkets, and books, spreading them out around the bare room to dry.

After about half an hour Morag's father came in, carrying a wooden box filled with a few muddy vegetables and some lumps of peat for the fire. Like Morag in the dining room at Glendarvie, he pushed the door open with his back, wheeling around as he entered the room. He gasped in shock as he saw the odd scene before him. Whatever he'd said was obviously a rude word on Tarimond, and Morag's mother snapped a rebuke at him. Morag tried to introduce the unusual visitors, but her father was already embarrassed and unsure of how to behave. He merely nodded at them, then gave his daughter a restrained greeting, pleased to see her but determined not to seem too soft. He found a space to put down his drab package amongst all the finery belonging to the two strangers, and sat down in silence at the table.

Morag gave him a bowl of soup, and tried to lighten the atmosphere again. She babbled on about the men, their journey, and life at Glendarvie Castle.

Suddenly, up against the thick accents of her parents, Morag's voice seemed clear. She was to act as interpreter for the Londoners throughout their stay. When Morag explained that Farcett's first name was Robert, her mother stroked his cheek, in tender memory of Robbie, her lost son. When Morag added that he was a doctor, her father flickered with suspicion, and then glanced towards his wife, whose hand passed quickly over her belly as she changed the subject. She asked for Montmorency's Christian name. Morag didn't know it, and he didn't volunteer one. So he was Mr. Montmorency for the duration of the visit.

Farcett and Montmorency were both wondering where they were going to spend the night. On the way to Tarimond, Farcett had imagined a little inn with a roaring fire, a sleepy cat, a dog or two, and brimming tankards of some local brew. In Montmorency's fantasy, after a hot rustic meal they would be shown to their rooms by a hospitable landlord, thrilled at the prospect of payment from two prosperous visitors. Now they both realized sadly that no such establishment existed. Morag's cottage had only two rooms: the bustling kitchen where they sat and a smaller, darker place with straw-filled mattresses on the floor.

They could see in through a gap in the curtain covering the doorway. It didn't look very inviting. Morag's mother shooed her father off the chest he was sitting on and lifted the lid. She brought out a pile of itchy-looking blankets and carried them into the next room, chatting to Morag as she went. Morag came back into the kitchen and explained that her parents insisted that Montmorency and Farcett should have their bed.

"Come through," she said. "I'll show you." They followed her next door and watched her open what looked like a wide closet, at waist level, running almost the length of the opposite wall. Inside was a mattress wide enough for two.

"You'll have to say yes," she chuckled, "or they'll be awful offended."

Farcett and Montmorency tried to look pleased, but the expressions on their faces only made Morag giggle more.

"I had to get used to your ways, you know. Now you'll have to get used to ours!"

Suddenly the men realized how much Morag had had to learn when she traveled from Tarimond to work at Glendarvie Castle. Far from being awkward and shy, she had in fact been quick-witted and adaptable, changing her ways to suit her employers' with a minimum of instruction. They had a new respect for her, and each resolved not to make a fuss about the bed.

But their polite resolution didn't make them any more comfortable. They were both taller than Morag's parents, and couldn't stretch right out. Their bent elbows and knees stuck into bellies and backs with every turn and shuffle as they tried to settle down to sleep. One embarrassed apology followed another until they realized that the family sleeping on the floor outside the closet could probably hear every word they said. For most of the night they just lay there, staring at everything except each other, willing themselves to sleep. Neither thought he had slept at all, yet both were snoring when they were woken by a terrifying screeching and clattering on the roof. They sat up together, the force of the movement opening the closet doors and displaying them to their hosts.

"Don't worry, gentlemen," said Morag. "It's just the pickens. They're seabirds. They come in for shelter when there's going to be a storm."

"A storm!" cried Montmorency in despair. After that rough night he wanted to get back to London, or at least Glendarvie, as soon as he could. "But we've got to go home!"

"No one will be going anywhere in this weather," growled Morag's father. "Come through for some porridge, and then Morag will show you the island before the wind hits."

Montmorency and Farcett shuffled into the kitchen. Farcett had never eaten anything like that solid porridge before. Montmorency had, in prison. He tried to look grateful as he polished off his bowl, despite the memories it stirred.

"Come on then, you two," called Morag, whose confidence seemed to be growing as theirs sagged. "You can have a mug of tea when we get back."

So Montmorency and Farcett were dragged around the island. As Morag kept reminding them, it was not looking its best in the gloom of the approaching storm. At each house the occupants stared out a cold, suspicious greeting. Farcett soon realized that the families who gaped at them all consisted of a mother, a father, and grown children. No one seemed to have offspring under the age of seven or eight. There were plenty on the verge of adulthood, strong and healthy, clearly built for hard work, but a whole age group was missing.

When they reached the churchyard they had confirmation of what Morag had told them on the boat. High on the cliff, with the waves crashing against the rocks beneath, ranks of little crosses marked a series of tiny graves. Each was carved with a name and an age. A pair of twins had been stillborn, a girl had died just two days old, but most had lived for about eight weeks. Morag knelt by the mound marked with the name of Robbie, her latest lost brother. Doctor Farcett took a scrap of paper and a stubby pencil from his pocket and turned with his back to the sea and the wind to note down the details. He caught sight of a strange figure striding from the church across the stubbly grass towards them. The man's black robes fluttered in the gathering storm, and wild white hair framed his head. He was waving his arms and mouthing something, urgently.

Farcett turned to Morag. "Who's that?" he asked. Morag saw the agitated man and jumped up, suddenly looking scared, as if she was in trouble.

"It's Father Michael," she said. "We'd better go."

The man came closer, still shouting something, but the noise of the wind and the waves sucked away his words as he spoke. Finally he was close enough for them to make out a few words.

"Go away home, Morag!" he yelled. "Get away! Go now."

"Aye, we must go. Follow me," gasped the girl,

starting to run away from the shouting, waving priest. Farcett and Montmorency were not going to argue. The fearsome instruction from the sinister man was not to be ignored.

"Go, go!" he intoned after them, his arms outstretched like some huge prehistoric bat.

The first fat raindrops had begun to sweep in, sideways, from the sea. The three of them ran through the rain to Morag's house, where her mother was fastening the shutters tight across the windows to keep out the weather. Montmorency was aching to get away from the hardship and menace of Tarimond to the comforts of Glendarvie. But Doctor Farcett had lost the urge to go back to the mainland. He wanted to stay and find out why the babies had been dying.

CHAPTER 18

NEW LIFE

The storm on Tarimond lasted for four days. The visitors had never seen weather like it. Rain slapped across the rocks, and even the locals struggled to stay upright against the force of the wind. But the animals had to be attended to, and the meager crops had to be saved. The islanders took turns venturing out to see that everything necessary was done, and on Sunday they all fought their way to the church, where Father Michael led them in prayers for better weather, while impressing on them that the tempest must be a divine judgment of some sort and therefore all their own fault.

The priest was not a local man. He had been sent, or had chosen to come, from Glasgow. He did not speak the native dialect of Tarimond, and didn't try. Most of the service was in Latin, anyway. But Father Michael had made plenty of changes to the traditional Catholic rites. In Glasgow, he had seen the ferocious passion of radical Protestant preachers, with their threats of Hellfire, and his words about the wrath of God and the islanders' unworthiness for salvation would not have been out of place in the freest of the free churches. High in the pulpit, he was a scourge and a bully to the wet and weary islanders in the pews. Sitting in the back, Montmorency and Farcett wondered how much of his sermon the congregation really understood. But the message was mainly in Father Michael's tone, his facial expression, and his passionate arm waving, which left his flock feeling guilty and judged by the Lord to be wanting. They chanted and sang to the drone of a wheezing harmonium. Morag, so calm and jolly with Montmorency and Farcett in her own house, was back to her timid, Glendarvie self as soon as she entered the church. She could hardly bear to raise her eyes to look at the priest. This was a God-fearing community — with the emphasis on the fear.

After the service, Montmorency and Farcett shook hands with Father Michael at the door. To their surprise, he greeted them warmly.

"Ah," he said. "Our English visitors. I was hoping you would come today. Have you got time to come home with me for a chat?" he said, as if they might be overwhelmed with other things to do. He turned to

Morag's mother. "Do you mind if I steal your guests from you for the afternoon?" he asked, not really giving her the option to say no.

"Of course not, Father," she replied, meekly. "It will give me a chance to tidy up." She blushed, realizing the unintentional criticism of her visitors, whose possessions were crowding her little home. Montmorency and Farcett realized for the first time as she spoke that they might be a burden to her, and they were embarrassed, too.

The priest said good-bye to the last of the old ladies, warning them to take care in the rain, then the three men ran the few yards to his cottage. Father Michael put the kettle on, and they gathered around the fire to dry off.

Father Michael, the terrifying figure from the churchyard, defied their first impressions. He seemed to be educated, charming, even witty.

"The worst of the storm is over," he said. "Lucky for me. They'll think it was the prayers that did it!"

Montmorency was shocked. This was rather like visiting an actor in his dressing room after a show, and being given an insight into the tricks of the trade. Father Michael seemed to read his mind. "It's not easy, you know, coming here from the mainland. I have to ratchet up the drama to keep their respect. It looked as if I frightened young Morag out of her skin in the churchyard the other day. I was only trying to warn you all to get under cover before the storm. You could have been swept off that headland and into the sea. This island can be a savage and dangerous place in some weather. More dangerous than you outsiders could know." He paused and laughed at himself. "Mind you, the islanders still see me as an outsider. After all, I've only been here ten years!"

"Ten years," said Doctor Farcett. "So you've seen all the infant deaths?" He was excited at the prospect of a conversation about the problem.

"Yes," said Father Michael. "I've buried every one of them. I've seen agony strike at almost every household on this island. For the past seven years not a single child born on Tarimond has survived to see its third month on earth."

"But why?" asked Montmorency.

"Of course we didn't realize it was anything strange for quite some time," the priest continued, "but there have been too many tragedies now for us to accept that it's a coincidence."

"And what do you think is the cause?" asked the doctor.

Father Michael paused and crossed himself. Then in a deep rumbling whisper he gravely declared, "Divine wrath!"

Montmorency spluttered into his tea, thinking that Father Michael was joking again. But he wasn't, and he snapped back, showing once more the fearsome force that had scared Morag in the graveyard and gripped the congregation in the church.

"Young man. I can tell you are not a believer, but I meant what I said in church today. I have the skills of my craft. I know how to kindle the spirit in these people's hearts, but my message is genuine. And the loss of our children needs more explanation than the playing out of a summer storm!"

Montmorency had no idea what to say next. Father Michael made him feel by turns very relaxed and very uneasy. He was saved by the doctor, who butted in, pursuing his own theme.

"What if there were a medical explanation for the deaths? What if there were a cure?"

"Then I would say that the God who sent the problem sent the solution, too. I have myself been considering contacting experts in Glasgow, to see what they make of it all. God may have sent us troubles, but it is for us to help ourselves."

"Would you help me investigate the deaths?" asked Farcett.

"I will do everything I can," said Father Michael, adding with dark seriousness, "Doctor Farcett, I don't think your presence here is an accident. If I ignored the gift of your visit I would be failing in my duty."

The doctor and the priest continued their discussion. The church had a register showing the date of every birth and death, going back at least a hundred years. Father Michael promised to make it available. He suggested that Farcett and Montmorency should move in with him. He had a spare room with two beds, and supplies of paper and ink so the doctor could keep proper notes. Both men were thrilled by the thought of escaping Morag's parents' closet-bed. Father Michael said he would come with them to explain the reason for their move, to avoid any offense being taken.

They were buttoning their coats, ready to brave the rain, when a young girl, aged about eight (and therefore one of the youngest on Tarimond), rapped on the door and gave Father Michael a note.

"It's from Maggie Goudie," he said as he read it quickly, reaching for his hat.

"She's the local witch doctor, is she not?" said Montmorency, jauntily.

Father Michael corrected him sternly. "Doctor, nurse, midwife, and teacher. She's kept this community together through its troubles. If anyone can help you in your task, Doctor Farcett, it's Maggie."

"Was she in church?" he asked.

"No, she's with Jeannie MacLean. A young wife, having a difficult labor. Maggie wants me there in case the baby dies."

"Then I must join you," said Farcett, pulling on his boots. Father Michael understood, and led the way.

The wind had died, the rain had softened, and outside the MacLeans' cottage a few chickens had come out from their shelter and were scratching for worms. The priest knocked lightly on the door, which swung open under the gentle pressure of his hand. Montmorency had seen a lot in his life, but never a birth, and he was nervous of what might await them inside. He hung back, letting Farcett go in next. A searing scream came from the back room.

"I must go to her," cried Farcett, pushing his way past a bemused John MacLean.

The priest hurriedly explained to MacLean the doctor's professional right to intrude on his wife at such an intimate moment, and then introduced Montmorency. The three men stayed in the kitchen, talking awkwardly, their polite exchanges punctuated by Jeannie's gasps and moans.

"It won't be long now," said Father Michael, though there was no way he could have known what was going on next door. "You'll soon be blessed with a child."

"Aye, but for how long?" said MacLean, all too well aware of the fate of Tarimond babies.

"Doctor Farcett wants to put an end to the deaths," said Montmorency, trying to reassure, but MacLean just gave a resigned shake of the head.

"We'll see," he muttered. "We'll see." Then he raged at Father Michael. "Why does Jeannie have to go through all this just to lose her child? If she doesn't lose it now, it will die in a few weeks' time!" He stared at the priest accusingly, and tears welled in his eyes.

Montmorency was overwhelmed by the force of such anger and despair at what should have been a time of joy. His own eyes were starting to sting, too. He told himself it must be the acrid smoke from the peat fire. Father Michael stumbled over a consoling reply.

A long screech from Jeannie silenced the men. Then there was a new noise, a powerful yell from tiny lungs.

Montmorency's cheeks were suddenly wet, and Father Michael spoke a short prayer of thanks. The curtain between the two rooms parted, and a tall, strong woman stepped forward. Blood and grease were spattered across her clothes, up her arms, on her face, and in her hair, which had once been tied out of the way on top of her head but now hung in tendrils plastered here and there to her neck by sweat. This was Maggie Goudie. She strode towards MacLean and handed him a bundle of gray cloth.

"Take your son, John. I have to go back to Jeannie." John MacLean clumsily balanced the precious load in his arms. A tiny fist punched out from the wrappings in the startled gesture of the newborn. Baby MacLean was taking a hold on life, and the weeping men around him were sharing one wish: that it should be a long one.

Farcett joined them, demanding hot water. He took a jug through to Maggie Goudie and returned to wash his own hands in the kitchen sink. Montmorency thought back to when he had been Robert Farcett's patient, and the many times he had seen the doctor perform that ritual of scrubbing his fingers and gouging under his nails. When he had finished, the doctor gently took the baby from the new father's arms and bathed him in the sink, as delicately as if he had been a piece of priceless china. Montmorency looked at the child, and sensed at once that something was wrong. He was alarmed by the enormous size of the baby's head in relation to the rest of his body. He was horrified by the wrinkled skin, the bulging belly, the blueness around the fingers and toes, and the fat shiny umbilical cord trailing from the belly button. He was amazed when Farcett wrapped the child in a towel and passed it back to John MacLean with the words, "Congratulations, sir. You have a fine, healthy baby boy. Absolutely perfect."

CHAPTER 19

MAGGIE GOUDIE AND THE LOST CHILDREN OF TARIMOND

When he had first heard of Maggie Goudie, Robert Farcett had imagined a wild and wizened native woman, steeped in the superstitious ways of her people, muddling through with ancient local remedies. No doubt, like Father Michael, she had won the confidence of her patients with a mixture of hocus-pocus and fear. He had even suspected that her amateur attempts at midwifery and child care might be the cause of the infant deaths. That was one reason he had moved so fast to get to the MacLeans' house. It was why he had burst through the kitchen, so alarming poor John MacLean. He had been surprised by the woman he found at Jeannie's bedside. Maggie Goudie was not old. Thirty, thirty-five perhaps, but not much more. She was fit and capable. Even more surprisingly, she had a stethoscope around her neck and a special trumpetlike device for listening to the unborn baby's heartbeat. The scene in the bedroom was as orderly and calm as it could be in the circumstances, and the breathless doctor faced none of the contempt he had expected.

"Ah, Doctor," said Maggie in a soft voice. "I am glad you are here. I would welcome your help."

"Robert Farcett," he stuttered, holding out his hand, taken aback.

"I know who you are," she laughed with a nod, her hands too busy to return his greeting. "The whole of Tarimond has been talking about you. Now get your coat off and give me your opinion of the situation." Then she mopped her patient's forehead and added soothingly, "See, Jeannie, what a privileged wee girlie you are. You have a grand doctor from London to look after you. Everything will be all right." The panic-stricken young mother said nothing, but stared frantically at Maggie and then at Doctor Farcett, pleading for help.

The two of them had worked together to get Jeannie's baby safely into the world. Then through the long night, as they struggled to save Jeannie, too, Maggie told her story. She had been born and raised on Tarimond. Like Morag she was a clever girl, and like Morag she had been sent away to the mainland to work. Father Michael's predecessor had found her a job in a hospital in Glasgow, where she had been trained as a nurse by nuns. She had been tempted to stay, to earn money to send home to her family, but the pull of the simple island life had been too strong for her, and so when she heard that her mother was ill she had returned and brought her new skills home. After her mother's death she had started a little school. It was there that Morag had learned to read and write English. Sadly, there were no new pupils joining now, and it would not be long before the last ones would be leaving to help their families on farms.

"You know about the babies of course?" she asked. Doctor Farcett nodded silently, and Maggie surprised him with a request. "Will you help me find out why they are dying?" Until then, Farcett had imagined himself taking charge of any investigation. He had been thinking of asking for her help, but now he realized that she knew far more than he about the mystery. He could assume no authority here.

"Of course. I am at your service," he replied, watching her tidy the bedroom while Jeannie slept. She arranged everything meticulously, washing herself and her patient, removing any possible source of infection. She was as careful as any matron he had encountered in the best-regulated hospitals. But she was gentle, kind, and thoughtful, too. The soap she used was delicately perfumed with aromatic herbs.

"I make it myself," she told him, "from local oils and leaves. I haven't abandoned all the folkways of my youth, and some of the plants we have here are as healing as anything you'll buy in a bottle at an apothecary on the mainland." She showed him the greasy lump, dotted with leaves and petals, before tucking it safely back into the pocket of her apron. "I have to be sparing with it. It takes a long time to collect all the ingredients; but I don't like to see my ladies washing themselves with the harsh stuff they use on the kitchen floor. I give them each a bar. I like to think it helps them to feel feminine again."

She was combing Jeannie's hair, and the pale, tired girl looked quite beautiful lying in the neat little bed. She rubbed sweet oil on Jeannie's temples and took some for herself.

"Would you like some, Doctor?" she asked. "It's very calming. I use it on my mothers and their babies."

He declined, but sniffed the bottle, and liked the scent. And everything was calm. No one entering the room now could have imagined the messy struggle that had taken place there a few hours before. Maggie

Goudie had created an atmosphere of comfort and dignity for Jeannie, who was battered and exhausted. Doctor Farcett and Maggie stayed there through the night, struggling to keep Jeannie alive. In the early morning they lost her, and John MacLean's howl could be heard a mile away. He clasped his newborn son to him, rocking to and fro. Father Michael tried a few words of comfort, but was repelled with an animal-like hiss. Montmorency looked on, unable to do anything to help. Farcett took charge of the baby, Maggie prepared Jeannie for her funeral, and the people of Tarimond started waiting. Waiting for Jeannie's baby to die.

CHAPTER 20

≫

STAYING ON

Back in the comfort of Father Michael's house, Farcett persuaded Montmorency to stay on Tarimond a little longer. He wrote a letter to Gus at Glendarvie Castle, explaining why their return would be delayed. He addressed it carefully, and it waited on the hall table for a few days, until a fisherman offered to take it to the biggest island. There the fisherman passed it to a friend of the harbormaster, who promised to see that it reached the next ferry to Oban. When he got home he put it on the kitchen table and, for a week or so, it picked up tea stains and grease. Eventually he remembered to put it in his coat pocket on the way to the pub. But the harbormaster wasn't there that night, and the barmaid who was supposed to hand it off forgot about it. Weeks later, when she came across it wedged between two bottles, she was too embarrassed to own up, and put it on the fire.

While the letter made its journey to nowhere, Maggie and Doctor Farcett put together a full picture of the babies who had died. She had kept records of every case, quite rudimentary at the beginning, when the deaths were seen as natural misfortunes, but much more detailed once a pattern seemed to be emerging. Together they drew up charts cross-referencing the circumstances of each labor, the health of each child at birth, the condition of the mothers, the position of their houses, the families' diets, habits, and medical histories. Doctor Farcett came to look forward to Maggie's arrival at the priest's cottage, and to the soapy fragrance of her presence. But they were rarely alone. When Father Michael heard Maggie arriving he stopped whatever he was doing to join them, adding his own recollections and ideas, often correcting Maggie gently over an age or a date, and pulling out the old church registers to look for similar bursts of catastrophe in the past. Babies had always died. Birth was risky everywhere, and on Tarimond a year of famine or harsh cold might cost a cluster of little lives. But nothing on this scale had ever happened before. They could find no reason for the recent deaths. There were no common factors of gender, condition, time of year, or behavior. When all their rational researches failed, Father Michael would fall back on the supernatural explanation, and lament God's terrible will — a punishment perhaps for long-past transgressions by the islanders. At the end of each session, he would insist on walking Maggie home, leaving Farcett to ponder the inconclusive documents on the kitchen table.

Montmorency took an occasional interest in the mystery, and now and then chipped in with a theory over supper, but much of his time was spent fishing and enjoying the Tarimond landscape. After the storm the sea had calmed to a gently lapping pool, bright blue or green when Montmorency looked away into the distance, but absolutely clear when he looked down. He had never seen anything like it. Certainly not in the filthy Thames, which had once almost taken his life, and not in the rushing water of the salmon stream at Glendarvie, which was flecked with peaty brown foam. If such tranquil beauty had been there on his foreign trips with Fox-Selwyn, he had never taken the time to notice. Now, on Tarimond, Montmorency could stand in the water at the edge of the beach and count the hairs and freckles on his feet. He could see tiny fishes flicking between the brightly colored pebbles around his toes. Yet when he looked back to the cliffs, he had a reminder of the wild force that the sea could unleash in stormy weather. Strangely shaped rocks towered above him, with deep curves and startling slopes carved out of them by wild waves. Sometimes he would climb up high and look across to the other islands spattered around before him. They looked as if they might once have been joined together. It was as if the ocean had deliberately torn a path between them, leaving little clumps of rock that it could continue to lick away over time. He had seen grand buildings in London and all over Europe, but he had never seen anything as magnificent as this. And he was growing to like the rough, uncomplicated life that went with the scenery.

He made himself useful. He helped Morag's father repair the barn, hauling great logs into position, and learning how to saw special grooves along their sides so that they stayed in place. It reminded him of the building work he had done in prison long ago. When they'd finished the barn, they got to work on a small boat, planing planks of wood so that they could be bent across the frame, and hammering them into place, close and watertight. Montmorency's shoulders grew stronger with the work, his skin tanned by the sun and wind. In time he came to look more like one of the islanders, his scars seeming to be marks of manhood rather than injury. At night the men of the island got together in one another's houses to drink and sing. Farcett was usually too embarrassed to join in, but Montmorency soon knew all the tunes, and most of the words, even if he wasn't always certain what they meant. Doctor Farcett watched Montmorency's progress with interest, and not a little pride. They never talked of the drug, and Farcett felt that very soon Montmorency would be fit to return to his old life again.

Like Farcett, Montmorency was very taken with Maggie Goudie. On his walks across the island he would drop in at her home, which like the others on Tarimond was a simple stone rectangle on the outside. Inside it was quite different. Maggie had books from her time in Glasgow. She even had a few pictures, and brightly colored fabrics, bought long ago in city shops, were draped across the gray stone walls. When she had time she would make Montmorency welcome with tea and freshly baked scones. More often she was busy, tending to a patient or collecting the ingredients for her homemade remedies. Sometimes she let him help her, teaching him how to tell the difference between the leaves of plants, and how to extract their fragrant oils. She collected and stored them in tiny watertight sacs made from the stomachs of sea birds and animals. They dangled like balloons from a long pole, hung across her kitchen ceiling. As time went by, she even trusted Montmorency to help her mix the oils, leaves, and petals together to make her medicines, lotions, and soap. And while they worked she told him more about her past. Although their backgrounds were quite different, Montmorency was secretly fascinated by the similarities between them. Both had reinvented themselves.

"Did you find it hard when you first went to Glasgow?" he asked her, as he stripped the petals from some purple flowers in a basket on the kitchen table.

"Oh yes. Everything was different. I'd never been on a train, or seen hot water coming out of a tap. I had to watch all the time to see how the people behaved: how they ate, how they dressed. I had to observe and imitate all the simple things you probably take for granted. . . ."

If you only knew! thought Montmorency, who had put in so much effort over the years doing exactly that.

". . . And at first no one could understand what I was saying. I had to lose my accent. In those days hardly anyone here spoke English."

"You mean they do now?" he teased. He still found

it hard to communicate with most of the islanders, especially the older ones.

"Oh yes!" she laughed. "Father Nicholas, who was here before Father Michael, started the classes, and I've carried them on since. And not many people could read then. Now most of us can. I've taught all the children . . ." Her voice trailed off as she considered how small her class was becoming, and how long it was since a new pupil had joined. She composed herself again. "Morag was one of the best. I bet over there at Glendarvie she's just like one of the locals!"

"Yes." Montmorency fibbed kindly, remembering how much difficulty Gus had understanding Morag. "Did you know Father Michael in Glasgow?"

"I did indeed. I persuaded him to come here when Father Nicholas died. He was the chaplain at the hospital where I trained." She paused, and her tone changed as she remembered those years. "I don't think he really suited a city parish. Some people didn't like him. There was a bit of trouble with his style. . . ." Then she smiled again. "But he was kind to us nurses, always bringing sweets when we were on long shifts. He'd come and chat with us for hours. He can be quite funny, you know, when you get him out of the pulpit! I used to tell him about Tarimond. He said it sounded like the perfect place to be a priest."

And indeed, in many ways it was. There was no money in it, of course, but Father Michael lived well on Tarimond. Poor though they were, the grateful, fearful islanders brought him gifts of meat, milk, bread, eggs, and vegetables. Once word got around that Montmorency and Farcett were staying at his house, the people made sure that he had enough for three. Montmorency was comfortable in the priest's house, even if he sometimes found Father Michael's mixture of worldly wisdom and fiery spirituality unsettling. Sometimes Father Michael could be seen standing in the churchyard, staring and muttering over the babies' graves. Sometimes he went right to the cliff edge and shouted prayers and curses out to sea. But at other times he would sit and joke with his lodgers over fresh fish and whisky, and ask them to talk of their lives in London. Occasionally, Montmorency felt homesick at the reminders of races and balls, but mostly he rejoiced in feeling truly healthy for the first time since the trip to Turkey. For the moment, at least, he was happy to stay.

CHAPTER 21

FOX-SELWYN ON A MISSION

While Montmorency and Farcett were getting to know Tarimond, Lord George Fox-Selwyn was doing his best to track down the London bomber. He was a very experienced investigator, but for five years now he had rarely operated alone. He and Montmorency were a great team, each making up for the other's deficiencies. They instinctively knew what each of them was good at. Fox-Selwyn, for example, could charm the aristocracy of Europe with his intimate knowledge of their family histories; he knew how to tempt diplomats into indiscretions, and to flatter petty officials and persuade them to bend the rules. Montmorency could understand the street life of an unfamiliar city and adapt his mannerisms and speech to fit in with new surroundings. He could blend into the background, so that sometimes even Fox-Selwyn wasn't entirely sure where he was. Fox-Selwyn had come to rely on his partner's skill. He had rather lost the knack of hiding in doorways, of doing deals in dark and dirty places, or of making himself invisible as he observed the world around him.

He didn't realize this until he found himself sitting in a Covent Garden pub, trying to look like a market trader, so that he could eavesdrop on the conversations around him. Perhaps his trousers were a little too well cut. He had chosen them for the loud check of the weave, which even the undemonstrative Chivers had described as "slightly vulgar" when pressed for an opinion. He had bought them two years ago for a sporting weekend, and since then he had put on rather a lot of weight around the backside. They were stretched almost to bursting point, and the cuffs hovered way above his ankles, showing his cashmere socks. Or could it be the shirt that was wrong? It was dirty, which was a good thing, but the weave of the cotton was too fine for a working man, and the neckerchief tied so carefully to project a nonchalant image was too obviously made of silk. He sat with his beer, conscious that the other drinkers were sizing him up with speedy glances whenever they thought he wasn't looking. He turned his eyes downward, and drummed on the grubby wooden table with his carefully manicured hands. He was so tall that he was bound to attract attention whatever he wore. In fact, his long legs stuck out beyond the other side of the table. And there, on his dainty feet, were his shoes: soft leather loafers from an expensive shop in Mayfair. He hoped no one had noticed them. He sat in the hot room for another quarter of an hour. There were plenty of customers, but the silence only grew with time. He wasn't going to pick up any information there. He decided to leave, and clumsily knocked over a stool as he rose to go.

"Oh dear, I do apologize!" he found himself saying, his distinctive posh voice bouncing off the walls. As the door closed behind him he heard a mighty roar of laughter. Before he was across the street, singing and shouting had begun. Everyone in the pub had seen him for what he was: a spy, and not a very good one. Oh, how he longed for Montmorency!

He sent a telegram to Glendarvie Castle that night. Gus wired back to say that he had heard nothing from Montmorency or Farcett since their departure for Tarimond. He didn't even know if they had survived the trip.

CHAPTER 22

≫

PRIORITIES

Doctor Farcett's tie to Tarimond was growing stronger. He confided in Father Michael about his disaster in the operating theater, and how he had killed a man to further his own career.

Father Michael was appalled. "That was a sin. It is wrong to kill. You must pray for forgiveness."

"I do, Father, but I fear that God will forgive me before I forgive myself."

"You are not the first to think that, my son. Believe me, I know what you mean." The priest looked grave and distracted. "I know what it is to break divine law. You must do what I try to do, and earn your forgiveness by helping others. Look at the good you are already doing here on Tarimond."

And it was true. Doctor Farcett had become a popular figure on the island. Any early caution among the locals had turned to curiosity and then to trust, and they had begun to consult him about a range of ailments. With Maggie to help him he treated broken bones, chesty coughs, itchy eyes, and aching backs.

Caring for the islanders, he began to remember why he had become interested in medicine in the first place. Secretly, he played with the idea of staying for good and setting up an infirmary where he could use his modern skills alongside Maggie Goudie's traditional remedies. He imagined them working there together, happily, every day. Sometimes he let the fantasy go a little further: a joyous ceremony in the church. Children perhaps. But then his mind rushed back to the harsh realities of family life on Tarimond. He concentrated once more on the mysterious deaths, and didn't tell anyone of his private dreams.

He took a special interest in little Jimmy MacLean, spending hours with him while his father saw to the crops and the animals. In days gone by, when a Tarimond woman died in childbirth, some other recent mother would take on the task of feeding her orphaned child. Now, of course, no other mothers were suckling children, and there was no human milk to be had. So Doctor Farcett and Mr. MacLean took it in turns to give the baby diluted goat's milk from a special jug with a tiny spout, made by the local potter to the doctor's specifications. Doctor Farcett explained to John MacLean all about germs, and why he should always scrub out the jug and rinse it out with boiling water. He showed him how to make sure the milk was at just the right temperature for the baby, and together, the two men made sure that Jimmy had every chance of survival.

He didn't know that as he settled into a routine, and Montmorency worked and watched the tides, Morag's Uncle Harvey was on his way to fetch them back to the mainland. The Marquess had received a series of frantic telegrams from Lord George Fox-Selwyn, insisting that he should trace Montmorency and see that he returned to London at once.

Harvey's arrival was difficult for everyone — not the least, it seemed, for Harvey himself. He was pleased to see his family again, but embarrassed for them to watch him in the role of a servant: diffident and respectful in the presence of the Londoners. Unlike Morag, he had been at Glendarvie for years, and he had been changed by the experience. He no longer felt at ease in the rugged informality of Tarimond. He wanted to collect Farcett and Montmorency and leave as soon as possible, and not just because of the urgency of Fox-Selwyn's summons, or the Marchioness's insistence that he should be quick.

Farcett had seen his boat arriving, and went down to the beach to find out who it was. He guessed that Harvey must be bringing news from Glendarvie, and Harvey got straight to the point.

"I've come to get Mr. Montmorency, sir. Lord Fox-Selwyn needs him in London."

"Oh dear," said Farcett, who was already debating in his own mind whether Montmorency could be trusted to return to his old life. "Let's get you dry and warm, Harvey. Come up to Father Michael's. Montmorency and I are staying there."

Harvey was reluctant to follow the doctor up to the house, but he felt he couldn't argue, and walked a few paces behind him, stopping at the threshold as Farcett burst into the kitchen, where Montmorency and Father Michael were trying to mend a broken clock. Montmorency had just fastened the glass in place, and was winding the key.

"You're here for the moment of truth, Robert," he said, triumphantly, holding the clock up and giving it a shake to start it ticking. Nothing happened. He shook it again, and the hands both dropped, limply, to point at the six. The priest howled with laughter.

"That must be what this thing was for," he cried,

holding up a screw that had failed to make it back into the mechanism. "Open it up again, Montmorency. Let's have another look."

"Come in, Harvey," called Farcett. "Montmorency will be pleased to see you again." He beckoned Harvey to enter. "Father Michael, this is Morag's uncle, Harvey. . . . But perhaps you two know each other already?"

The atmosphere changed in an instant. Father Michael's giggling was swallowed into a glare. He turned his head away and said sternly: "Aye, we know each other. Harvey left Tarimond soon after I arrived."

Harvey said nothing to the priest. He turned to Montmorency. "I have a message for you, sir, from Lord George Fox-Selwyn. He wants you to return to London, sir. I gather it is a matter of some urgency."

"Well, we can talk about that in a minute, Harvey," said Montmorency jauntily. "Will you have some tea? You must be tired after your journey." He sensed at once that he had offended Father Michael by offering hospitality to this unexpected guest.

And sure enough, the priest butted in curtly: "We must not keep Harvey from his family. They have been parted from him for years."

Harvey picked up the tone: "Indeed. My sister will

want to see me, and there is not much time. We must get away tomorrow at first light."

Farcett broke the awkward atmosphere, trying to sound relaxed. "Yes, Harvey, Father Michael is right, you must put your family first. And Montmorency and I will need to pack. You get on, and we will be ready in the morning."

Harvey hurried away before Montmorency had a chance to ask him more about why Fox-Selwyn wanted him so urgently, and Father Michael challenged Farcett straightaway.

"You are leaving? Why? What can be so urgent that you have to go like this?"

"Montmorency has business in London. Something extremely important must have happened for him to be recalled in this way."

"If Lord George Fox-Selwyn has gone to all this trouble to get me," said Montmorency, "it must be pretty serious. I will have to go." He tried not to betray the sudden rush of joy he felt at the idea of returning to city life.

"But Robert," said Father Michael, "you don't have to leave, too. We need you here now. Won't you stay?"

Farcett was pacing the kitchen. In the short time

since Harvey's arrival, his mind had been whirling around the decision he knew he must make. He desperately wanted to remain on Tarimond, but he knew he must make the trip with Montmorency.

"I don't want to go," he said. "But I've been thinking. This is the best opportunity I'll have to get expert advice about the babies. I can take all our research to London and get it properly analyzed. I must go with Montmorency. If I leave it much longer the weather will make the journey impossible till spring."

"I beg you not to, Robert," pleaded Father Michael. "You belong here now. Stay. We can solve this mystery together."

But Farcett insisted he had to go. He had to do it for the sake of all the grieving parents on Tarimond, and for Morag's mother, who was pregnant again and dreading the loss of another baby. But most of all he wanted to do it for the sake of Jimmy MacLean, who was already regarded by the islanders as a little miracle. For Jimmy MacLean was three months old, and Jimmy MacLean was still alive.

CHAPTER 23

BACK IN TOWN

The next morning, Harvey loaded their bags into the boat. Morag and her family had come to the beach to see him off, and they gave Montmorency and Farcett warm hugs, too. Maggie Goudie arrived with some gifts for the journey, and Farcett coyly brushed her cheek with his lips. Then Harvey began calling them to hurry. Farcett smiled.

"It seems strange that Harvey should be so keen to get away, when we don't want to go," he said.

"Harvey has his reasons," said Maggie, pulling away from the doctor as Father Michael arrived to join the group.

"Come on, sir," shouted Harvey. "We don't want to miss the tide." And he pulled on the oars as soon as the doctor was settled in the boat. They waved goodbye, and then the little party on the beach climbed up to the top of the cliff and waved some more. Farcett watched Maggie until she was no more than a black silhouette in the distance. Then Father Michael put an arm around her, and guided her away from the cliff edge. Harvey rowed even harder, and soon Tarimond was out of sight.

During the long journey to Glendarvie and then on to London, Montmorency and Farcett gradually transformed themselves back into smart metropolitan men. The beards went first. Montmorency wondered if he would ever get used to shaving again, but by the time he was home he was beginning to feel uncomfortable when his stubble was too thick. They were both glad that the reentry into their old lives was so gradual. They were tired when they reached Glendarvie Castle, and were tempted to stay for a while. Gus's children were fascinated by their stories of Tarimond, and didn't want them to go; and even the Marchioness, who was thrilled that Harvey was back, didn't mind having the doctor and Montmorency under her roof as well. The dogs, Mac and Tessie, seemed to recognize them, too, diving into their bags and stealing shoes to bury in the garden, as if they were trying to stop the visitors from leaving. But Farcett and Montmorency knew they had to press on. Still, the brief rest at Glendarvie, where they collected the rest of their luggage and reacquainted themselves with the complications of large meals and expensive clothes, set them up for the rail journey south. At Aberdeen they encountered traffic and crowds for the first time in months, and rattling towards London on the sleeper they each prepared themselves for the mental adjustments needed for the tasks ahead.

Farcett knew he would have professional problems. He had resigned from the hospital suddenly, and felt he owed his former colleagues a personal explanation. The patients he used to treat at home might have found new doctors they preferred; but some might want to come back. Should he see them, even if he wasn't entirely certain that he was going to stay in London permanently? People would probably be polite enough to his face: asking if he had enjoyed his holiday, but he knew that behind his back they would be gossiping about him, speculating that he had lost his professional nerve after the botched operation, or despising him for deserting them and putting his own interests first when they had let him into the most intimate parts of their lives and depended on him to get them through their illnesses and personal crises. But he hoped for enough patients to finance his investigations into the Tarimond mystery, and that the experts he needed to help him with his research would still respect him enough to give him their time.

He had no desire to return to the flashier side of his old life. The idea of demonstrating his surgical skill in public now scared and slightly repulsed him. But he desperately wanted to find out why so many children had died. He had brought all his notes from Tarimond. Reading through them transported him back to the stark beauty of the place. Here and there, the sight of Maggie Goudie's handwriting conjured up the image of her hard at work, trying to improve the health of her people; and the earthy fragrance of the bar of soap and the pot of relaxing oil she had given him as keepsakes reminded him of her every time he smelled them. He kept the oil on his desk, and he knew he would never use the soap. Instead he tucked it in amongst his clean clothes, so that every new shirt carried a hint of that faraway island, of Maggie, of Morag and her family, of Father Michael, and of little Jimmy MacLean.

Montmorency was excited about going home. He had enjoyed the simple life, but he had fought hard to win his place in the world of parties and fun, and towards the end of his time on Tarimond he had sometimes found himself looking out over the waves at a golden sunset and wondering who had won the 3:30 race at

Sandown Park. Once or twice, drinking the cool, clear spring water of the island, he had imagined a bottle of champagne in an ice bucket at Bargles, and when Morag had trimmed his hair because it had started to flop over his eyes, he had balanced on the wobbly wooden stool longing for the black leather swivel chair at his London barber's, the sharp click of the shiny silver scissors, the hot towels, and the comfort of relaxing and listening to "society" gossip as someone gently manicured his nails. He didn't like to think about it too much, but he had noticed that his craving for the Turkish drug had gone. He imagined how thrilled Fox-Selwyn would be that he was his old healthy self again, and was delighted when he saw his friend waiting on the platform at King's Cross, ready to whisk them back to his house where Cook had prepared a welcome breakfast.

"I had to get you back, Montmorency," said Fox-Selwyn. "I've been getting nowhere with my investigation, and now it seems the government is going to call off the hunt."

"Hunt for what, exactly?" asked Montmorency, and Fox-Selwyn realized that his friend knew nothing of the bomb and the shambles of the search for the culprit. (It was worse than that: Montmorency couldn't even remember the explosion, though he pretended to when Fox-Selwyn described the start of that terrible night on the train.)

Fox-Selwyn told them all about the King's Cross blast and its aftermath. "The problem is," he said, "that the government has done too good a job persuading everyone that it was gas. It seems they've almost convinced themselves. Now they want to wind down the investigation and just hope for the best. But we can't let this go. There's a bomber out there, and he might act again. I need you to help me track him down."

"But surely whoever planted the bomb did it for publicity. Hasn't there been a note to the police or the papers or anything?" said Montmorency, piling extra scrambled eggs onto his plate.

"Not a sausage," said Fox-Selwyn.

"Oh, sausages, too! Lovely."

"No, I meant there hasn't been a squeak from anyone, that's what's so strange. The Foreign Office says that points to a continental anarchist group out to destabilize all bourgeois societies, just trying to spread panic and uncertainty. The War Office boys have their eye on agents working for foreign governments, but they haven't got anywhere. The Home Office thinks there might be an Irish link."

"Or of course just a nutcase working on his own," Farcett chipped in, buttering his toast.

"Yes, and I suppose if that's true, it's just as bad as the others until he's under lock and key. You're the medical man, and I'll bow to your opinion, but I've never heard of a fanatic who acted only once."

"Even if he's sick, he must be caught," said the doctor.

"So what have you been doing to try and find the culprit?" asked Montmorency, placing a large spoonful of buttery mushrooms alongside his deviled kidneys.

"Well, for a start, I've been talking to people in the Home Office, the Foreign Office, and the War Office. Unofficially, of course. They won't have anything to do with each other, so I've done a bit of wining and dining to try to get up to date on all the investigations, and to see whether they agree on anything."

"And do they?" Montmorency's mouth was full, but Fox-Selwyn knew what he meant.

"No. The only things the three inquiries have in common are their omissions."

"Which are?" asked Farcett.

"No one has talked to the people who were at King's Cross that night. At least not since the morning after, when Scotland Yard took some very basic statements. And all three are relying on paid informants for news of the usual suspects. No one is out there trying to find out if this is something new."

"Well, you can't blame them. Where would they start?" said the doctor.

"There is one lead." Fox-Selwyn's voice dropped into a more confidential tone. "Actually, we can't criticize the authorities for not following this one up. I'm the only person who knows about it." And Fox-Selwyn told them about the Home Secretary's night out after the opera, and his conversation with the painted lady.

"I've been trying to find her. Unfortunately, the Home Secretary's description seems to fit most of the women you find hanging around outside the Opera House. I must admit that until I started this project I hadn't realized how many of them there were. Anyway, I've been working my way through them." Montmorency had to grab his napkin to stop a laugh from showering food across the table. Fox-Selwyn blushed, realizing he'd given the wrong impression. "Just taking them for a few drinks and so on," he stuttered. "Just talking. But I haven't found her yet."

"So that's why you've sent for me."

"That's the bit you'll enjoy, yes," said Fox-Selwyn, "but I need you for other things, too. You can get inside the world of these people — the passengers at the station, and these Irishmen, anarchists, and bombers. I've tried, but frankly, I don't seem to be able to blend in." Now Farcett was giggling, imagining his huge aristocratic friend trying to meld into the underworld. Fox-Selwyn carried on, "I've worked out where we need to go, and who we need to watch, but I'm going to need you to do the fieldwork."

Montmorency slapped the table enthusiastically. "Well, I'm all for tracing the girl," he said, "though she may not remember anything. It's been months now. Still, let's give it a go. What's on at the Opera House tonight?"

"*Don Carlos.*"

"Oh, Verdi! Wonderful!" cried Montmorency, but Fox-Selwyn interrupted him sternly.

"It's sold out. But dress up anyway, and I'll see you there after the performance when the girls gather."

"Can I come, too?" asked Doctor Farcett. "There are people I want to see this afternoon, but I should be free this evening, and I'm getting interested in your little hunt."

Fox-Selwyn, usually so affable, darkened and snapped back at the doctor. "Little hunt! You're just as bad as the officials. Just because there hasn't been another bomb. Just because the people who died were nobodies. Just because the station is still there, spic and span as if nothing happened, you think this is all a bit of fun. Well, it isn't. Think about it. Montmorency and I walked past that tramp. We may have seen that woman just before she died. Who knows, we may even have brushed against her skirts as we made our way to the sleeper. She might have stood on our platform and waved our train away. We passed the fatal spot only minutes before the bomb went off. We could have been killed. Anyone could have been killed. And the bomber is still out there. We have to stop him from doing it again!"

Doctor Farcett looked crestfallen. "I'm sorry, I didn't mean to be flippant. I apologize."

Fox-Selwyn was calming down. "All right." He paused and regained his composure. "You can come. But remember, however much fun we have tonight, this is a serious business." His eyes started to twinkle again as he poured them all some more coffee. "Now, tell me more about what you got up to on that island of yours!"

CHAPTER 24

GREAT ORMOND STREET

After breakfast, Robert Farcett went home, bathed and changed, and then set off on his own mission. He knew who he wanted to talk to. Doctor Donald Dougall had trained with him years ago. They had rowed crew for their college together, and though they had specialized in different areas of medicine, they had always enjoyed each other's company when they met up. Doctor Dougall now worked at the Hospital for Sick Children in Great Ormond Street. When it had opened thirty-three years before, the very idea of having a hospital especially for children seemed bizarre. Most doctors thought children were simply smaller versions of adults, suffering from the same illnesses, which needed the same treatments. The founders of Great Ormond Street Hospital had proved that wasn't true. They had successfully won support for their institution, which was growing all the time. It treated, and did research on, poor children who couldn't pay for their care elsewhere. The doctors who worked there knew more about the workings of children's bodies than anyone else in the world. If anyone could help Robert Farcett solve the mystery of Tarimond, Donald Dougall could.

Doctor Farcett presented his card at the entrance to the hospital and asked to see Doctor Dougall. He was shown to a waiting room, where a couple of worried parents were sitting with sickly children. One girl of about four lay listless in her mother's arms, her skin and eyeballs discolored yellow. *Liver,* thought Farcett instinctively. *Or possibly kidneys, or some sort of blood disorder.* He knew that Great Ormond Street specialized in all three. An older boy played happily with a toy train, taken from a box of playthings in the corner. *He looks fine,* thought Farcett. *Perhaps he's her brother.* Then the child turned, revealing an ugly growth across the side of his face.

The door opened, and Doctor Donald Dougall strode in. He was chubby and enthusiastic, with bright red hair and freckles. Farcett rose and put out his hand, but Dougall went straight to the child on the floor.

"Hello, Sid!" he boomed, taking the boy's face gently in his hand and inspecting the grotesque shape. "I say. You are doing well! I'll be with you in a minute, but first I must see this young lady." He turned to the worried mother. "If you'll go in with the nurse, Mrs. Mills, I'll be there right away." Only then did he acknowledge Doctor Farcett. "Robert. Good to see you. Can you hang on for half an hour or so? Busy clinic. Lunch?"

"I'd love to."

"Right, see you later." And Doctor Dougall disappeared. But not before Farcett noticed that he was putting a glove puppet on his hand, ready to tease the little girl out of her fear.

While he waited for Donald Dougall to finish his work, Farcett went for a walk. The hospital was not far from King's Cross, and he thought how the patients there must have heard the bomb. He wondered if they had been scared. That area of London probably had more children in it than any other. He walked past houses and shops to Guilford Street where the proud entrance of the Foundling Hospital stood before him. This was one of the oldest orphanages in the country. Children were taken in as babies, their names were changed to protect them from their past, and they were brought up in an atmosphere of adequate, kindly, but unloving care. It was an imposing building right in the middle of London, but the children inside knew hardly anything of the world around them. Farcett stopped and looked through the gates. A bell rang. A line of girls emerged from one wing, a line of boys from the other. They were all dressed in brown uniforms, the girls in dresses with little white aprons, the boys in short jackets and trousers ending well above their ankles. None of them spoke. One glanced at Farcett, but turned away quickly as if he had been breaking a rule. Then the children marched off in parallel lines towards the dining hall. It was lunchtime there, too. It looked grim, but Farcett knew that these children were the lucky ones. They were being fed and given enough education to get themselves jobs when they left in their early teens. Many London children who lived with their parents did less well than that, and some of them, victims of illness or malnutrition, ended up at the Great Ormond Street Hospital around the corner.

"Sorry to keep you, Robert," said Doctor Dougall as he waved his last patient from his consulting room. "Come in." He gave Farcett an inquisitive but understanding smile. "I heard you'd had a spot of bother."

"Yes. I had to get away for a while. But I haven't come to talk to you about that. I've come across an interesting case in Scotland, and I wondered if you could give me some advice."

"Thank goodness, Robert. There was a rumor that you were packing everything in. Medicine can't afford to lose people like you, you know. Let's talk about it over lunch. I know a little place around the corner where we can be reasonably private."

So off they went, and Farcett told the story of the Tarimond children. Donald Dougall asked all the questions that Farcett himself had put to Morag and Maggie Goudie. He was intrigued.

"And you've brought back some notes?"

"Full details, and samples of the local water for analysis. I'm not sure how well it has survived the journey."

"Well, it will be better than nothing," said Dougall. "I'll certainly take a look at it all for you." But then he surprised Farcett by adding, "I wonder if you would consider doing something for me in return?"

"Certainly," said Farcett, uncertain of what Dougall would ask for, but mentally preparing to offer a generous donation in exchange for his advice.

Dougall looked Farcett straight in the eye. "How about coming to work here?" he said with a note of excitement in his voice.

The suggestion took Farcett completely by surprise. "But it's not my field," he sputtered apologetically.

"Not yet, perhaps, Robert. But you seem like a man who needs a change, and we need a surgeon with your skills and your kind of mind. The patients who come here don't pay, Robert — in fact, at the beginning, you would pay us for the privilege of working with them and learning our techniques — but it's rewarding work, and we're making advances all the time. Think about it. Children are the future, Robert. If we can keep the next generation healthy, the country will thrive as well."

Farcett was completely thrown. He couldn't think of a way of stalling Dougall's enthusiasm. He wasn't ready to reveal his secret dream of a hospital on Tarimond, and anyway, this enterprise of Dougall's seemed to offer much of the satisfaction that might give him, plus the comforts of London. He played for time. "It's tempting," he mused aloud. "But I'd have to keep on what I've got left of my own practice."

"Understood. Just a couple of days a week would be enough to start with. Come back with me now and I'll show you around the wards."

They went. And Farcett was surprised by what he saw. He was used to hospitals with regimented beds and grateful patients lying in silence. The wards at Great Ormond Street were clean enough to satisfy his obsession with hygiene, but the atmosphere was quite different. There were toys. There was laughter. As Doctor Dougall pointed out, many of the children got better care and more attention there than they were used to at home. There was crying and sadness, too, and Dougall warned Farcett of the agony of losing young patients. Doctor Farcett thought of Maggie Goudie and the anguish she had suffered as each baby died. But he already sensed that the Great Ormond Street Hospital might well become his professional home. He could think of nothing else as he changed into evening dress, ready to meet Fox-Selwyn and Montmorency at the Opera House.

CHAPTER 25

WHO'S THAT GIRL?

Montmorency had caught the opera bug early on in his London life. In his travels he had visited opera houses all over Europe. It had become a standing joke between him and Fox-Selwyn that even when they were chasing bandits across Hungary or undermining assassins in Austria, Montmorency would drop everything for a good production of *The Marriage of Figaro* or a quick *Lucia di Lammermoor*. In Paris, Montmorency had lured Fox-Selwyn into his first experience of queuing. They had stood all day outside L'Opéra for tickets to see a great tenor in *Il Trovatore*, taking turns going to shops for supplies of baguettes and wine. Fox-Selwyn had to admit afterward that it had been worth it, if only for the rousing Anvil Chorus, which had stuck in his head for months; though often he had found it difficult to remember exactly who was who in the silly story; and unlike Montmorency, he hadn't cried.

Looking back, Fox-Selwyn realized that the first sign of Montmorency's slide into drug addiction had been the death of his passion for opera. On their painful journey back from Turkey, Montmorency had not once inquired about performances, or sloped off to read the posters on a foreign opera house's wall. So it was a delight to see him excited again, even if tonight they would only be watching the audience leave, and looking for the Home Secretary's mystery girl. They dined at Bargles, where Montmorency's sparkling health was much admired, and arrived at the Opera House just before the curtain fell. Doctor Farcett joined them, and they stood, stamping their feet in the early winter cold.

"You look happy, Robert," said Fox-Selwyn. "Have you solved your mystery?"

"No, but I've found someone who can help me. If there's a medical solution, he'll find it."

"What do you mean 'if'?" said Montmorency. "You're not starting to believe all that stuff from Father Michael about divine judgment, are you?"

"No. Well, not exactly," said Farcett. "But running through it all again today I couldn't think of a scientific reason. And you have to admit, Father Michael did have a very special quality to him, a sort of spiritual magnetism."

"Sounds as if I got you back from Tarimond just in

time," Fox-Selwyn chortled, "or the two of you might have ended up in a monastery. And then who would help me with these Covent Garden girls?" They all laughed, Montmorency louder than any of them after his first night back on Bargles booze. But Fox-Selwyn shushed him to be quiet, whispering loudly, "Look, there's one now."

"Shall I go and talk to her?" said Montmorency, eagerly.

"No. No need. I've checked that one," replied Fox-Selwyn, as if he was talking about examining the drains. "I haven't seen this one before, though."

A woman of about twenty was lazily walking up the slope towards them. Her ill-fitting dress couldn't disguise her slim figure, and despite the heavy makeup, Farcett noticed her pretty face. Montmorency stared in silence, and then found himself saying, out loud and to the amazement of the others, "Good Heavens. It's Vi."

Montmorency's guard was down. Had he been thinking straight he might have held himself back and not done the one thing that would force him to let Farcett and Fox-Selwyn into the past he had guarded so carefully. Perhaps something inside him knew it was time to let his secret go. In any case, his tipsy excitement at seeing the girl outweighed years of caution, and he strode towards her. A look of bemused recognition crossed her face. "Hello, Vi," he said, staring into her eyes. "Remember me?"

"Evening, sir," she said in a bored, routine way. But then she paused, and the puzzled look came back. The others watched as Montmorency repeated her name.

"Vi. Vi. Vi, it's me!" He took off his top hat, and rumpled up his hair. "Vi. It's me, Scarper! Remember?"

"Oh, Mr. Scarper! Remember? How could I forget you? You was so good to me and my mum. Oh, Mr. Scarper, she's terrible now. You wouldn't know her if you saw her. I've been stuck at home for months looking after her. This is the first night I've been out in ages."

"Oh, Vi, it's so good to see you!" cried Montmorency, genuinely thrilled.

"But Mr. Scarper! Look at you!" She grasped the edge of his cape and fingered the fabric. "You've had more than a little bit of luck, haven't you? Where've you been?" She looked at his companions. "Ain't you going to introduce me to your friends?"

Farcett and Fox-Selwyn had been standing back, embarrassed and shocked by the encounter. Fox-Selwyn had recognized the name "Scarper." It was the name Montmorency had called himself in the depths of his drug-induced depravity. He had wondered if it might be a key to that dark part of Montmorency he had never understood. Yet here was someone who liked Mr. Scarper, someone who knew him, and whose mother he knew. What was going on? Perhaps tonight he would find out more.

Montmorency had a split-second decision to make. Was he going to try to ignore Scarper's exposure, or use tonight to complete the picture of his past he had painted for his friends? Inspired by the fun of the evening, the thrill of meeting Vi, and a sense that she might be able to help them, he decided to let them in on his secret. He beckoned Fox-Selwyn and Farcett to join him.

"Vi," said Montmorency, bowing slightly in an exaggerated burst of social etiquette, "Miss Vi Evans, meet Lord George Fox-Selwyn. Lord George Fox-Selwyn, may I present my dear friend and former landlady, Miss Vi Evans. Miss Evans, this is Doctor Robert Farcett. Doctor Farcett, Miss Evans." They all said "Pleased to meet you" as if they were being introduced at a royal garden party.

The doors of the Opera House opened, and the first of the audience rushed out. Montmorency despised these early leavers: the people who prided themselves on making a quick getaway and dodged the curtain calls to do it. He thought them rude not to acknowledge the work that the singers and musicians had put into entertaining them all evening. He pitied them, too, for cutting themselves off from the last bit of drama and fun, when the conductor welcomed the applause, the cast came to the footlights and bowed, and flowers were thrown to the star performers, who clutched their hearts to demonstrate their love for their public. They missed all that, just for the fleeting, smug satisfaction of getting to the cloakroom first, or grabbing a cab before anyone else. Montmorency wanted to get out of their way.

"Vi, you may be able to help us. Can we come home with you?"

"No need for that, old boy!" said Fox-Selwyn, worried about where Montmorency might be leading them. "We could go to a bar nearby."

"Oh, it's not far," said Montmorency. "And I know the way."

He put his arm through Vi's and walked off in the direction of the lodging house where he had found a room on his first day out of prison, all those years ago. He remembered then how he had first seen Vi, squatting by the front door, barely more than a child. He remembered her doing a grand impression of her loud, blowsy mother, Mrs. Evans, and showing him to the dirty upstairs room that had become the nerve center of Scarper's criminal activities while Montmorency had lived in style at the Marimion Hotel. He knew that he would have to explain all this to Fox-Selwyn and Farcett, and he was filled with a heady feeling of relief. Scarper's existence had been the one big secret between them, even after all the revelations that had followed Farcett's reintroduction into his life. Now the strain of keeping that secret would be removed.

But first there was a shock. For sitting on the doorstep of his old home was the slumped and snoring shape of Vi's mother. Montmorency recognized her tattered yellow dress. He had seen it often, five years before. She was still large, perhaps even larger than she used to be, but her bulk, which had once bulged and billowed over the top of her clothes, had now settled lower down, in a heavy heap. Her unnaturally bright hair had turned a dirty white and thinned almost to baldness. Her teeth had gone. She smelled of alcohol, and worse. As they approached, she jerked awake. She stared at the group coming towards her and started shouting, over and over again.

"Where's my Vi? She's a good girl. Good Evans, we call her. Good Evans!"

Poor, demented Mrs. Evans was stuck forever in a very old joke. Above her head was the old chalk sign: "Vakensees." Vi saw Montmorency looking at it.

"We don't have many lodgers now," she said sadly. "Just people passing through, desperate for a place to stay."

Montmorency was horrified that the Evans family fortunes had fallen even lower since he'd left them. He approached Mrs. Evans. Fox-Selwyn was horrified to see him sit on the step beside her.

"How do you do, Mrs. Evans?" he said gallantly.

The old lady recoiled from him with a look of wild suspicion. "Where's my Vi?" she repeated. "She's a good girl. Good Evans . . ."

"She won't recognize you," said Vi. "And she won't say anything else. Lost her mind. Talks about me all the time, but doesn't know who I am." Vi bent to help her mother up.

"You get off me," cried Mrs. Evans, wriggling away from her. "I want my Vi! Get me my Vi!"

"It *is* Vi, Mum," said the girl, but the old woman still fought against her grip.

Fox-Selwyn had never seen anything like the

desperate violence of this once-loving mother towards her exhausted daughter. Farcett had come across senility before, but never so raw: usually in the sanitized setting of an institution, or in a household where servants could take the strain. They were both wondering how to get away, when Montmorency drew them deeper into the scene.

"I'll give you a hand," he said. And with kind concern he helped Vi guide the protesting woman inside, settling her into an old armchair by the window.

"Is there somewhere we can talk?" he asked Vi.

"Choose a room. They're all free," she replied, in a mixture of resignation and shame. Montmorency called Farcett and Fox-Selwyn in from the street. They all went into the back bedroom. It was as bare and grubby as Scarper's attic lair had been. Fox-Selwyn brushed the dust off the only chair and sat down. Vi sat on the table. Farcett and Montmorency sat side by side on the sagging, squeaking bed.

"Now, Vi," said Montmorency. "We're looking for someone. Perhaps he's been here, or perhaps one of the other girls has told you about him."

Fox-Selwyn butted in. "We heard about him from an acquaintance who met a young lady outside the Opera House. He is a distinguished gentleman, of about average height. He's smartly dressed, with a refined manner."

"Blimey, sir," laughed Vi. "That gives me plenty to choose from! They're all like that!" She eyed Montmorency quizzically. "Even Mr. Scarper now, it seems."

"Well," said Fox-Selwyn, "the gentleman we're talking about has connections with the government."

"That won't narrow it down much!" she scoffed. "We get all sorts — judges, admirals." She started giggling again. "I even had one who said he was the Home Secretary!"

Fox-Selwyn dived in, asking, "When was that?"

"Oh, months ago, now," she replied, casually. "He was in a terrible state. All worried about that explosion at King's Cross. You know, the one that killed Molly Mead. I told him, 'You should be grateful you're not the Head of the Gas Company! Her family is after his blood! I'd stick to being Home Secretary if I was you, love.' That's what I told him!"

"You knew the dead woman?" asked Fox-Selwyn, excited at this new lead.

"Molly? Of course. She worked in the flower market."

Fox-Selwyn was exasperated that that simple detail hadn't made it to the police report. He was soon to find that Vi was a treasure trove of new information.

She carried on: "Everyone around here knew her. She ran a whole load of stalls. Inherited them from her husband. She did all the ordering. Wasn't short of a bob or two either. She'd just forked out for her daughter's honeymoon. That's what she was doing at the station, seeing them off on the sleeper. Do you know, they actually have beds on those trains. You can lie down. You can sleep all the way to Scotland!"

Fox-Selwyn realized, sadly, that he had guessed correctly. The jolly woman with the handkerchief had been one of the bomber's victims.

"You should have seen the flowers at her funeral," said Vi. "The very best, all sent up by her suppliers from the country that morning."

"But what about the man?" Montmorency interrupted. "The one who said he was the Home Secretary."

Vi thought back to her talkative client, and out came another torrent of words. "I remember him because he was so drunk, and how he just went on and on about the explosion. He got really interested when I told him I'd heard it. I don't know why. I mean it's not that far to King's Cross from here as the crow flies, is it? Though you'd be lucky to see a bird of any description around here, wouldn't you? Apart from those disgusting pigeons, I mean. Rats with wings, that's what Mum used to call them. Anyway, I was telling him how I remembered the explosion because of this man who was staying here that night. Or he should have been staying here but he went out just before the bang and he never came back, and I was wondering if he'd been killed or injured or something, because he never came back for his stuff. And I was telling him all this, and he kept asking me more and more about it: you know, 'What was his name? What did he look like?' And I was just sitting here thinking, 'Why is he asking all this? How much is he going to pay me for sitting here talking about a gas explosion?' He just went on and on and then he fell asleep in the kitchen." She laughed as she thought back to the morning after: "Ran away pretty quick when he woke up. Probably came as a shock when the drink wore off and he realized he wasn't the Home Secretary, and had his own life to get back to!"

The three men were temporarily silenced by the heap of information that had been dumped before them. There were so many leads buried in Vi's chatty account that nobody was sure what to ask. Fox-Selwyn spoke first:

"And he never came back?"

"Oh no," said Vi. "Well, they don't, you know. They're too ashamed."

"No, not the Home Secretary." (Fox-Selwyn paused and rephrased the question to protect the honor of his friend.) "I mean the man who *said* he was the Home Secretary. No, I wasn't asking about him. I meant the man who was staying here on the night of the explosion. Did he ever come back?"

"No, he never did. But his friend came to collect his bag. Lucky I hadn't thrown it out. It just had some bits and pieces in it, some string and some candles and a load of old dirt."

Montmorency and Fox-Selwyn exchanged glances, recognizing the possible components of a bomb.

Vi jabbered on. "Anyway, I put it under the stairs in case he came back, and I forgot about it. Then his friend turned up yesterday . . ."

"Yesterday!" exclaimed all three men at once.

"Yesterday. About seven o'clock at night. He seemed really relieved to get the bag back. I suppose they'd be in trouble for taking it from work."

Fox-Selwyn was confused. "From work?"

"Yes, it had it written on it, see. 'Property of the Royal Botanic Gardens, Kew.' I thought the first man must have stolen it, but his friend said no, they were working there."

"And this was yesterday?"

"Yesterday, yes. But why are you all so interested? It was only a bag."

Montmorency tried to make up an explanation that didn't sound too complicated. In the end he opted for a version of the truth. He reached over and took hold of Vi's hands.

"Vi," he said. "The explosion at King's Cross wasn't caused by gas. It was a bomb, and we are wondering whether the man who stayed here might have been the bomber. Somewhere in everything you have told us tonight there might be a clue. We need to talk a lot more, and I need to explain to you how I come to be here now, dressed like this." He paused, overawed by the task. "But it's late." He looked at his friends. "Why don't we go home and get some sleep and we'll come back and start again in the morning."

"You can stay here if you like," said Vi cheerily. Fox-Selwyn looked horrified, but she continued, turning to Montmorency: "You could have your old room," she said, "only the floor fell in. I should tell you about that as well. . . ."

"No, thank you, Vi," said Montmorency, afraid of setting off another rambling story. "You've told us quite enough to be getting on with already. Get some rest, and we'll be back in the morning. But whatever you do, don't mention any of this to anybody."

"Can I help you get your mother into bed?" asked Doctor Farcett, appalled at the pitiful conditions in which the women lived.

"She just sleeps in the chair," said Vi. "I can't lift her, see."

"Well, just for tonight, let's get her comfortable," said the doctor. And he and Montmorency carried the slumbering old woman into the bedroom. As they dropped her onto the mattress, a low rumble shook the room.

"That's just what it sounded like!" shouted Vi. "The explosion, I mean."

"Another bomb?" said Doctor Farcett, catching Fox-Selwyn's startled reaction.

"Probably, yes," said Fox-Selwyn.

"And not far away," added Montmorency.

"You stay here with Vi, Robert," shouted Fox-Selwyn as he ran to the door.

Montmorency pulled Farcett to one side and whispered to the doctor, "If Vi's visitor planted this one, she could be in danger. He might want to silence her. Don't tell her. We don't want to alarm her. But don't leave her, and don't answer the door. We'll go and see what's happened."

Montmorency and Fox-Selwyn ran through to Bow Street in time to see a group of policemen leaving at speed. They followed them in the direction of Waterloo Station.

CHAPTER 26

≫

WATERLOO STATION

This time the bomb hadn't killed anyone, but the damage to the building was worse. When Fox-Selwyn and Montmorency arrived, Waterloo Station was full of swirling dust. The front wall of the main ticket office had been blown out, and cardboard tickets, pages from timetables, and assorted pieces of official paper were fluttering around the concourse. The water pipe to the Gents had been severed, and a gushing torrent was pouring out onto mailbags leaning against the wall. It was late. The station had been closed at the time of the blast, which was registered by the hands of the huge shattered clock as 1:37 a.m. It seemed that the bombers had wanted to avoid hurting passengers, but to create the maximum disruption in the morning.

With hardly any staff on the premises it was a while before anyone took charge. Montmorency and Fox-Selwyn, along with assorted tramps and late-night revelers, were able to wander amidst the devastation at will. It was exciting to be there, but unproductive as an exercise in detection. There was nothing to see but rubble, nothing that gave them an instant clue to the identity of the culprit. So when the police finally organized a guard on the site and started ordering all civilians to leave, Fox-Selwyn put up only the minimum resistance. The two of them walked back to Covent Garden, grubby, but not much the wiser. They had noticed that there was no gassy smell. This time the authorities would have to admit it was a bomb.

Vi and Doctor Farcett were still awake, waiting up for news. Farcett had persuaded Vi to let him help her wash Mrs. Evans, and she was lying tucked up in bed, snuffling and occasionally mumbling about Vi in her sleep. Farcett had promised to visit and give her a proper examination in the morning. Vi offered around a bottle of gin. There were no takers.

"I think we should go back to our plan for some sleep," said Fox-Selwyn. "This is all very exciting, but my guess is that we're in for a busy time. Tomorrow we can find out what the police make of it all and take it from there."

"George, I don't think Vi should be left on her own," said Montmorency. "Why don't I stay here with her? I think she deserves an explanation of what's been going on, and why we think she might be in danger."

"Me, in danger!" shrieked Vi. "Don't be ridiculous. I know how to look after myself."

Farcett sat down alongside her, and spoke calmly. He knew how Montmorency's mind was working. "Vi, it's possible that the bomb at Waterloo was planted by the man who came here yesterday. If it was, he might want to stop you talking to the police."

"But you're not the police!" she said, looking at Montmorency with a smile that dropped into shock. "Are you?"

"Not the police, no," he replied.

"But on the same side," added Fox-Selwyn. "We may be able to help the authorities piece all this together and stop the bombers. Montmorency . . . or should I say Scarper . . . will explain it all to you. I'll come around in the morning and we'll work out what to do next." He looked at Montmorency like a schoolmaster challenging a naughty pupil: "Then perhaps he can fill *me* in on one or two things."

Montmorency nodded. He knew that the time had come to reveal all about Scarper and the thieving that had gotten him from this seedy house to the height of London society. "Yes, I will, George. Tomorrow, I promise."

"I look forward to it," said Fox-Selwyn, picking up his hat and brushing off the dust with the back of his hand, "at last!" He turned to the doctor: "Come on, Robert, let's go."

With the exception of Mrs. Evans, they all slept badly that night. Early the next morning Fox-Selwyn asked Chivers to go out for a newspaper, and had the presence of mind to send him to Bargles, to get a change of clothes for Montmorency. He himself paid a private visit to the Home Secretary before breakfast. As he expected, he found a scene of despair. Early reports on the bombing indicated the usual confusion and lack of leads. The Home Secretary insisted that Fox-Selwyn and Montmorency should continue investigating without reporting to the police. They should report directly to him. They could use whatever methods they pleased, so long as they didn't look to him for support if it all went wrong. He needed to be able to wash his hands of them if necessary, but he assured Fox-Selwyn that the "very highest authorities" would be made aware of their role in any successful outcome. *Yours, too, no doubt*, thought Fox-Selwyn as he took his leave of the unhappy man.

When Fox-Selwyn arrived at Vi's house, Farcett was already there, with his doctor's bag, listening to Mrs. Evans's failing heart and testing her reflexes.

"She really shouldn't be living in these conditions," he whispered. "It's too damp, and too cold."

Montmorency took Fox-Selwyn upstairs to his old room. They shuffled around the hole in the floor. They had been close friends for more than five years, and on one level they knew each other inside out. But they had never mastered the kind of intimate conversation they needed now. Neither could bring himself to look into the other's eyes. Fox-Selwyn sat, picking at a hole in the filthy mattress, while Montmorency began to get changed, and started, with false joviality, to tell the full story of his life of crime. He recalled their first meeting, outside his other home, the palatial Marimion Hotel. Fox-Selwyn had long ago guessed that the money sustaining that lifestyle came from a shady source. At Glendarvie, Montmorency had admitted as much. But Fox-Selwyn had not suspected that Montmorency's criminal career had extended well into the time of their friendship. He didn't know that night after night Montmorency had bade him farewell after a party or a game of cards and hurried back to the Marimion to change into rough working clothes.

In that outfit, as Scarper, he would make his way to this very room in Covent Garden. It was the base from which he robbed all corners of London.

"I used to come here and get into my sewer gear," said Montmorency.

"Your what?" asked Fox-Selwyn, bemused.

"I used to go down the sewers almost every night. Did you know there are underground tunnels right across London? I could go anywhere, and no one knew I was on the move."

Fox-Selwyn could guess why he did it. "And when you came up from the sewers?"

"I stole things. Lots of things. Good stuff. Better and better as time went by. I used to hide it under the floorboards where that hole is."

Fox-Selwyn stared at the floor. "Did it pay for the Marimion?"

"Yes. And my membership at Bargles," said Montmorency, with a nervous laugh.

"And did you ever steal from me?"

Montmorency was appalled that his dear friend could think such a thing. "Of course not, George. I wouldn't do that, believe me, I couldn't do such a thing." He paused, and then tried to lighten the atmosphere with a confession he thought his friend would enjoy. "I did steal from Sir Gordon Pewley, though." And Fox-Selwyn smiled at the thought of the corrupt Bargles bore suffering at Montmorency's hands.

"And the police never caught you?" he asked.

Montmorency was relaxing now, and enjoying his tale. "No, I was too clever for them!" he laughed.

Fox-Selwyn could believe it, recalling his friend's exploits abroad.

"I was lucky, too," Montmorency continued jovially. "They stopped looking actually. They arrested somebody else."

Fox-Selwyn was suddenly appalled. The mood changed again as he asked, slowly, "And you let someone else go to prison for you?"

Montmorency slumped with guilt. His voice grew softer. "It's worse than that," he said. There was a pause as Montmorency drew up the courage to tell everything. "George, I let him hang. He's dead. And I knew him, George. He taught me so much in prison. We shared a cell. He showed me how to change myself, how to copy other people's movements and speech, how to build a new identity. Without him I couldn't have done any of it. Without him I wouldn't be here now."

"Who was he?"

"In prison we called him Freakshow."

"I've heard that name."

"Yes, it was in all the papers."

"I've heard it on your own lips, Montmorency. When you were delirious in Turkey, and at Glendarvie. It's why you took the drug, isn't it? To get away from the shame?"

"Yes. To stop the dreams. But it didn't work, George. I think about Freakshow every day."

"And so you should, Montmorency!" Fox-Selwyn spat out the words.

"But George . . ." Montmorency's voice was appealing for sympathy and understanding, as it had so often recently. But this time he wouldn't get it. Fox-Selwyn was disgusted. He had been prepared for much of Montmorency's story. He was willing to turn a blind eye to some of Montmorency's crimes. He could even accept his life in the sewers. He had always suspected that his friend had used some nefarious skill on his first mission for the government, when he had infiltrated a foreign embassy and trapped Pewley in the very act of betraying his country. Now he knew how Montmorency had gotten in there. Perhaps he could even forgive Montmorency's deceit in the early days of their friendship, when he had pretended to be a gentleman while still working as a thief. But letting another man hang! That was too much.

Fox-Selwyn turned his back on Montmorency. He had stood by that man through the horrors of drug addiction. He had let him into the very heart of his family. And Montmorency was despicable. No better than a sewer rat. The room was silent. Montmorency sat with his head in his hands, waiting for his closest friend to turn on him with words of rejection. But it was worse than that. There was silence. Fox-Selwyn just stood there, with his back to him, biting into his fist, thinking.

Fox-Selwyn felt disillusioned and betrayed. And yet . . . and yet . . . hadn't Montmorency acted with honor and bravery on their trips abroad? Hadn't he been loyal? Hadn't his friendship been fun? He couldn't erase the memory of their happy times together in the past. They had been a great team. Perhaps Montmorency should be given the chance to earn his place on that team again.

Montmorency was in despair. Since that moment, last night outside the Opera House, when he had decided to tell Fox-Selwyn everything, he had lost sight of why he had kept his secret for so long. He had actually been looking forward to unburdening himself by telling his friend about his double life: about Scarper, and the sewers, thinking only of the relief he would feel when everything was out in the open. He hadn't thought about Freakshow. He had been so happy, returning to London and meeting his jolly friend again, that he hadn't considered how Fox-Selwyn would react to the news that he had let another man take the blame for his crimes. And of course, Fox-Selwyn was right. He was contemptible. Not fit to be allowed out of the sewers he had inhabited for so long. He deserved to be rejected by his friend. Perhaps even turned over to the police and returned to prison. He waited in agony for Fox-Selwyn to speak.

But after what seemed to him like many minutes, it was Montmorency who broke the silence, still not daring to look at Fox-Selwyn directly.

"Do you want me to go?" he said. "I could just disappear. I know how to do that. I wouldn't blame you if you never wanted to see me again."

Montmorency was surprised by Fox-Selwyn's response.

"No, don't go. What you did to this 'Freakshow' was disgraceful. But running away won't bring him back. I won't pretend that I'm not shocked and disappointed, Montmorency. More shocked and disappointed than the many, many times you've let me down since Turkey. But I'm going to give you a last chance. And I mean last. It's final. You've pushed me right to my limit. Montmorency, if you want to atone for your crimes, do it by achieving something good. Use the skills Freakshow gave you to help catch this bomber."

"What do you mean?" asked Montmorency, his tearful eyes fixed on Fox-Selwyn's back.

Fox-Selwyn turned to face his friend. "I mean, Montmorency, that you are going to have to transform yourself all over again. But this time you won't be doing it on your own!"

CHAPTER 27

TRANSFORMATIONS

Sometimes Lord George Fox-Selwyn's mind worked rather slowly, particularly after a good dinner and a couple of bottles of wine. But sometimes, as exasperated school reports had pointed out year after year, he was capable of moments of intellectual clarity and brilliance. It was a shame, his teachers had said, that he seemed so reluctant to put this capacity to good use. That morning in Scarper's room in Covent Garden the schoolmasters would have been proud of him. Listening to Montmorency inspired the instant formulation of a complex plan for securing Vi's safety and catching the station bombers.

This time Vi and Mrs. Evans would be at the heart of the scheme, with new identities and a new way of life. Up in the top bedroom, Fox-Selwyn sketched out the idea to Montmorency, and with a few refinements what he suggested is what they did.

Montmorency was to return to the Marimion, and warn the hotel manager that his elderly aunt and her daughter were coming to England from their home in Italy. His aunt, the recently widowed Contessa Evanista, was sick and was not to be disturbed. She would be attended to by her daughter, Violetta, and her personal physician in London, Doctor Farcett. The Contessa and Violetta (Mrs. Evans and Vi) would share a ladies' maid, Susanna (Vi again, in the female equivalent of Scarper's old role). None of them could speak any English. Montmorency would, as before, have Scarper at his side. They would all move into the hotel. An improvement on Montmorency's old arrangements would be their ability to use Fox-Selwyn's home as an extra base to change clothes and compare notes, though the Covent Garden house would remain for use in emergencies, too.

Fox-Selwyn outlined the merits of his scheme. If all went according to plan, Mrs. Evans would be looked after, Vi would be out of reach of the bombers, and Scarper could circulate in the underworld trying to track them down. But only Vi knew what the bombers looked like. She would have to go out with Scarper or Montmorency from time to time, dressed as Susanna or Violetta according to the nature of the occasion. The plan would have to be implemented quickly. They would start that very day.

"What have you two been up to?" said Vi as Montmorency and Fox-Selwyn came down the stairs. "You've been up there for ages."

"Vi! Robert!" called Fox-Selwyn. "Come and hear this. We've got a plan."

"Put the kettle on, Vi," said Montmorency, "and George will explain."

"Put the kettle on!" said Vi, mockingly, in a posh voice. "What do you think this is — the Grand Hotel?"

Fox-Selwyn laughed: "Not the Grand, Vi. The Marimion. That's where you and your mother will be living by the end of the week. And I'm glad to hear you can do accents. You're going to need some acting skills."

"You don't live in Covent Garden without learning to act," said Vi, striking a dramatic pose. "And Mum was on the stage, you know, before she had me. Though you wouldn't believe it now."

They looked across at the slobbering figure in the armchair by the window.

"She's a good girl, my Vi," she shouted. "Good Evans, we call her. Good Evans!"

We'll have to do something about that, thought Fox-Selwyn. *Perhaps Robert can give her a sedative.*

When he outlined the plan, Vi raised the obvious problem.

"Where are me and Mum going to get clothes to make us look like this Contessa and this Violetta, then?" she asked. Fox-Selwyn, not used to worrying about the practicalities of life, hadn't thought of that.

"Well, who makes your clothes normally?" he asked. "Perhaps they could be persuaded to do something a little special. I'll pay, of course. . . ."

"Don't be silly, I've never had anything made for me in my life!" said Vi, spreading out her arms to show her dilapidated frock. "All our stuff comes off the secondhand stall in the market. They're not likely to have anything grand enough for a countess, now are they?"

"Well, do you know any girls who work as seamstresses, Vi?" he asked. "*I've* never actually had need of one before, either!"

"None as could keep a secret," she said. "And none as would work as fast as we need them to."

Montmorency interrupted them: "I know someone who might help." He was thinking of his tailor, Mr. Lyons. "He's friendly and discreet, and well connected in the trade. If I could just have a list of the ladies' measurements, I should be able to sort something out."

Fox-Selwyn took out his notebook and a pencil,

and looked towards Doctor Farcett. "Robert, have you got a tape measure in that bag of yours?"

"I'm not sure," said Doctor Farcett, who was unconvinced by the plan so far, and was reluctant to get involved in measuring the women.

"He has, you know, I've seen it!" said Vi. "It was in there this morning when he was doing his tests on Mum." And she opened his bag, pulling out a tape measure. Montmorency recognized it as the very one Farcett had used to measure his own body in the prison, years ago.

"Oh, of course," said the doctor, flustered.

"Well, go on then," said Fox-Selwyn. "Measure them. You can't be expecting one of us to do it. You're the professional!"

"I'm just not sure if this is the right thing to do," stuttered Farcett. And Fox-Selwyn was glad he hadn't yet asked him to drug Mrs. Evans.

"Come on, man!" he said. "We both know you've faced bigger challenges to your principles than this. Montmorency and I will leave the room if you like."

They went into the kitchen, where Fox-Selwyn composed a letter in Italian, using handwriting he was pretty confident no tailor or dressmaker would be able to read. As he wrote, they could hear Vi hooting with laughter as Doctor Farcett measured both the women. The letter was from the "Contessa." It warned of her arrival, and asked Montmorency to arrange for clothes in the best London fashion to be waiting for herself and her daughter when they got there.

"Show this to the tailor, and tell him a tale of woe," he said to Montmorency. "Say that the letter was delayed, the women are already on their way, and the dresses must be made up in a hurry."

As he spoke, the door to the front room opened, and Farcett emerged, red in the face and holding a neat list of figures.

"What about my maid's uniform?" said Vi, who seemed to have been enjoying herself. "Where am I going to get that?" The men looked at Fox-Selwyn.

"You're the one with a houseful of maids," said Montmorency. "You'll have to steal one and hope your housekeeper doesn't notice."

"All right," said Fox-Selwyn, reluctantly. "But Heaven help me if she does!"

Montmorency had not visited his tailor for a year. His last visit had been to collect lightweight traveling clothes for his trip to the East. Mr. Lyons was thrilled to see one of his favorite customers again, hoping for one of Montmorency's large and costly orders. He clapped his freckled hands with glee as the shop door opened.

"Such a delight to see you, sir. And looking so well, sir. What can I do for you today?"

"Well, Lyons, I'm going to need a new winter suit."

Lyons clasped his hands joyfully.

"But not today, I'm afraid. Today I need your advice."

The tailor was used to being a confidant for his clients. He held the secrets of scores of unsuitable liaisons, bad debts, and family feuds. He was intrigued. Montmorency took the Italian letter from his pocket and explained the problem of the imminent aunt.

"She will be furious that I haven't sorted something out, but I have no idea where to start. I know nothing about women's clothes."

"Ah, sir, but I do! My sister, Madame Lyonnaise, has a shop not far from here." He bent towards Montmorency confidentially and whispered, "She isn't really French, you know. The name's just for effect. Her ladies expect it."

"Really!" gasped Montmorency in mock surprise.

Mr. Lyons got his hat and coat, locked the shop, and led Montmorency to his sister's establishment.

She emerged from the back as the bell over the door announced their arrival. Like her brother she was festooned with freckles, though she had taken great pains to disguise them with layers of chalky white makeup.

"Albert! What are you doing here?" she began, in an irritated London accent, before noticing the distinguished figure following Mr. Lyons into the shop. Then she turned on the refinement. "Good morning, sir. Can I be of assistance?"

Her brother answered: "Dolly, this is Mr. Montmorency. He's a very valued customer of mine. He has a problem, and I told him you're just the person to help." Mr. Lyons told the story of the Contessa and her daughter, and passed on the list of measurements, stressing the need for speed. His sister cast a professional eye over the piece of paper.

"Absolutely no difficulty with the young lady, sir. I'm sure I have a display gown of the highest quality I could let you have straightaway. The Contessa may require a little work" — she hummed thoughtfully — "though she does seem to be about the same size as Lady Harvington, give or take an inch. We are working on a day dress for her ladyship at the moment, and I know she won't be needing it for a couple of weeks. Perhaps I could adapt it for your aunt and make a new one for Lady Harvington. If I took away a few ribbons, added some buttons, and possibly an extra frill around the hem — though that would take time, and we don't have time, you say — no, we'll just raise the neckline a little instead."

Montmorency was intrigued. He was already obsessive about the world of male fashion, and felt privileged to be given this insight into the female version.

Dolly Lyons carried on. She was convincing herself it was all possible. "Yes. If we do all that, Lady Harvington could meet the Contessa and never know that she's wearing the same dress! My ladies are quite particular about that, you know, sir."

"Oh, I understand completely," said Montmorency, quite genuinely. "The last thing I would want to do is cause any trouble. Could I possibly see the designs?"

"Well, sir, if you don't mind coming through to the workroom you can see the dresses themselves."

Montmorency was thrilled, and couldn't hide his excitement as Dolly led him and Mr. Lyons through the curtain and along a passageway to a large room where six girls were stitching away by the light of enormous windows. Bales of brightly colored cloth leaned against the walls. Dressmakers' dummies in all shapes and sizes were clothed in costumes at various stages of development. Dolly put her arm around the shoulders of a turquoise and pink confection in the corner.

"The Duchess of Frogmore!" she exclaimed proudly. Then she brought a hand to her mouth and whispered to her brother conspiratorially: "Just needs a little easing on the hips."

In the middle of the room, on a long sturdy table, some scarlet satin was marked out with chalk scribbles, paper, and pins. A huge pair of scissors lay alongside, ready to cut. Mr. Lyons cast a professional eye over the scene, and fondled the shiny fabric.

"It's lucky you arrived when you did," said Dolly. "I was just about to start cutting. I don't like to be interrupted when I get going."

"Can't be helped sometimes, though," said Mr. Lyons quickly, worried that his sister might be making Montmorency feel uncomfortable. But Montmorency was in heaven, and oblivious to the Lyons family chemistry.

Dolly had made her way over to one of the larger forms. "This is Lady Harvington!" she cried, like a helpful hostess. Montmorency playfully held out a hand and shook the empty sleeve. The sewing girls giggled, and Dolly swiftly put them in their places with a sharp "Shh!" She ran through the proposed alterations again, and Montmorency nodded his approval, suggesting the addition of a shawl. Dolly Lyons was most complimentary about his idea, and not only because it would increase the bill without creating any extra work. She had plenty of shawls in the stockroom.

"And now for the young lady. May I suggest this?" Dolly pulled out a long-sleeved dress in mauve and black striped cotton. "Striking, I think, but not too loud."

"Perfect," said Montmorency, imagining the elegant figure Vi would strike in her new clothes. "My cousin will be delighted with it, I'm sure."

Dolly drew him to one side, and dropped her voice so her brother and the girls could not hear. "Will the ladies be needing anything else, sir? Nightwear, or anything for" — she paused and went even quieter — "underneath?"

Montmorency felt himself blushing. "Quite possibly," he mumbled. "May I leave all that to you?"

"Of course. I know what to do," she said, squeezing his arm a little. "We have everything in stock. They can always send things back if they are unsuitable."

Montmorency smiled to himself at the thought of Vi and Mrs. Evans complaining about lavish replacements for their meager (possibly nonexistent) underwear, and asked for the order to be sent to Lord George Fox-Selwyn's home as soon as possible. Mr. Lyons led the way back through the curtain and into the shop.

"I'm extremely grateful, Madame Lyonnaise," said Montmorency. "You have been most accommodating. And you have spared me from the wrath of my aunt! I'm sure she and my cousin will come straight to you if they need any more clothes while they are in London."

Dolly beamed. Montmorency left the shop first, and Mr. Lyons turned back to peck his sister on the cheek.

"You're on to a good thing there, Dol. Big orders, no nonsense, and always pays on time, in cash. You get those dresses off as fast as you can, girl."

"Don't worry," she said, "he'll have them tonight." Then she turned back to the workroom to get her girls into action.

CHAPTER 28

SHOPPING QUEEN

When Madame Lyonnaise's parcels arrived at Fox-Selwyn's house, Vi was having a bath. Chivers and the housekeeper had been told as much as they needed to know about what was going on, and were reluctantly, but efficiently, making their master's extra guests comfortable. Mrs. Evans was already clean, and tucked up in the spare room. Montmorency, Fox-Selwyn, and Doctor Farcett were discussing their plan of campaign. They all agreed that a trip to Kew Gardens was an urgent priority, and that Vi should go in her grand clothes, so as not to be recognized. They unwrapped the packages straightaway, and Montmorency proudly showed off the fruits of his morning shopping trip. He picked up Vi's new dress and held it in front of himself, mincing around the room and kicking out the skirt. The door opened.

"Very fetching! But I think that would look better on me!" laughed Vi, grabbing the dress as Montmorency hurriedly dropped it to the floor. She was tightly wrapped in one of Fox-Selwyn's silk dressing gowns, with a towel around her hair in a turban.

"I think you might need these as well," said Montmorency, shyly, passing her the box of assorted underwear. She peeped inside, and brought out an enormous corset, wrapping it around herself in front of the embarrassed men.

"I think this must be for Mum!" she giggled, and swept out of the room with her arms full of clothes.

Five minutes later she was back, almost unrecognizable, asking for help with the buttons up the back. She paraded up and down the room, looking like quite a lady, answering any questions in an incomprehensible foreign-sounding gibberish. Fox-Selwyn was most impressed.

"Perfect," he said. "My dear, you will be a credit to the Marimion! You are ready."

"Not quite!" said Vi. After a dramatic pause, she slowly lifted up the hem of her dress. There beneath it were her gnarled and knobby feet.

"Oh dear," said Montmorency. "I forgot about shoes. Where can we get them?"

"You'll have to take me shopping," said Vi excitedly. "But they'll be closing soon, so we'd better be quick." And she slipped on her old battered pumps, ready for her first outing in her finery. "What about Mum? Her feet are all swollen, you know. She'll need special shoes."

Doctor Farcett came to the rescue.

"I've got a wheelchair in my consulting room. I'll bring it round in the morning, and we'll take her to the Marimion in that. She needn't have any footwear at all."

So the shopping trip was just for Montmorency and Vi, and it turned out to be the first of many — fitted in between their more serious duties and, if anything, rather overequipping Vi for both her new roles.

It was raining, so they took Fox-Selwyn's carriage. This time, there was no point in going to the fancy part of the West End, near Montmorency's tailor. There, the shoes were made to measure, and delivery could take weeks. Instead they made for one of the newer, cheaper shops, with ready-made shoes from the factories in the Midlands. They found one not far from Leicester Square. The window was full of little wooden stands, displaying everything from slippers to stout walking boots. Montmorency went in first. Inside there were comfortable sofas and chairs, and more samples of the shoes on offer. The manageress had had a quiet day. The weather had kept the customers away, and she was tidying up, getting ready to close for the night. But she greeted the well-dressed man politely enough.

"We don't sell men's shoes, I'm afraid, sir. We have a branch in Charing Cross Road that will be able to help you."

"Actually, it's ladies' shoes I require," he said. For a moment the manageress wondered if he was one of the more exotic men who lived in the neighborhood, but he quickly came out with his explanation: "My cousin has had an accident in the wet, and needs a new pair urgently."

On the way to the shop, Montmorency and Vi had realized that she couldn't be seen in such a fine dress with her terrible shoes, and they'd concocted a story to explain why Vi was sitting outside in the carriage in her stockinged feet.

"She slipped on some muck on the pavement, and the heel of her shoe came right off. Not a very pleasant introduction to London, I'm afraid. She's here on a visit from Italy, and I fear her delicate shoes were not quite up to our climate."

The manageress was intrigued; and quick to see

that since this was an emergency, and it was nearly closing time, she was definitely going to make a sale.

"Perhaps I could take some shoes out to her," she suggested. "Of course, we don't know the size." She picked out a smart pair with a low heel. "Let's give these a try."

Montmorency was relieved that she was entering into the spirit of things, and held his umbrella over her head as she bustled out to the carriage. Vi was already under strict instructions to say nothing during the transaction. Now he made sure she wouldn't be asked any questions: "My cousin is rather embarrassed, of course, and she doesn't speak English."

"Don't worry, sir. I'll do my best," said the lady, climbing up into the carriage, and settling herself down alongside the mysterious lady with a fan to her face. She was impressed by the quality of her clothes, and the silkiness of her stockings. She tried to be gentle.

But there was no hope of the foot fitting the shoe. It was like the scene after the ball in "Cinderella," when all the girls in the land tried on the glass slipper. Vi pushed as hard as she could, but it was no good.

"I'll have to go and get some more," said the manageress.

Montmorency, tired of standing in the rain, had a different idea. He gave the manageress the umbrella, and carried Vi, like a new bride crossing the threshold, across the puddles and into the shop. She had never been anywhere like it in her life, and squeaked in delight.

"Blimey . . ." she gasped, quickly correcting herself to something that sounded like "blimioni" and fanning herself fast. Her eyes were glowing at the sight of all the shoes. Montmorency squeezed her a little tighter, and put her down on the sofa a little harder than he need have, just to warn her to keep her mouth shut. He was determined to stay in charge.

The manageress disappeared into her stockroom and came out with some sturdy shoes in a range of larger sizes. While she was gone, Vi whispered a quick, "I'll need two pairs, you know," and though Montmorency shut her up with a furious look, he did send the lady back again, to bring some additional styles.

"Will that be all, sir?" she asked, when they had found three pairs that fit.

Montmorency said, "Yes, thank you," and reached for his wallet.

The woman looked pleased that she might at last get the chance to go home, but then a moaning noise started up somewhere deep inside Vi.

"Nooo, norre, nono, nori, nori, nooo," she rumbled, pointing at one of the stands. "Sleepperdoodo, sleepperdoone, sleepearsi, sleeepears . . ." Montmorency turned to silence her, but the manageress had worked out what she wanted.

"We do have some lovely styles in slippers!" she said. "Shall I get some?" Montmorency said yes, but only to get the woman out of the room so that he could hiss a rebuke at Vi. "I told you to be quiet!" he whispered angrily. "Do you want to ruin everything?"

Vi started to defend herself, but only got as far as "But . . ." when she caught sight of the manageress coming back. She changed the "but" to "Buttonioni . . . butterono . . ." trying to signal with her fan to Montmorency that they were not alone. The manageress had heard her, and thought she was picking out a particular pair from the display.

"Yes, we have some with buttons on them!" she said, cheerily.

Montmorency just wanted to get away. "I'm not sure that's what my cousin meant," said Montmorency, snarling at Vi. But Vi was nodding and smiling at the woman, so he gave in. "Very well. Let's sort out the slippers, and we'll be on our way."

Somehow they ended up with two pairs of slippers,

one with buttons and one without. He thought of them as Vi's reward for not saying a word as she was trying them on. Then while they were being wrapped up, she couldn't resist one more request.

"Bootto . . . bootie . . . bootini," she cried, miming pulling on boots and tying long laces. The woman understood at once.

In the end, they needed her help to carry all the shopping out to the carriage. Montmorency was charm itself until the door was closed and the driver had shaken the reins to make the horse set off. Then he let rip at his companion.

"What on earth did you think you were doing? I've told you to keep your mouth shut, and I mean it!"

"But it didn't do any harm, did it? And we're not going to have to buy shoes again, are we?"

"Not for years, by the look of this lot," Montmorency grumbled, though of course he, the champion shopper, had far more pairs tucked away in his room. "We mustn't take chances. People have got to believe that you can't speak English."

"I wasn't speaking English," she said, bundling herself up to one side of the carriage in a sulk. "Lord George Fox-Selwyn told me all about Italian. Everything ends in 'i's, 'e's, and 'o's. I was talking Italian."

"Huh!" he scoffed, sullenly.

"My own kind of Italian. And it did the trick, didn't it?"

Montmorency looked at the parcels. He looked at the charming shoes that transformed Vi's feet from a working girl's to a lady's. He softened. "All right, Vi. You got away with it this time. But it won't be so easy at the Marimion. They've seen real Italians there. From now on you leave all the talking to me."

Vi shuffled in her seat, and pulled out one of the old shoes she'd hidden under the cushion when they'd arrived at the shop. They were crossing the park, and she pulled down the window and hurled it outside. Montmorency was appalled, then amused, and dug down under the seat for the other shoe.

"This won't be of any use on its own either!" he cried, sending it on its way across the wet grass. By the time they reached Fox-Selwyn's house they were both giggling like children.

CHAPTER 29

≫

BACK TO THE MARIMION

After he had dropped Vi off at Fox-Selwyn's for the evening, Montmorency made his way to the Marimion. Five years ago the hotel had been his home, but he had been out of touch since then, not even visiting the bar, for fear of encountering the manager's daughter, Cissie, whose crush on him had blighted his life there. He wondered if her father, Mr. Longman, was still in charge of the hotel, and found himself, to his surprise, hoping that he was: Longman would be far more likely than any stranger to believe the story of the aunt from Italy. He was accustomed to Montmorency's desire for privacy, and knew Scarper, his taciturn servant, even if he didn't like him very much. Montmorency climbed the wide marble steps up to the Marimion's grand front doors, which he was alarmed to see had been replaced with a revolving contraption. *We'll never get Mrs. Evans through here,* he thought as he spun inside, jumping out into the lobby only just in time to avoid having to go around twice.

The lobby was deserted, but loud hammering and

shouting were coming from the direction of the dining room. He went over to look, and saw that the already elaborate décor was being enhanced with swags, ribbons, and flower arrangements. Tables were being laid for a grand banquet. In the middle of it all stood the thin figure of Mr. Longman, still the manager, barking orders and criticism at his weary staff, obviously in the despairing, panic-stricken stage of preparing for a major event. He turned and saw his old resident guest in the doorway. For a moment his face betrayed his real feelings: *Oh Lord. What now?* Then he got a grip on himself, pulled his body into the military bearing that characterized him when he was front-of-house, and strode towards Montmorency, bowing humbly to the man whose regular payments had kept the hotel solvent when its finances had been at their most precarious.

"Why, Mr. Montmorency, how wonderful to see you! What can I do to help? Have you come for a drink?"

"No, Mr. Longman, I called to see if you had a room available from tomorrow." And he took out the Italian letter, repeating the story of the Contessa's unexpected visit, which he found even he was beginning to believe.

"Tomorrow is a problem; I'm up to here with

Americans!" Longman indicated with a simple gesture that he found his transatlantic customers too demanding for words. "But most of them are going after the wedding; then I could give you and your family the large suite on the top floor. We call it the Parkview Suite, sir. It has a splendid view of the park. Would that be suitable?"

"Ideal," said Montmorency, realizing at once the convenience of his whole team being together, somewhat isolated from the other guests. "So you have a wedding tomorrow. Looks like a grand affair."

"Only the best for my little girl!"

It took Montmorency a moment to register what he had said. "Cissie's getting married?" he spluttered, hoping that his voice had not betrayed his amazement at the idea that someone would want to wed her.

Mr. Longman smiled proudly: "Mr. Montmorency, tomorrow Cissie will become Mrs. Cornelius Delahaye Newhaven Junior. Her fiancé is the heir to one of the largest pig-meat processing enterprises in the United States!"

So Cissie had finally done it. The pushy, vulgar glutton, so despised by the staff of the Marimion, had finally trapped one of the guests. And what a catch! Cissie would be able to eat as much bacon, pigs' trotters, and cracklings as she wished. He remembered how she used to scavenge among the remains of meals as dirty plates arrived in the kitchen from the dining room. He pictured her wide cheeks, her tiny eyes, the carbuncle by her nose, and the springy yellow hair tied in bunches on either side of her prominent ears. Then there was that squeaky babyish voice she reserved for male guests: a wheedling, ingratiating whine, always delivered with her face slightly too close. And of course there was the smell of her breath, a smell he could sense even now as he recalled that sing-song "Mithter Montmorenthy."

"Mithter Montmorenthy!"

There it was again. Loud now, right in his ear.

"Mithter Montmorenthy!"

He turned, and there she was, almost on top of him.

"You've come back! Oh, Daddy! What am I going to do? I can't marry Cornelius now!" Suddenly she was gripping on to him, sinking to her knees, and howling. Right there in the middle of the grand lobby of the Marimion.

Poor Cissie. Her timing was never good, and this time it could not have gone more spectacularly wrong. Just as she was threatening, purely for effect, to call off her lucrative marriage, a vast American matron swept down the stairs. Montmorency guessed who it was. Mrs. Cornelius Delahaye Newhaven Senior, no doubt. She joined in with more raucous screeching and a few well-aimed prods at Montmorency with her parasol, demanding to know what was going on. Longman skillfully steered the writhing bundle of Montmorency, Cissie, and her future mother-in-law into the back office, where an unhappy hour was spent defusing the drama. Cissie, enjoying the emotion, and unable to see what else she could do, continued to rant about the impossibility of going ahead with the wedding. Montmorency, seeing the risk that Mrs. CDN Senior might flounce off with her wealthy son, leaving Cissie free to pursue him, decided to lie. He said he had come to the Marimion to release Cissie from any obligation she might feel towards him, to free her to marry the fine man who, he was sure, loved her with a noble passion he could never match. Mrs. CDN Senior glowed at his praise for young Cornelius, unaware that Montmorency had never seen or heard of her son. In fact, on the evidence before him, Montmorency judged CDN Junior to be a fool with an unhappy future. Cissie fell for the false romanticism of being the object of two admirers, one of whom was prepared to give her up to make way for a finer (and richer) love. She collapsed into luxurious tears, relieved that her American dream was back on again. For effect she dismissed Montmorency with a flamboyant cry of "I never want to see you again!", hoping to restore herself in the eyes of her fiancé's mother as a worthy partner for her son. They were words Montmorency had been longing to hear from the first day he met her.

Rejoicing inside, but for Cissie's sake looking like a man whose world had crumbled, he marched away to look for another hotel for the Contessa. But behind him, in the next segment of the revolving doors, came Mr. Longman, rapping on the glass partition, and pleading with him to stop. Mr. Longman was a doting father, but he was also a good businessman.

"One moment, sir," he shouted as Montmorency took to the steps. "I just wanted to confirm your booking, sir. The Parkview Suite will be ready for you and your aunt's party the day after tomorrow, sir." He paused. "The wedding guests will have departed by then, sir."

So it was fixed, and Montmorency looked forward to another stay at the Marimion, but this time without the attentions of Mrs. Cornelius Delahaye Newhaven Junior (née Longman) to cramp his style.

CHAPTER 30

KEW AND COVENT GARDENS

On Cissie's wedding day, Fox-Selwyn lent Montmorency and Vi his carriage, so they could travel westward to Kew to look for the station bombers. He went with them as far as Doctor Farcett's house. He wanted to see the evidence about the Tarimond babies.

The doctor had cleared a huge space on the floor of his untidy study so that he could spread out the paperwork in what he regarded as orderly piles. There was a chart, set out like a calendar, to show the precise date of every death. Like Farcett, Fox-Selwyn could see no seasonal pattern there. There were family trees, illustrating the relationship between all the affected households. They pointed nowhere. Each dead baby had a file of its own, giving full details of its short life. There were lists of symptoms, cross-referenced to show the course of every child's decline. Fox-Selwyn was fascinated. But he had no more luck at finding a solution than Farcett, Maggie Goudie, or Father Michael.

"Perhaps they're just unlucky," suggested Fox-Selwyn. "Perhaps Tarimond's just going through a bad patch."

"It can't be that," Farcett insisted. And he took a huge reference book from a shelf. It contained medical statistics from all over Europe, including infant mortality rates. "Look at this!" he said to Fox-Selwyn, flicking through the pages. "Tarimond has worse figures than all these places. If they weren't so cut off, there would be a public outcry."

Fox-Selwyn picked up the idea. "Who knows," he said. "If they weren't so isolated whatever it is might be spreading through the whole British population."

"Exactly, George," said Farcett. "We've got to find out the cause. I'm hoping to get one of the best experts in the country to make sense of it all."

"He'll need a bigger brain than mine," Fox-Selwyn replied.

"And mine," said Farcett. "I've been through all this paper a thousand times. I'm getting nowhere at all."

In the carriage on their way to Kew, Vi told Montmorency as much as she could about the two men they were looking for. She had only the vaguest memory of the visitor who had stayed at her house on the night before the King's Cross explosion, but she gave Montmorency a full description of his friend, who had collected the bag on the eve of the Waterloo blast. He was the one they had the highest hopes of spotting today. He'd told her the other man had gone missing, and she believed him.

They gave him the nickname "the Bag Man." He was of above-average height, suntanned, and healthy, all of which suggested that he might, indeed, have an outdoor job. He had dark hair on his head, and on the backs of his hands, too. She had particularly noticed that. He spoke indistinctly, with a pronounced accent. She couldn't say whether it was Irish or something more exotic. He had kept his words to a minimum, and hurried to get away when she tried to engage him in conversation about his missing friend. She was sure she would recognize him if she saw him again. And sure, too, that he would not recognize her in her fine clothes, and with the handsome Montmorency at her side.

Their plan was to walk around the gardens like any other day trippers, in the hopes that they would spot the man among the gardeners there. Neither had been there before. In fact, Vi had never heard of the place until she read its name on the bag. Fox-Selwyn had to explain to her how it was a huge open space by the river, home to some of the world's most exotic plants. It had been founded by the Royal Family for their own amusement more than a hundred years ago, and now it was open to the public. Vast greenhouses had been constructed there, so hot inside that you believed you were in the tropics. There was a Chinese pagoda, a lake, and a new gallery housing paintings donated by a lady explorer. Vi was dying to have a look. The driver took them over the river and then through the quiet villages of Putney, Barnes, and Mortlake where the road followed the sweeping curve of the Thames. At Richmond they turned onto Kew Road.

"Do you want the main gate, sir, or will one of the side ones do?"

"Oh, I think we want the main entrance," said Montmorency, not sure what difference it would make.

"Yes," said Vi, "the main gate. Let's do this in style!"

So they plodded on, past a cricket field, and then alongside an apparently endless brick wall.

"Is this all Kew Gardens?" asked Montmorency.

"It certainly is," said the driver. "Big, isn't it?"

Too big, thought Montmorency, wondering how they would ever trace one person on such enormous grounds.

The carriage eventually turned left to Kew Green, past the pretty redbrick church of St. Anne, once a plain little chapel, but all curves, arches, and bulges now, thanks to extensions added by its royal patrons. Finally, where the road relaxed into a crescent in front of the grand iron gates, they arrived at the Botanic Gardens.

"Pick us up here at four," said Montmorency, hoping that by then they would have tracked down their suspect.

"Is this where you get into the countryside?" asked Vi innocently, as Montmorency paid the entrance fee at the turnstile. And he realized that, like him only a few years ago, she had never been outside the center of London in her life.

It was another overcast day. Heavy rain had fallen throughout the previous month, and the grass was soft and muddy underfoot. Vi was glad she had persuaded Montmorency to buy her the boots, and kept saying so, somewhat to his annoyance. The grounds were even bigger than she had imagined. They wandered from path to path, looking for the men. There were hardly any gardeners to be seen. Whenever Vi and Montmorency spotted one or two at work, they went up close until Vi could be sure she could rule them out. Sometimes they were so near that Montmorency had to fake an interest in the plants to explain their presence. They learned a lot, chatting to the gardeners about leaf shapes and soil types, but they didn't find their man. At half past three a bell rang and the staff of the gardens set up a general cry of "Going home!" The last few visitors ambled towards the gates in the fading light.

Montmorency bought a guidebook on the way out. It was obvious they were going to be coming back, maybe more than once. But if the bombers were gardeners, they would be leaving now, and they might be moving on to look for Vi in Covent Garden. Tonight Montmorency would have to risk taking her back there, in the hope that she could spot the Bag Man before he noticed her.

In town, back at Fox-Selwyn's house, they changed their clothes and their identities. It was a long time since Montmorency had dressed up as Scarper, though his old alter ego had visited him unbidden often enough. In the early days of his transformation from convict to gentleman, Scarper's personality was the one in which he felt most at home. Scarper's movements, voice, and attitudes were the ones that had come naturally then. Now, Montmorency felt more like an actor, re-creating the rolling walk, the downcast eyes, and the accent that went with Scarper's rough clothes. Standing in the spare bedroom at Fox-Selwyn's, the newly bought jacket and boots felt too clean. He ripped a few seams, and rolled around on the floor to try to make the clothes a little more convincing. Grabbing a bite to eat before he left, he made sure the gravy trailed down his shirt. As he reached the front door he wiped his nose on his sleeve. Vi pulled his cap farther down to cover his too-clean hair. She was back in her old clothes, ready to risk one more trip to Covent Garden to look for the Bag Man and to find the Mead family, whose matriarch, Molly, had been killed in the King's Cross explosion.

Fox-Selwyn saw them off. "I'll wait up for you," he said, making some last-minute adjustments of his own to their costumes. "Be careful."

"There's nothing to worry about," said Vi. "I know my way around there. I know what I'm doing."

But Fox-Selwyn wouldn't let it rest. He didn't want to frighten Vi, but he was genuinely worried for her safety. "Remember, you're just there to point the Bag Man out to Montmorency — I mean Scarper," he corrected himself, seeing the scruffy figure at her side. "If you see the Bag Man, don't confront him. Don't speak to him. Leave that to us. Once you have identified him, you can step back from this investigation. He's looking for you, but he doesn't know about Montmorency and me. We can pursue him when we know what he looks like."

Vi laughed: "Don't get in such a state, your lordship. I'll be all right. He's not going to bother with me!"

As she left the house the two men exchanged concerned glances. They both wished they shared her confidence.

Vi and Scarper went from pub to pub. Vi found an acquaintance in each one, but it was not until Montmorency had drunk a few pints and she had gotten through a good deal of gin that they came across Joe Mead, Molly's brother, playing cards with some market porters in the corner of one of Scarper's old haunts. Joe nodded in recognition as Vi positioned herself close by. She waited till he had played his hand, then used one of the opening lines they had rehearsed on the way.

"Evening, Joe. How's the family?"

"Fair to middling, Vi. Though I don't think Edna will ever get over it. She can't bear to think that she was larking around on her honeymoon while her mum was lying dead in the morgue."

Vi turned to Scarper, and for effect spelled out the background to what Joe Mead had said. "Joe's sister was killed in that gas blast. You know, at King's Cross, in the summer. Joe, this is my friend Bert."

Bert? thought Scarper. Surely she could have come up with something better than that. He tried not to let his disappointment at his new name show as he worked his way into the conversation. "Shocking business. Were you there, too?"

"We all were. The whole family. Gone to see Edna and Archie off after their wedding. Molly had saved for ages for them train tickets." Joe warmed to a tale he was obviously used to telling. His brush with death and danger had given him a certain celebrity in the area; it had made him someone people wanted to talk to. "I should never have given Molly that cigarette," he continued. "Must have been that what set off the gas. Course, if she hadn't had so much to drink, she'd never have tripped over that bloke with the suitcase. I reckon that's what made her drop her cigarette down near the broken pipe. You should have seen it. A great big flash, and so much smoke you couldn't see your hand in front of your face. And you could smell the gas. It's a wonder the whole station didn't go up. And when the dust cleared, I just couldn't look. Molly had gone. Nothing left of her, just blood and guts everywhere. My cousin lost an arm, and his wife lost a leg. The rest of us were lucky. Cuts and bruises, that's all.

If you don't count the broken hearts of course. Gas. I ask you. Shouldn't be allowed."

"And did the police talk to you?" asked Scarper.

"Oh yes, they were there at the station, and took statements while we were being patched up at the hospital, but they haven't done anything about it though, have they? I mean you won't see the Gas Company in court for killing my sister Molly. That's because they've got money, and influence." He was getting really angry now. "Makes you sick," he snarled into his glass.

Scarper was left in no doubt that the wedding party was convinced, possibly with the encouragement of the police, that gas had been to blame for the explosion. But something in Joe Mead's account of the blast had set him thinking. Maybe the bomb hadn't been planted at the station, waiting to go off or to be detonated from afar. Perhaps someone had been carrying it when it exploded. In his concern for his own family Joe seemed to have lost sight of the fate of the man with the suitcase, the man who had collided with Molly just before the explosion. He obviously hadn't been mentioned to the police or to the press. Was he the culprit? Had he gotten away? Or had he, too, been killed? Blown to pieces so small that the railway officials, cleaning up quickly to get the station back into action, had been quite unaware of his existence, unable to tell his remains from those of the old tramp who had died?

It had been a mystery why he had left the incriminating bag at Vi's house. Perhaps he had intended to return for it, possibly to use the contents to construct another bomb. Perhaps his friend at Kew (the man he and Vi called the Bag Man) had waited for his reappearance, and only much later guessed his fate. Maybe the Bag Man had spent months worrying that his co-conspirator had been caught, and might spill the details of their plan. Or he might have been cursing his friend, suspecting him of cowardice, and of running away, leaving him in the dark as to what to do next. Scarper imagined the Bag Man picking up the paper, day after day, month after month, half expecting to find news, and never hearing even an acknowledgment that the explosion was a crime. Imagine how galling that must have been for him, risking so much to make a point, and then finding that no one realized the gesture had even been made. Scarper thought how the Bag Man must have wrestled time after time against the urge to trace his friend's movements, to find out where he had been on the fateful night. When he found Vi, and she had told him about the disappearance, and about the bag, he must have panicked and made an instant decision to take the bag away, getting the material for the Waterloo bomb, but also laying the trail that Montmorency and Vi had followed to Kew. So far they hadn't found him there. But might he not also be operating here, in Covent Garden, looking for Vi, who could give evidence against him; or even, if their story had reached him, for the Meads, who might know what had become of his friend? Scarper realized that for as long as it took, he would be seeking the Bag Man in these two very different gardens. As Montmorency in Kew Gardens by day, and as Scarper in Covent Garden by night.

While he had been thinking this through, Vi had been engaged in sympathetic chatter with Joe, letting him milk his story some more. She wasn't taking much notice of anything else in the pub. All at once, she jumped up and ran towards the door. "It's him!" she whispered to Scarper on her way past. A man with hairy hands pushed through the crowd after her. He didn't see Scarper following behind.

CHAPTER 31

≫

VI ON THE RUN

After her day out at Kew, Vi's feet had been aching. She had found it hard just slogging around from pub to pub with Scarper. But now that her life was threatened she found she could run, dart, and dive in her desperation to get away from the Bag Man. She had one big advantage over him. This was her home territory. She knew all the little lanes and courtyards; she could lead him through mazes of barrels and carts in the sleeping market. Scarper kept his distance behind the Bag Man, trying to make sure that Vi was always in sight. Passersby watched the chase with amusement, imagining that the furious man was after a pickpocket or a treacherous lover. The Bag Man himself never looked back. He followed Vi's every move, getting closer to her all the time. Following her route, Scarper guessed where she was aiming for. It was late, and the audience would soon be leaving the Opera House. She was going for the protection of that crowd, ready to dive in amongst them where the Bag Man would not dare to strike.

But she was too soon. The road outside the Opera House was still dark and deserted. A line of cabs had pulled up, waiting for business when the doors opened, and she weaved between them, gasping for breath. The Bag Man followed, but in the press of carriages lost sight of her, got ahead, then came back, checking in, around, and under each one. Scarper dodged and ducked, trying to keep Vi in his eyeline, without letting the Bag Man see he was there. The horses pawed the ground and snorted as the commotion disturbed their rest. For a moment, Vi leaned against the wheel of one cab, winded, hoping she had shaken the Bag Man off. Then she looked up, and saw his ferocious face staring at her, not six feet away. He raised his arm to grab her, an expression of pure hate and savage violence burning in his eyes. She screamed. The horse alongside her whinnied, and the cabbie jumped down into the road. The Bag Man turned, punching the driver with his flailing fist, and in that second, as the Bag Man was distracted, Scarper caught Vi and dragged her between the wheels into the darkness at the side of the Opera House. They squashed themselves against the wall and shuffled to the shelter of the scenery storehouse at the back. From there they could hear the last triumphant climax of the performance inside.

The Bag Man was still dashing from cab to cab, looking for Vi, shouting and swearing now. They could see him through a tiny window, spinning around, getting angrier and angrier as he yelled out threats to Vi.

"I'll find you, and I'll kill you! Don't think you're going to get away from me!" he shouted, turning and racing away from them just as the audience burst into tumultuous applause.

Vi lay on the ground in the scenery store, desperate for air, but almost unable to breathe.

"Go after him!" she panted.

"No, I know what he looks like now. I can come back for him another time." Scarper was rummaging among the props and tools, looking for something: "I've got to take care of you, Vi," he said. "The Bag Man's out to get you. Surely even you can see that now. He's not going to stop looking now that he's seen you. We've got to get away from here before he comes back." Scarper found a metal bar amidst a pile of fake armor, swords, and guns. He held it out, judging its weight and thickness. "This will do," he gasped in triumph. "Come on!"

He pulled Vi to her feet, but she was tired, and wanted to stay and hide. "You won't be safe till we get you well away from here," he said sternly, tugging her by the arm. "Come with me, and do just what I say."

He dragged her down a side street and in the darkness found the familiar shape of a manhole. He used the bar to lever the iron disc up and away to one side. "Get in," he ordered, pushing her towards the hole in the road. "Find the ladder with your feet, and work your way down. I'm coming after you."

Vi was paralyzed by the billowing stench that enveloped them as the lid came off the hole. Scarper had to lift her and force her feet down into the darkness. He could hear footsteps from around the corner. They couldn't risk being seen. He leaped onto the ladder after Vi, and pulled the manhole cover down on top of them. A loud resounding clang rang around them, echoing for what seemed like minutes before Scarper could make himself heard to the terrified girl clinging to the ladder below him.

"Are you all right?" he whispered. He got his reply with the sound of Vi vomiting into the sea of filth beneath them. "Hold on," he said. "I'm coming down. You'll get used to it, I promise you." He worked his way down the ladder carefully, until he was hanging off the side alongside Vi. She was grasping the rungs tightly, shaking with fear and disgust.

Scarper reached into his pocket for a box of matches. He found a handkerchief and felt for her hand. "Here, hold this over your mouth, it might help. Now I'm going to strike a match. It won't burn for long, but you'll be able to see where you are. Look down, now, and when the light comes you'll see a ledge at the bottom of the ladder. That's where we've got to get to. But don't worry if you slip into the water. It's not deep. Just go carefully and you'll be safe."

He struck the match. The wide arch of the tunnel was suddenly lit up, all the tiny bricks glistening in reflection beneath them, where a stream of sewage ran slowly along. He just had time to glimpse Vi's ashen, startled face before the flame died. He shook the matchbox. There were only a few matches inside. He would keep them for later. For now he had to get Vi moving. He pried her fingers from the metal and coaxed her downward, talking soothingly all the time.

"We're in the sewer, Vi. Don't worry. I know my way around here. We can get right across London without anyone seeing us. You're safe, Vi, that's all that matters. The Bag Man can't get you now."

"It stinks," she said, her voice muffled by the handkerchief.

"I know, but the Bag Man isn't going to think of looking for you here. I'll hold on to you. Now you try to stay on the ledge, and I'll walk in the stream. I know how to do it." He put his arm around her waist to steady her as she took her first, terrified steps.

Even after years of absence, the layout of the sewers was clear in Scarper's mind. In the darkness he felt his way along the walls, leading Vi out of danger. She couldn't see the rats, but she could feel all sorts of objects bumping against her legs in the water as they waded and slithered their way underneath central London, and their motion made the liquid lap up the walls. Sometimes it was hard even for Scarper to keep his footing. The base of the tunnel was curved, to keep the slurry moving on its way east to the mouth of the Thames, and it was slippery. Scarper wasn't wearing his special boots. Their clothes were soaked with the foul liquid that sloshed against them as they walked against the flow, westward, to safety.

"Have you been here before?" asked Vi, as she calmed down, and let Scarper guide her through the nightmare.

"Yes," said Scarper. "When I lived in your house, I used to come down here almost every night. I know every inch of this stretch. We're lucky it's not raining or it would be deeper. Good job it's late, too. No one's cooking or having a bath. Sometimes the drains up there are pouring with foam." He struck another match, and she watched the shadow of his arm point out the places where some of the most illustrious effluent in London joined the general flow.

"Not far now," he said, reassuringly. "You've done very well. I'm proud of you. When I first came down here I didn't get to the bottom of the ladder."

She was encouraged by his confidence, and asked him more about why he had spent so much time underground. He told her everything: about the thieving, about the time he had been caught in a storm, and about his daring raid on the Mauramanian Embassy. They trudged on for miles, until Scarper stopped and felt along the wall for a ladder.

"Where are we now?" she asked.

"Not far from Fox-Selwyn's," he said, striking another match to show her the way to the surface. "You follow behind me. I'll tell you when it's all right to come out." He climbed up, and pushed on the manhole cover above him, letting in a cool blast of pure air. Even though it was the middle of the night, to his eyes the pavement seemed awash with light. He waited a moment for his vision to adjust. Then he swung himself up to ground level and lay down to pull Vi up, too. After the warmth of the sewer she shivered in the winter air. She crouched against a wall on the lookout while Scarper pulled the cover back over the hole. Then they ran in their sopping clothes back to Lord George Fox-Selwyn's house.

George was waiting for them when they arrived, smelly and bedraggled, at his front door. Fortunately Chivers and the rest of the staff were asleep in their attic rooms, unaware of the frantic bathing that took place through the night. Once their bodies were clean, Vi washed their clothes over and over again.

"Shouldn't we go to the police?" she asked, wringing out her dress over the kitchen sink.

"No," said Fox-Selwyn. "While you were in the bath, I thought the whole thing through. At the moment we have no concrete evidence at all. We don't even know who this man is. But we can be pretty sure that he thinks his main problem is you, Vi. He imagines that all he has to do is silence one girl in Covent Garden. From what you say, he didn't notice Scarper, and while he's after you, we know where he's likely to be and we can keep an eye on him. If he gets wind of the police being on his tail he might disappear, only to bomb and bomb again." He looked at the tired, brave woman up to her elbows in soapsuds at the sink. "Don't worry,

Vi," he said. "We'll make sure the Bag Man can't catch you. But we're going to do our best to keep him looking for you. We have to."

Vi hung the torn and stained garments over the kitchen range. Fox-Selwyn looked at the tattered rags and laughed. "Well, Montmorency," he said. "You needn't worry about Scarper looking too smart now!"

"Just as well," said Montmorency. "He'll have to get back to Covent Garden tomorrow. But you, Vi, will be staying put in the Marimion."

CHAPTER 32

INSTALLED

Fox-Selwyn's cook was appalled at the state of her kitchen the next morning. After years of putting up with her master's strange comings and goings, she knew better than to ask for an explanation, but she made her displeasure clear, banging around and scrubbing everything with caustic soda and some pungent carbolic soap donated by Doctor Farcett when he arrived to catch up on the events of the night. He insisted that no food should be prepared there until all germs had been eradicated, and he gave Montmorency a stern warning against venturing into the sewers again. Chivers was sent out for some bread and fruit for the ladies' breakfast, and Fox-Selwyn, Montmorency, and Farcett set off for an early-morning visit to Eats Minor, the small dining room where breakfast was served at Bargles. Montmorency had to go to Bargles anyway, to pack for his stay at the Marimion. Sam, who helped him sort out his luggage, seemed offended that Montmorency was leaving them.

"Don't worry, Sam," said Montmorency. "It's only temporary." And he told the story of his aunt the Contessa and her daughter, of their unexpected visit, and urgent need for accommodations.

"Now we couldn't have them staying here, Sam, could we?" he said.

Sam was scandalized by the very idea. "Women at Bargles? Oh no, sir. Absolutely out of the question! I quite understand."

While the men were at Bargles, Vi was upstairs at Lord George Fox-Selwyn's house, busy preparing her mother for the move. It was quite a struggle getting the corset on. The old lady couldn't stand up long enough for Vi to get it around her. If she sat down, the rolls of fat were too vast to stuff inside. In the end, Vi laid the corset out on the bed and rolled Mrs. Evans across it, ending with her facedown, screaming dissent into a pillow while Vi pulled the laces tight along her back. Only with the stiff corset in place was there any chance of getting Mrs. Evans into the dress. But the dress needed to go over her head, so Mrs. Evans had to sit up again. Vi tried to roll her onto her back to get started, but she pushed too hard, and with a loud thump her mother hit the floor. Vi despaired of lifting her from there, but managed to prop her up for long enough to pull the black taffeta construction as far as her waist. Then there was more rolling and pummeling to get the skirt down over her legs. That final maneuver left the old woman lying on the carpet, staring at the ceiling with her arms outstretched like a corpse in an opera. But this corpse was shouting and swearing at the top of its voice.

When the men got back, Doctor Farcett prepared the wheelchair, and they bumped it down the stairs with Vi's mother inside. By the time they reached the bottom, her shouting was so loud and so obscene that Doctor Farcett overcame his ethical objections to drugging her into silence. He administered a quick injection, which brought forth a final expletive, and then Mrs. Evans slumped into the docile, pitiful form of the Contessa Evanista. While all that was going on, Vi had dressed herself. She had gotten the hang of it now, and needed help with only the last two buttons. As he gently fastened them, Montmorency reminded her of the need for silence, and that if she had to talk she should try to sound Italian. He picked up the bag containing Scarper's clothes and the maid's outfit, and escorted her to the cab that would take them to the Marimion. Lord Fox-Selwyn's carriage followed behind, heavily laden with the doctor, Mrs. Evans in her wheelchair, and a mountain of luggage. They made a strange but imposing sight as they trundled along the edge of the park. It was easy to believe that they had come all the way from Italy.

Mr. Longman was there to greet them, glad that Montmorency hadn't had second thoughts after Cissie's performance two days before. It turned out that the fiendish revolving doors could be manipulated so that they folded back, leaving an opening big enough for the Contessa's chair. Even better, the improvements at the Marimion had included the installation of a lift, so her passage to the top floor was less of a nightmare than Montmorency had envisioned, even though the sudden effect of gravity on all their stomachs as the car lurched upward brought from her a spectacular and very unladylike burp.

Vi loved the suite, and had fun opening and closing the wardrobes, leaning precariously from the balcony, and picking at the grapes in a bowl on the table. Montmorency was staggered at how quickly she was adapting to the high life, and suggested that they should both change into their new servants' clothes and go down to meet the rest of the staff. Mr. Longman recognized Scarper straightaway, and greeted him with the old, ill-disguised contempt. He was rather taken with Susanna, if irritated that she spoke no English. Nobody else in the backstairs world had been there long enough to have any recollection of Scarper and Montmorency's last stay. Mr. Longman's shortcomings as a manager, and Cissie's disgusting habits, had chased them all off. Scarper was glad. There would be no one to make claims on an old acquaintance, demanding updates on their lives. He would play it cool, coming and going to suit himself, silently avoiding any camaraderie that might have built up among the new staff. And he would start now. He sent Susanna up the back stairs, then ducked out into the street through the dustbins, and off to Covent Garden. He was back on the trail of the Bag Man.

CHAPTER 33

POST

After the excitement of the morning, Doctor Farcett left the Marimion and went home to pick up his post. There was a bill from his tailor, a reminder that his subscription to the Scientific Society was due, and two really interesting letters. One was from Donald Dougall, reiterating his invitation to Farcett to become involved in the work at Great Ormond Street Hospital, and offering to go over his Tarimond notes, when time allowed it. The other was from Tarimond itself, the envelope in Maggie Goudie's confident, flowing script. Farcett was reluctant to open it, fearing that it might bring bad news about Jimmy MacLean. But as it turned out, the letter had taken a while to get to London. It had been written very soon after his departure. Then, at least, Jimmy had been thriving, and seemed well set to face his first winter. In addition to Morag's mother, two more Tarimond women were confirmed to be pregnant. They had been persuaded to let Maggie keep detailed records of their progress, of what they ate and what they did before their babies' births. Like her, they wanted Doctor Farcett to find out why the children of Tarimond had been dying, and would do anything to help. Maggie promised to forward details of little Jimmy, and of the expectant mothers, regularly by post. There was little other news. Father Michael had remembered Farcett and Montmorency in the prayers on the Sunday after they left, wishing them a safe journey. Had they arrived safely? She implored him to write and let her know. He sat down at his desk straightaway, telling her about Doctor Dougall, certain she would be pleased that the London expert at work on the Tarimond case was a Scot. Then he set about sorting through the evidence he and Maggie had compiled together, ready to take it to Great Ormond Street for analysis.

CHAPTER 34

TACTICS

Scarper decided to go from the Marimion to Covent Garden on foot. He enjoyed looking in the shop windows, and reading the billboards outside the theaters and galleries along the way. The town was busy, with horses, carts, and pedestrians trundling in all directions. At Oxford Circus he was waiting for a gap in the traffic so that he could cross the road, when a cab pulled up alongside him. It was Lord Fox-Selwyn, on his way to Bargles for lunch.

"Scarper!" boomed Fox-Selwyn, alarming Scarper himself, to say nothing of the bystanders who thought he was telling someone to get lost.

"Jump in, I'll give you a lift."

The driver was surprised when the smart man in his cab invited the scruffy fellow on the pavement to join him. He was bemused, too, at being redirected to Covent Garden. He would expect a big tip.

"So you're off to look for the Bag Man?" said Fox-Selwyn.

"Yes. I reckon that after what happened last night he'll be out there again, looking for Vi."

Fox-Selwyn's tone grew serious. He wanted to discuss tactics. "Go carefully," he said. "He's the only lead we've got, and if you scare him away, we're back where we started. Remember, the priority is to find out exactly who he is. We still don't even know his nationality. If we can establish where he's from, why he's bombing, and where he lives now, we should be able to let the police do the rest."

"Understood, George," said Scarper. "I'll hang back a bit. No confrontations."

"Absolutely not," said Fox-Selwyn, sternly. "It's bad enough that he already knows about Vi. We don't want him working out that you're on his tail. He's obviously prepared to kill for whatever this cause of his is, and don't forget: If Scarper's killed, good old Montmorency dies as well." Fox-Selwyn watched his companion's face. Even though he was wearing Scarper's ratty clothes, his eyes had the depth and nobility of Montmorency at his most thoughtful. There was a pause before he spoke.

"I sometimes wish Scarper *was* dead, George," he said. "But I've got to be Scarper today, and perhaps it's just as well. Scarper's a lot braver than Montmorency, you know."

"And more foolhardy," warned Fox-Selwyn. "He's gotten you into trouble more than once."

"I just can't help listening to him sometimes."

"Well, I suppose that's understandable," said Fox-Selwyn. "After all, he was there first."

Scarper looked down at his clothes. "But I don't really like him, you know," he sighed.

"I'll tell you something," confided Fox-Selwyn. "I've only met him a few times, and I don't like him either. But we both know we need him to catch this man."

As Fox-Selwyn spoke, the cab came to a halt at the edge of a mess of traffic where seven roads met at a tiny junction. Drivers were shouting at one another. It was clear no one was going to give way.

"I'll walk from here," said Scarper.

Fox-Selwyn noticed that his friend's voice had dropped into a cockney drawl. "Come to my house afterward, and tell me what you've found," he said. "Even if it's nothing. I want to know. And be careful."

"OK," said Scarper. As he put on his cap, his shoulders dropped, and he swung down from the cab with a cry of "See yer, boss!" He shambled away without looking back, his hands in his pockets, his shoulders hunched, and his backbone curved.

"Good luck," Fox-Selwyn called after him, wondering what news his friend would bring him later. Then he tapped on the roof of the cab and shouted to the driver.

"You can turn around now. I'm going to Bargles after all."

CHAPTER 35

»

STALKING

Scarper guessed that the Bag Man would be watching Vi's house. He was right. As Scarper came around the corner from the market he caught sight of him leaning on a cart, pretending to wait for someone, but flicking his eyes to Vi's front door time and time again. Scarper stood in a shadow and studied the Bag Man from the front for a few moments. He was wearing a thick black wool jacket and dark green trousers. Perhaps they were part of his working uniform, assuming of course that he really did have a job at Kew. His boots were not new, but they were sturdy and well repaired. He was not a poor man. Scarper noted the boxlike shape of his head, and his black springy hair: luxuriant except at the front where it had receded, making his forehead seem high, even a little distinguished and intelligent. It wasn't a young face: It bore the marks of experience and troubles, but Scarper remembered how the man had run through the streets the night before, and guessed that in spite of his grave expression, he couldn't have been much more than about twenty-five. His features gave no clue to his origins. He could have been British, Irish, or from any one of a number of countries specializing in dark good looks.

Having committed the image to memory, Scarper moved around behind the Bag Man to watch him without risking being seen himself. Like the Bag Man, he had bought a newspaper to while away the time, and to make himself less conspicuous. He was glad he had. It was a long wait. Of course, Scarper knew that there was no one in the house, but the Bag Man had been hoping that someone would come or go. Ideally Vi herself would be there, but at the very least one of her lodgers might tell him where she was. The Bag Man was surprised not to see the old lady slobbering at the window. Eventually, towards the end of the afternoon he cracked, and walked over to knock on the door. There was no reply. He stomped off angrily, with Scarper following close behind.

The Bag Man made his way to the river, walking purposefully, obviously with a destination in mind. The streets grew narrower and dirtier at each corner, until at last he came to an ancient group of houses whose upper floors bulged out above their lower rooms, so that the top windows on either side of the little lane almost touched, and the alley below became like a dark tunnel. Scarper couldn't risk getting too close. The Bag Man's footsteps rang out on the cobbles, and he would notice at once if another set followed behind. Scarper cowered against a wall, waited, and watched. In the gloom, he couldn't see exactly where the Bag Man went, but before long the footsteps stopped. He must have gone into one of the houses. Just as Scarper was about to set off in pursuit, he heard a noise in the street behind him. A man appeared, looking around guiltily as he walked past, failing to notice Scarper tucked into the deep frame of a doorway on the corner. Scarper's eyes were getting used to the dark now, and he saw this new man knocking nervously on a door halfway down the alley, and sidling inside. Again Scarper tried to follow. Again the sound of footsteps froze him in position as another figure shuffled by him and into the house. This time Scarper walked a few steps behind. He reached the door and listened.

A low murmur of voices seeped out, but that meant less to Scarper than the smell that stole into his nose. It was sickly sweet: tempting and offensive at the same time. He identified it instantly. It was the devastating Turkish drug. Another figure rounded the corner and started walking towards him. Scarper slipped around the side of the house, to a narrow passageway leading to the water's edge. He listened as the newcomer knocked on the door, using a rhythmical pattern that Scarper realized was a code for gaining entry. *Tap, tippety tap. Tap. Tap*, it went. The door opened, and the smell of the drug grew stronger. Scarper had assumed himself to be free of its power. He had been clear of it for so long that whole days passed without him even congratulating himself on not thinking about it. And yet here, now, he had the chance to try it again, just once. *Should he go in?* He hid again at the sound of two new arrivals. There was more tapping, and another blast of stench into the street.

His conscience wrestled with his love of danger. *Surely he must explore this house. He knew the code to get inside, and once there he would find the Bag Man, too. He'd have to pretend he'd come for the drug, of course, but so what if he had to take a little of the forbidden substance to catch his man? He would be doing it for the sake of a greater good.*

But no. He mustn't. Doctor Farcett had warned him that even the smallest lapse could set him back on the road to despair. He thought back to the agonies and indignities of his trip home across Europe and the hideous embarrassments on the way to Scotland. He must not go in.

He sank down into a crouch beside the wall, frantically trying to persuade himself to go away.

Then he heard the splash of oars in the river. He looked to his left, and saw the unmistakable shape of the Bag Man rowing across the water. So he hadn't been in the drug den at all! He was on his way somewhere else, and Scarper, delayed by the lure of the drug, had lost the trail. He ran down to the riverside. There were no other boats, nothing in which he could pursue the Bag Man, whose little rowboat was well away in the darkness. Even the sound of the oars faded in the distance. The Bag Man could be going anywhere, and he still could be anybody. Scarper had failed to get anything more than a basic description of him. And meanwhile the Bag Man could be up to anything. He might let off another bomb tonight, and if he did, if anybody died, it would be Scarper's fault: all because of his weakness for the noxious drug.

Dejected, Scarper walked up the shingle, back to the road, ready to set off to face Fox-Selwyn and tell him about his failure. Then he stopped, catching the horrible aroma in the air once more.

So what, he thought, basking in self-disgust. *I might as well go in and get some.*

Tap, tippety tap. Tap. Tap. That was it. *Tap, tippety tap. Tap. Tap.*

But he mustn't. He would be letting down all the people who had believed in him: Fox-Selwyn, Farcett, even Morag and Chivers, who'd cared for him when he was at his worst. What would Vi think if he didn't make it back to the Marimion to see her through her first night there? He must go.

But his head played out the rhythm again. *Tap, tippety tap. Tap. Tap.* He slumped back down on his haunches. *That was the code. He was sure. He could just get in and have a look. Perhaps the Bag Man had something to do with the drug den. After all, his boat had been moored just alongside it. That could be a clue, couldn't it? Tap, tippety tap. Tap. Tap.*

He rose again. Then leaned against the wall with his eyes shut. The lapping of the water, the filthy water of the Thames, reminded him of the clear cold water of Tarimond, and the sparkling unfamiliar healthiness he had felt there. He pushed himself away from the wall, around the edge of the house, and forced himself past the front door. The staccato code pounded in his head all the way to Fox-Selwyn's house.

Scarper let himself in and called out for his friend. He wanted to tell him how he had resisted temptation. But Fox-Selwyn wasn't there. He had grown tired of waiting for Scarper's return and had left a note saying simply: "At Bargles. Do come."

Scarper went upstairs and changed into Montmorency's evening clothes. But as he reached down wearily to fasten his shiny shoes, he decided not to go to Bargles. He scribbled "No luck" underneath Fox-Selwyn's message. His friend would have to wait till the morning to hear from him. For now he was tired. He packed Scarper's working clothes into a suitcase and went back into the Marimion through the front door.

Upstairs in the Parkview Suite, all was quiet. The Contessa and Violetta were both asleep. Montmorency slumped into an armchair. He noticed Doctor Farcett's bag on the sideboard. He started reading a book, but every now and then his eyes found their way to the bulging leather case. *Tap, tippety tap. Tap. Tap,* went the unforgettable code in his inner ear. *Tap, tippety tap. Tap. Tap.* He found himself opening Farcett's bag. He found the sedative the doctor used to pacify Mrs. Evans.

When Doctor Farcett arrived to examine her early next morning, he found Montmorency lying unconscious on the floor.

CHAPTER 36

>>

IN DISGRACE

"How could he?" shouted Fox-Selwyn furiously.

"Quiet, George," hissed Doctor Farcett. "He'll hear you."

"I hope he does hear me," yelled Fox-Selwyn. "I want him to know how he's let me down."

"Oh, he knows that, all right," said the doctor, quietly. "I've never seen him so remorseful. Not even in Scotland. Go easy on him, George. It's my fault for leaving my bag here."

"Well, that wasn't exactly brilliant of you, was it?" Fox-Selwyn snapped.

"No. I'm partly to blame."

Farcett's humility calmed Fox-Selwyn down a bit: "And me, too, I suppose," he said, throwing himself down into an armchair. "I should have waited for him instead of going to Bargles."

"So give him another chance," Farcett pleaded.

Fox-Selwyn would have none of it: "How? Another trip to Scotland? Gus would love that! I can hear the Marchioness nagging now!"

Farcett tried to reassure him. "There won't be any need for that. The stuff he took last night was not as strong as whatever that Turkish muck was. I've given him something to wash it through his system. He's just exhausted and very, very sorry."

"Can I see him?"

"If you promise not to shout."

Fox-Selwyn gently opened the door to Montmorency's bedroom. His friend was lying on his side, staring at the wall.

"I'm sorry," said Montmorency, without looking around.

Fox-Selwyn fought back the lecture he was formulating in his mind. "I know," he said, sitting down on the bed. "You seemed fine when I dropped you off at Covent Garden. Do you want to tell me what happened after that?"

Montmorency slowly turned over, sat up, and accepted a cigarette. He told the story of the night before. His version of events centered on the drug den, and how he'd lost the Bag Man on the river. "So you see," he said sadly, at the end of his tale, "it was all a waste of time. Has there been another bomb?"

"No, no bomb," said Fox-Selwyn. "And yesterday

doesn't sound like a total waste of time to me. Don't forget all that time you spent outside Vi's house. You say you got a good look at the man?"

"Yes, I'd know him again if I saw him."

"And you didn't go into that drug den."

"No, but George," Montmorency added, in a voice weak with shame, "believe me, I so nearly did. I wanted to."

Fox-Selwyn corrected him: "Scarper nearly did. Montmorency came home."

Montmorency rejected the implied praise: "And raided Robert's bag."

"Which was unforgivable. You must make amends."

"How?"

"By carrying on the hunt for the Bag Man. As soon as Robert gives you the all clear, you and I are off to Kew."

Doctor Farcett was standing in the doorway, listening. "If you promise to keep an eye on him and don't let him exert himself too much, he can go tomorrow afternoon."

Montmorency saw a chance to blame himself for the delay: "And if there are any bombs in the meantime, it's all my fault."

Fox-Selwyn could see that Montmorency wanted to use self-pity to cancel out his guilt. He wasn't going to let him off the hook: "Yes, Montmorency. All your fault. I may be under instructions not to upset you" — he cast an eye at Farcett — "but I'm not going to pretend that I'm not angry. I am. Angry, offended, and disappointed!"

His voice grew louder as he spoke, his whole body started to shake, and Doctor Farcett tried to restrain him as he stormed from the room, still shouting.

"You keep an eye on Violetta and the Contessa," barked Fox-Selwyn. "I'm going to the club."

Montmorency turned his face back to the wall again, and sobbed.

In fact, it was Vi who kept an eye on Montmorency, sitting by his bed and, as Farcett instructed her before he left, encouraging him to drink as much water as possible. She had had a hard day. Her mother was at her worst. Montmorency had left the doctor with nothing to calm her down, and the old lady sat in her wheelchair, dribbling, ranting, and completely unable to control her natural functions. Once or twice Vi contemplated running off home to Covent Garden, but the thought of a killer out there looking for her made the luxurious hell of the Marimion preferable, just. She watched from the balcony as people came and went below. Sometimes she thought she saw a shady figure looking up at her from the park. Only two days ago she had thought her new friends were ridiculous when they warned that she might be in danger. Now she was seeing images of the Bag Man on all sides.

CHAPTER 37

MARY O'CONNELL

Doctor Farcett felt he had to leave Vi on her own with the invalids. He wanted to go to the hospital on Great Ormond Street, to deliver his Tarimond charts and tables to Donald Dougall. He stayed to observe Doctor Dougall at work. A stream of worried parents arrived, dragging reluctant toddlers to consult the experts about their ills. It was mostly the mothers who came. In fact, there was just one man: a striking, tall, dark fellow who carried a limp three-year-old girl into the room. The child had been dizzy and sick on and off for months, he said, and now she was getting worse. Doctor Dougall examined her and started making arrangements for her to be admitted to the ward at once.

"Doctor Farcett, would you mind staying with little Mary and Mr. O'Connell while I prepare some tests?"

"Perhaps I could take a fuller history?" Farcett suggested, anxious not to be left with nothing to do, having to make polite conversation with a worried adult.

"Yes, that would be most useful," said Doctor Dougall, grateful for the help, and glad that Farcett was getting involved in the work of the hospital. He handed Farcett a notepad and pen as he left the room.

Farcett had his own theories about what might be wrong with the girl, and there was a string of medical questions he wanted to ask. But he found it almost impossible to get a coherent account of the family's basic details. Even taking into account the stress of caring for a sick child, this burly Irishman was behaving oddly. In his time, Doctor Farcett had come across plenty of patients who were intimidated by hospitals or scared of illness, but Mr. O'Connell seemed unusually nervous and confused. He was uncertain even of his address, changing it from east to west London as if forgetfulness on such a matter were perfectly normal. He was unclear about Mary's date of birth, or of the Christian name of her mother, who had died when she was born. He appeared to know little of Mary's medical past, except to say that she had always been a "lovely little girl." Yet he was clearly worried about her, and Farcett tried to be sympathetic. He decided to move on to Mary's current illness, and asked, innocently: "Now, tell me. What's been going on?"

Mr. O'Connell hugged the child closer to him and started to rock to and fro. He tried to say something, but tripped on his words. He tried again, but his eyes grew wet, and he buried his face in the little girl's clothes.

"Doctor Farcett," he implored. "Do you believe in divine retribution? Can a child be punished for her father's crimes?"

Farcett's mind went back to Father Michael on Tarimond, and his opinion that the babies there were victims of God's judgment.

"I know some people believe that, Mr. O'Connell. I can think of one priest in particular who has told me so. But Mr. O'Connell, whatever you have done, Mary must not be allowed to suffer for it."

"It's not what I've done," said O'Connell, pausing as he struggled to find the courage to tell the truth. "Doctor Farcett, Mary is not my child." Farcett was unsurprised by this news after O'Connell's performance so far. "She belonged to my brother, who looked after her on his own after he lost his wife. But a few months ago, my brother . . ." O'Connell paused, and seemed to be groping for words. "My brother . . . left us. Mary's always been a sickly child, but since then she's gotten worse and worse. I have done my best in my brother's place. I have taken on his obligations in his family and in his work. Now Mary is suffering for my sins, too, and she is growing sicker and sicker."

Farcett found himself strangely moved by O'Connell's heartfelt speech, even though he thought the man was completely misguided in blaming himself and his brother for the child's condition.

"Mr. O'Connell," he said, soothingly. "Don't torture yourself. In taking on the care of your niece you have shown great humanity. I am sure you have done everything in your power for her. Illnesses come about for all sorts of reasons, many of them unknown to us as yet. We are trying to find out why children get ill, and to do something about it. Even that priest I told you of, the one who believed in divine retribution, told me he believed that God could work through doctors to find a cure. The God of judgment is a God of mercy, too. Mr. O'Connell, trust me. With God's help, we will make Mary well again."

Doctor Dougall returned to find O'Connell sobbing in Farcett's arms. He took over, passing Mary to an orderly, who carried her up to the ward. He saw O'Connell to the door, reassuring him that the child was in good hands, and passing him a slip of paper with details of the visiting hours and the hospital rules. As O'Connell left the premises Donald Dougall patted Farcett on the back.

"It doesn't do to get too involved with the patients," he said. "But all things considered, Robert, I think you've got a bit of a gift for this work."

CHAPTER 38

RETURN TO KEW

The next day, Doctor Farcett gave Montmorency permission to continue the investigation, and Fox-Selwyn suggested that they should travel to Kew by boat. He had a faint hope that Montmorency might catch sight of the Bag Man's vessel, and anyway he fancied the calm of a river trip after the stresses of the previous day. Up in the Parkview Suite at the Marimion he worked his way through Montmorency's guidebook, and with Vi's help planned a route around the gardens that would take them to all the major landmarks in the shortest possible time.

"Can't I come with you?" pleaded Vi, who was longing for a break from the hotel. "It's so lovely there. We could take Mum in her wheelchair."

Fox-Selwyn was appalled at the idea of wheeling Mrs. Evans around the Botanic Gardens all day, and was trying to find a polite way of saying no, when Montmorency reminded him of the real reason.

"No, Vi," said Montmorency kindly. "It's too dangerous. If we find the Bag Man at Kew, he might recognize you. We can't take the risk for your sake. You wouldn't be safe."

"And you wouldn't want to have to come home through the sewers again, now would you?" joked Fox-Selwyn.

Vi shuddered. The memory of the nauseating underground tunnel was enough to make her back off. For the first time, the men got a picture of how scared she now was. "It's all right," she said shakily. "I'll stay here."

Montmorency realized his friend had been insensitive. He tried to console Vi.

"You can help us, though. You know what the Bag Man looks like. Why don't you draw a picture of him, so George knows who to look out for? I'll do one, too, and we'll see how they compare."

The two of them sat at opposite ends of the long table in the sitting room, doing their best to show what the Bag Man was like. Neither Montmorency nor Vi was a great artist. Both went a bit over the top on the high forehead and the black bushy hair.

"Are you sure we shouldn't be visiting the zoo?" laughed Fox-Selwyn when he saw their efforts.

Vi pointed out that she hadn't meant to give the impression that the Bag Man's ears were at different heights, and Montmorency was unhappy with the way he'd shaped the chin, but in the end they produced two pictures that were similar enough to give Fox-Selwyn a rough idea of the kind of man he was after. He put the sketches inside the guidebook, and he and Montmorency set off to catch the boat at Westminster Pier.

The boat ride was rather more bracing than Fox-Selwyn had bargained for. Winter was getting a firm grip, and an icy breeze felt even stronger on the water. As they staggered from the jetty at Kew, Fox-Selwyn announced the first of many changes of plans. They would go straight to the Palm House to warm up. They could see it almost as soon as they entered the gardens, a vast structure of iron and glass, like the hull of a ship upturned on the grass. Nearby, an ornate chimney, cunningly disguised as a bell tower, belched out smoke from the boilers that were keeping the Palm House warm enough to sustain the tropical plants inside. On the brisk walk there, Montmorency and Fox-Selwyn kept an eye out for the Bag Man. They did see a bag, made of green canvas with "Property of the Royal Botanic Gardens" stenciled across it, but there was no man to go with it. At least not the one they were after. Fox-Selwyn noticed a skinny old gardener with a peaked cap watching as the two distinguished visitors took rather too close an interest in his tools.

Inside the Palm House, the hundreds of windows that formed its walls and roof were dripping with steam. After five minutes of standing over the iron grilles that let the heat of the boilers rise into the air, Fox-Selwyn took off his hat and mopped his balding head with his handkerchief.

"Beats the Xandan Baths," he chortled. "Gus should get one of these at Glendarvie. He might even persuade me to go up at Christmas if there was somewhere to get warm."

"It was terribly cold there. Especially at night," agreed Montmorency. "I thought it was just me. You know, with my trouble and everything."

"Dear boy, it's absolutely freezing," laughed Fox-Selwyn. "Even in the summer. And the Marchioness likes to keep it that way. Says it's character-building for the children."

"Perhaps she's right. Wasn't your character built there?"

"Only part of it, and I suspect it's the part that likes snuggling under the bedclothes or sitting by a roaring fire eating crumpets!"

"Would you like to live where these come from?" asked Montmorency, pointing out some spiky specimens from South America.

"We may have to if we mess this up!" laughed Fox-Selwyn, only half in jest, as he glanced across at a bald man with a hose, mentally crossing him off the list of suspects. "Now what's the quickest route to somewhere else that's warm?"

"Vi and I never made it as far as the new gallery. It's somewhere over there, near the road."

They left the Palm House and got their bearings. Fox-Selwyn didn't fancy taking off his gloves to turn the pages of the guidebook. "I suppose if we keep our backs to the river we should find it," he said. "Ah! Could it be that modern monstrosity, or do you think that's the lavatory?" He was pointing at a trim red-brick building, somewhat in the style of a suburban villa, with steps up to double doors. Montmorency took the guidebook and read the entry: " 'Built to house the collection of paintings generously donated by the artist, Marianne North, depicting plants encountered on her travels throughout the world.' "

"Oh dear!" sighed Fox-Selwyn. "A lady painter. Still, it's indoors. Shall we give it a go?"

He swept inside, with Montmorency a few paces

behind him. They were both expecting a handful of timid watercolors tastefully displayed against flocked wallpaper. What they found as they entered took their breath away. Hundreds of pictures in narrow black frames were crammed on the walls, each right up against its neighbor. Their livid colors shouted across the room. Beneath them the wall was inlaid with samples of wood from across the globe. Above, huge windows all the way around flooded the gallery with light, and a border was decorated with the names of faraway lands: Borneo, Ceylon, Java, New Zealand, America. It seemed that Marianne North had been everywhere, flourishing her paintbrush as she went. A few chilly visitors were studying the pictures, stamping their frozen feet to bring back the circulation; and in the corner someone was up a ladder, engaged in the demanding task of cleaning all the glass. He was powerfully built, struggling to treat the pictures with the delicacy they deserved. His hands were big and hairy. He was wearing dark green trousers. The collar of his shirt bounced against his wiry black curls as he breathed on the glass and rubbed with his cloth. Montmorency knew at once who he was. He discreetly nudged his friend, and pointed to the sketches he and Vi had drawn, which were nestling in the guidebook.

In the center of the room the architect had placed wooden benches, which would have been welcomed by weary walkers, had they not been so keen to keep moving to fight off the cold. The workman had hung his thick black wool jacket over the arm of one of the seats. Montmorency looked at Fox-Selwyn, and glanced at the coat in a pantomime gesture. Fox-Selwyn nodded, and Montmorency moved towards it, intending to pick its pockets for any clues to the owner's identity. As he touched it, the Bag Man up the ladder caught sight of the movement reflected in the picture glass. He looked around, and realized what was going on.

"Hey! Put that down!" he cried, attracting the attention of everyone in the room as Montmorency seized the jacket and ran out. The Bag Man followed, shouting and waving. Fox-Selwyn, puffing a little, brought up the rear, hoping that the respectable souls in the gallery would judge him to be a public-spirited citizen giving chase.

Montmorency turned to his left, vainly searching for a place where he could climb the wall and escape onto the road. Before long he saw the mighty form of the Pagoda rising before him. It was one hundred and fifty feet of sheer folly built in the Chinese style by

King George III as a surprise for his mother. From its broad octagonal base it rose up, each of its ten stories a little narrower than the one below, until it drew to a point with a huge golden spike at the top. Montmorency could have run around it. He could have run away from it, into some bushes at the side of the path. He could have ignored the Pagoda completely. Instead he did a very stupid thing. He wrenched open a door at the bottom and ran inside. The Bag Man was there in an instant. Like Montmorency he disregarded the warning signs that forbade the public to risk a climb on the rickety spiral stairs. There was nowhere to go but up, with giddy vistas of the river, the hothouses, the lake, the gallery, and then the road spinning before them through the windows as they climbed. At the top, the two men faced each other. The Bag Man's eyes flared with panic and hate. As his hairy fist swung towards Montmorency's face, Montmorency smashed a window and hurled the jacket out onto the sloping roof below. It slithered down from one story of the building to the next, occasionally catching on a loose roof tile, but eventually sliding down gracefully to ground level, where Fox-Selwyn caught it and dexterously transferred the contents of its pockets into his own.

At the top of the Pagoda, Montmorency and the Bag Man were wrestling, grabbing each other's arms to stop the punches, and kicking out with their feet. They were deadlocked until a mighty head-butt by the Bag Man forced Montmorency against the rotting banister with such force that the wood splintered and the two of them fell locked together through the air onto the floor below. Montmorency thrust his knee into the Bag Man's belly, leaving him writhing just long enough to clear his way to the remaining stairs. Montmorency leaped down them several at a time, and burst out through the doors at the bottom. A small crowd had gathered, attracted by the chase and then the noise of cracking wood and breaking glass. They gasped as Montmorency appeared before them. They gasped again as the Bag Man followed him. They cheered as Lord George Fox-Selwyn grabbed Montmorency's arm with one hand and twisted it in a half nelson behind his back. With the other hand he reached out to the panting Bag Man.

"Your jacket, sir!" he declared, with a triumphant flourish. There was applause. "Somebody see to his wounds," he commanded, with all his innate aristocratic authority, and a huddle of well-meaning visitors gathered around the Bag Man, blocking him in.

"Never mind this scoundrel," declared Fox-Selwyn. "He's coming with me!"

Fox-Selwyn frog-marched a shamefaced Montmorency to Lion Gate, a small side exit from the gardens, just a few yards away. Out in the street he let go of his arm. The two of them ran in the direction of Richmond, slowing down in time to look quite respectable as they entered the station to catch a train back to London.

In the train car, Fox-Selwyn emptied his pockets. The Bag Man had been carrying all sorts of odds and ends. There was a penknife, some string, cigarettes, matches, candy wrappers, and a couple of keys. There was also a printed sheet with writing that reminded Montmorency of a script he had seen on Tarimond, but Fox-Selwyn identified it as Irish Gaelic, rather than Scots. And there was one last folded piece of paper, newer and less crumpled than the rest. It was headed with the words "Great Ormond Street Hospital for Sick Children" and it listed the visiting hours and rules.

CHAPTER 39

PROFESSIONAL ETHICS

Farcett was at the Marimion when they got back, calming down the Contessa with a little something. When Montmorency came into the room the doctor screwed the lid tightly onto the medicine bottle and thrust it firmly into his own pocket for safekeeping. "Had a good day?" he asked, as Montmorency and Fox-Selwyn collapsed onto the sofa.

"One of the best!" said Fox-Selwyn. "Though Montmorency has a few bumps and scrapes you might want to look at. I seem to have escaped unscathed!"

Vi came into the sitting room. "Did you see him then? Does he really work at Kew?"

"We saw him, Vi."

"And so you know who he is, where he lives? Have you told the police where to find him?"

"Not yet, Vi. We're not quite ready. But we will. The police won't take any notice of us until we've got more evidence. We don't know where he lives, and we don't know what he's called. We could ask the management at Kew, but after today I doubt whether he'll be turning up for work."

"So why are you so pleased with yourselves, then?" Vi snapped. "He's still on the loose, and I'm still stuck here hiding from him."

"Yes, Vi," teased Fox-Selwyn. "I can see that life at the Marimion must be very tiresome for you. Please bear with us. You may not have to stay here much longer."

"Sorry," said Vi, repenting her ingratitude. "Only I can't see what you've got to be so happy about."

"Vi," said Montmorency. "We have reason to believe that the Bag Man will not leave London. In fact, we have reason to believe we know where he will be between the hours of two and four o'clock on any day in the near future."

"And what gives you that idea?" asked Vi, still unconvinced.

"This!" declared Fox-Selwyn, pulling the paper from his pocket. "It seems that the Bag Man visits a child at Great Ormond Street Hospital."

Doctor Farcett grabbed the paper. It was a printed sheet, and gave no indication of the patient's identity.

"What did this man look like?" he asked. After Montmorency's reply, and a glance at the two sketches, he was in no doubt. The Bag Man was none other than Mr. O'Connell. The tearful man he had comforted at the hospital was the Waterloo Bomber.

Fox-Selwyn interrupted his thoughts. "Robert, doesn't that expert who's looking at your Tarimond files work at Great Ormond Street?" he asked, innocently. "Couldn't you ask him about the Bag Man?"

"Yes," said Doctor Farcett, distractedly. "I think I will."

Farcett wanted to tell his friends about his trips to Great Ormond Street and his suspicions about O'Connell, but he said nothing. For he was wrestling with a professional dilemma. He knew Mr. O'Connell in his capacity as a doctor, a job that conferred on him special duties, including absolute confidentiality. He knew that O'Connell assumed as much. Why else would he have dropped his guard in such an emotional outburst? Yet O'Connell might be a criminal. Fox-Selwyn and Montmorency certainly believed so. Should Farcett take the initiative in turning him over to the authorities? He tried to console himself with the thought that perhaps there would be no need. After all, it sounded as if, guided by his friends, the police might find O'Connell for themselves. And yet, wondered Farcett, what if he stayed quiet now and there was a new bomb before Scotland Yard could track O'Connell down? Didn't Farcett have obligations to O'Connell's potential targets, too?

It was a problem Doctor Farcett had faced before. Quite recently he had discovered that another of his patients was a criminal. On that occasion his conscience had excused him for failing to reveal the man's crimes to the authorities. He lived every day quite comfortable with that decision. For the criminal patient in question then was in the room now, laughing and joking with his other friends. It was Montmorency.

"You're a bit quiet, Robert — aren't you going to congratulate us?" said Fox-Selwyn.

"Sorry. I've got something on my mind," stuttered the doctor. "A problem with a patient." He looked at Montmorency, standing there, proud and happy, totally at home in the world he had built out of the proceeds of crime. If he turned O'Connell over to the police, should he tell them about Montmorency, too?

Montmorency sensed none of his anguish, and carried on talking about the Bag Man. Farcett could bear it no longer. He got up to go. "I'll leave you to rejoice in peace," he said quietly. "Shall I get them to send you up some supper?"

"Oh yes!" cried Vi. "I'm starving!" And they spent

ages drawing up an order for Farcett to take downstairs.

"Get them to send some champagne, too," said Fox-Selwyn, as he left. "There's something else I want to celebrate."

"Really. What's that?" asked Farcett.

"I want to toast the fact that if they get the Bag Man, it won't be because of Scarper. The Bag Man was caught by Montmorency!"

CHAPTER 40

DOCTOR DOUGALL'S DIAGNOSIS

Farcett didn't sleep well. All night he debated with himself the pros and cons of handing O'Connell over to the police. Whenever he came down on the side of exposure he saw before him the image of little Mary, deprived of the one adult she loved, who might, for all he knew, be innocent of any crime. When he decided to keep quiet he imagined the sound of a bomb, tearing the life from a dozen little Marys, and showering untold others with grief and pain. At dawn, no nearer to a decision, he resolved to ask Donald Dougall's advice, and he skipped breakfast to make sure he could catch the doctor before he started his morning rounds. He was waiting outside Dougall's office when he arrived for work.

"Robert. I'm so glad you're here," said Doctor Dougall in a tone of excited relief. "Come in. Come in. This really is most serious."

Farcett wondered how he could know. Had Fox-Selwyn and Montmorency been in touch already?

Doctor Dougall continued: "There's no doubt about it, we'll have to call in the police."

"It's as straightforward as that?" asked Farcett, bewildered. He couldn't understand why Dougall saw no problem with confidentiality. But it turned out that Doctor Dougall was talking about something completely different.

"Absolutely. The evidence is all there in the notes. Robert, I can't come to any other conclusion. The children of Tarimond are being systematically poisoned!"

Farcett was dumbstruck with shock. The crisis over O'Connell faded from his mind as he thought through the implications of what Donald Dougall had said. Every child born on Tarimond for the past seven years had been murdered. He voiced his next thought aloud.

"The water? There was something in that sample I gave you?"

"No, the water was as pure as any I've seen," said Dougall. "I had thought it a possibility though. Small children can succumb to impurities that would have no effect on a healthy adult. But there's nothing there. No, Robert, the key is in the symptoms. If we only had some tissue from the dead children I'm sure we would find the slow-acting agent that has been used to kill them all."

"Used by whom? How? And why?" gasped Farcett.

"I was hoping you'd have some suggestions there. Obviously someone with access to all the babies, someone who could introduce a toxin into their milk . . ."

Farcett interrupted. "Not Maggie Goudie. Surely not! The woman's dedicated her life to helping the people of Tarimond. She's delivered all those babies herself. She helped me collect the information. She's still helping. I can't believe it could be her."

"Then who else? Who else could have the inclination and the means?"

"Nobody in their right mind could want to stir up all that grief." As Farcett spoke the words he recalled his first sighting of Father Michael, wild and shouting against the storm, towering over the tiny gravestones in his flapping robes. Then after church that Sunday, all civility and cheer after his searing sermon, he had joked about the need to keep his flock loyal with threats of fear and divine judgment. Father Michael himself had said the wrath of God was the cause of the deaths. Wasn't Father Michael God's representative on earth?

"What is it, Robert? Do you know who it is?" asked Doctor Dougall.

"I fear I do," said Farcett, punching his palm with his fist. "I stayed in his house, I shared his food, and I discussed with him every lost child. I saw him baptize Jimmy MacLean, the only survivor . . . if he still survives. Oh, Donald! I've got to get back to Tarimond before Jimmy is killed, too!"

"You spoke of a baptism. Is it the priest you suspect?"

"It has to be him. I know. I can feel it in my bones."

"Because you don't want it to be the midwife?" suggested Dougall with an eyebrow raised.

"It can't be her. I would know. Surely a doctor, of all people, would recognize a killer?" Farcett's voice trailed off as he pictured himself only the day before, comforting O'Connell and judging him to be a humane and noble man.

Doctor Dougall guessed from Farcett's silence that he was realizing the probable truth: "The priest and the midwife may be in this together," he said.

But Farcett's mind had jumped back to the other mystery. "There's something else," he said. "Something just as bad. I didn't come here to talk about Tarimond. Do you remember Mary O'Connell from yesterday?"

"Remember her? I'm about to go and examine her upstairs!"

Farcett told Doctor Dougall about his friends' suspicions, and his dilemma about turning O'Connell in. Dougall could see that Farcett was overwhelmed by the two problems competing for his attention. He offered to take half the burden.

"Leave O'Connell with me. Mary is my patient, so the decision is rightfully mine. You go away and pack. You must get to Tarimond without delay. It's a grim duty you leave to do, Robert, but even so I'd love to be traveling to Scotland with you! I will write up my report and send it to the police in Glasgow, but if what you suspect is true, you can't wait for that."

Farcett rushed home. A quick look at the train timetable showed there was no time to visit his friends to tell them what was going on. He sent a note to Fox-Selwyn's house giving the barest outline of the reasons for his flight. He didn't mention O'Connell. That matter was in Doctor Dougall's hands now.

On the train he reread Maggie Goudie's letter. It looked so very different in the light of his new suspicions, not at all the tender note he had treasured since its arrival four days ago. How was he now to interpret her apparent concern for his welfare? Was it all a bluff to throw him off the scent? What of Jimmy? Was he really thriving, or had he already started the pathetic wasting that had shriveled away all the others? And what was this about Father Michael praying for Farcett and Montmorency's safe return to London? No doubt he had! He'd have been glad to get the visitors out of the way so he could continue on his murderous career. Perhaps Donald Dougall was right, and they were in it together, Father Michael and Maggie. They had been friends since their days in Glasgow. They had spoken so highly of each other. They had both been so suspiciously eager to help, so apparently civilized by contrast with the rest of the islanders. They said they had been trying for years to get to the bottom of the deaths. Yet they had failed. Of course they had! They were not researching the cause of the deaths; they were disguising it behind a pretense of concern. Hadn't Father Michael said he had been considering calling in experts from the mainland? Why hadn't he? Hadn't he tried to stop Farcett himself returning to London with the facts? Hadn't he encouraged him to stay on Tarimond forever, where he couldn't publicize his concerns? And why was Father Michael always there, suddenly, whenever Maggie brought charts and documents for Farcett to study, gently correcting her on matters of fact, subtly guiding all their thoughts, always the first to point out that the only explanation was divine wrath. Hadn't the priest himself spoken of breaking divine law? What had he done? Was he hinting then that he had killed the babies? How could Farcett have been taken in? Had he and Montmorency not sensed on that very first day on Tarimond that there was some strange power in the man? Wasn't it obvious that the islanders felt it: Morag, the congregation, even Harvey, who had been away so long? Harvey would not even go near the priest. Did Harvey know something about Father Michael? Was that why he had left Tarimond? Was that why the atmosphere in the priest's house had changed so markedly when he came back?

The train trundled on. Farcett had convinced himself that Father Michael was behind the deaths, but he couldn't believe that Maggie was guilty, too. Was she another of his victims? The prisoner of his evil influence? Or was there, after all, far more to it than that? She had invited Father Michael to Tarimond in the first place. And one image was burned into his memory. It was of Father Michael with his arm around her as she waved good-bye to Farcett, Montmorency, and Harvey from the top of the cliff.

He willed the train to go faster. He must get back to Tarimond as quickly as possible before any more babies were born, to save them and little Jimmy MacLean from the murderous hands of Maggie and Father Michael.

CHAPTER 41

CAPTURE

When Farcett's note arrived Lord George Fox-Selwyn was out, and Chivers put it on the hall stand for later. His lordship was having another of his early breakfasts with the Home Secretary. This time the atmosphere was full of excitement and hope. The evidence against the Bag Man was flimsy, but it was the only lead anyone had about the bombings. Montmorency would have been happy to continue undercover surveillance a little longer: watching outside the hospital at visiting hours, following the Bag Man home, chatting to his neighbors and drinking companions about his background and habits; but Fox-Selwyn sensed that the time had come for the official operators to take over. The Home Secretary agreed. As far as he could see, the chances of success now outweighed the possibility of humiliation, and he wanted to be able to take full credit when the culprit was caught. The Home Secretary examined the sketches of the Bag Man drawn by Montmorency and Vi.

"It's good to have these. I'll pass them on to Scotland Yard and tell them they came in the post."

"You'll need some sort of anonymous letter to go with them. Shall I write it now?" said Fox-Selwyn.

The Home Secretary took a sheet of letterhead from his desk. Fox-Selwyn laughed. "It might be better not to use something with your address on it, don't you think?"

"Oops!" gulped the Home Secretary. "I really wouldn't be very good in your line of work, would I? Do you remember how I always used to get caught at school?"

Fox-Selwyn could indeed remember the exasperation of sharing a dormitory with that slow-witted boy. If it hadn't been for his clumsiness and need to be loved by the powerful, the sorry episode of the frog and the molasses would never have reached the prefects. And now that little boy was in charge of national security. Oh dear!

"Here," said Fox-Selwyn, "I'll tear a page from my notebook." He took a pencil in his left hand and, with deliberate misspellings, wrote:

> *This is the face of the Waterloo Bommer. He works at Kew Gardins. He*

will be visitinge the Childrens Ospital at grate Hormund Street in the afternoon. The Kings Kross job wasint gas. Ask Him.

"Shouldn't you explain a bit more?" asked the Home Secretary.

"No. There's enough there to get the police going. Best to let them think they've worked it out for themselves. Have you got an envelope? A plain one without any flourishes or crests?"

"Afraid not."

"Probably just as well. We don't want them interviewing the postman. Tell you what. You go out for a walk at eleven, and someone will pass the note to you in the park."

It was a good move. A detective, secretly detailed by his superiors to keep a discreet eye on the Home Secretary, saw Scarper run up and slip something into his pocket. Scarper got away, but the discovery of the note was taken all the more seriously by Scotland Yard when it was brought in by one of their own men. Within minutes a constable had been dispatched to ask questions at Kew. Yes, the man in the pictures worked there. No, he had not turned up for work today.

»»»

At Great Ormond Street Doctor Dougall was still agonizing over Farcett's suspicions about O'Connell when the police saved him from a decision by arriving unbidden. He identified the man in the sketches as the guardian of one of his patients. He begged the police not to confront the suspect on the premises, and so at two o'clock, assorted uniformed and plain-clothes officers were positioned in the street outside. O'Connell came around the corner holding a posy of flowers in his hairy fingers. He was still clinging to it after they had slipped the handcuffs on his wrists. Doctor Dougall watched it all from an upstairs window. Then he turned to look at little Mary, sleeping quietly, clinging on to life, not knowing that she had lost the only person left in the world who cared for her.

CHAPTER 42

INTERROGATION

The next week was eventful, in London and in Scotland. The police were pleased to have O'Connell in custody, but they knew that they would need more evidence than the words of an anonymous note if they were to be able to keep him locked up. Vi was terrified that she would be asked to stand up in public and say what she knew about him.

"I've never gone to court, and I never will," she told Fox-Selwyn. "Suppose this man's got relatives, suppose they hear about me. What do you think they'll do then? I might as well have let him catch me in the first place."

Fox-Selwyn tried lecturing her about her civic duty, but Montmorency took him aside. "She's right, you know," he said. "If she gives evidence, she'll never be safe in London."

"How else are the police going to be able to prove O'Connell bombed Waterloo? It's not as if he's going to admit it," said Fox-Selwyn.

"Ah, but he might. In fact, he has to. It might be the only way he'll escape the gallows."

"I don't follow you," said Fox-Selwyn.

Montmorency explained his thinking. His aim was to keep Vi out of the witness box, to find out the truth about both bombings, and to deliver to the police an informer against other Irish terrorists in London. It depended on the authorities maintaining the myth that the King's Cross explosion was caused by gas, but there was every reason to suppose they would be happy to do that. After all, changing their story would raise all sorts of questions about whether they could be trusted to tell the truth in the future.

"In fact," said Montmorency, "I don't see how anyone can lose under this plan."

"So what do we do?" asked Fox-Selwyn.

"First we tell the police exactly what we think happened. Vi, we'll have to tell them everything, but I'm sure we can keep you out of it. The Home Secretary should see to that."

Fox-Selwyn nodded. He knew the Home Secretary would not want to risk revealing the details of his night out with Vi.

"Then," continued Montmorency, "they interrogate O'Connell. They tell him that they're going to charge him with the King's Cross job, and that the charge will be murder."

"But he didn't do it!" exclaimed Vi. "It was the other man."

"We know that, and O'Connell knows that," said Montmorency. "But no one else does. The only way he can hope to get out of the murder charge will be to tell the whole story."

Fox-Selwyn was beginning to see where Montmorency's mind was going: "So then the police offer him a deal?" he asked.

"Exactly. They say that they'll cut the charge to something connected with the Waterloo bomb if he'll give them information about people, places, and plans. The better the information, the lesser the charge. And he pleads guilty at the trial, so there's no need for the full evidence to come out in public."

"But he'll still go to prison, won't he?" said Vi, anxiously. "There's no hope for me if he's on the loose."

"Oh yes, Vi," said Montmorency. "He'll go to prison, and for a very long time. Probably for the rest of his life. But he'll keep that life."

"Let's just hope he values it enough to make the deal," said Fox-Selwyn. "If he does, you're right. Nobody loses. I'll have a word with the Home Secretary and see what he thinks."

The Home Secretary was thrilled with the plan, and

added a twist of his own. Since Fox-Selwyn and Montmorency were the only people in full command of the details, they should conduct the interrogation. So they went with him to Scotland Yard, where the police had no choice but to agree (reluctantly) to the suggestion from their political master. The Police Commissioner and two senior detectives from the Special Irish Branch were to join the Home Secretary, listening in on the questioning from an adjacent cell.

It was a bizarre scene. The Minister and the top men in the London police force filed down to the basement and took up their places in the tiny bare room, sitting sideways in a line along a hard wooden bench. The Commissioner took four glass drinking tumblers out of a wooden box, and showed the Home Secretary how to place one against the wall and press his ear to it, so that he could hear what was going on next door. Fox-Selwyn and Montmorency were already in there, discussing tactics.

"I say!" cried the Home Secretary, in high excitement. "This is fun! Do you know, I can hear every word."

"That's the idea, sir," said the Commissioner, politely enough to cover up his contempt. "We have our methods, sir."

"This is marvelous," continued the Home Secretary.

"I mean, one could listen to anybody. I say! It's just like being a spy!"

"Indeed, sir," said the Commissioner, as if he were hearing the idea for the first time. "So it is." There was a series of clangs, as a distant door opened and shut. "The prisoner's on his way, sir. We must be quiet now."

The Home Secretary turned around to the detectives, put his finger to his lips, and let out a loud "Shush!" When he turned back, they rolled their eyes at each other in exasperation, and then settled back into position, pressing their own glasses against the wall, ready to listen. They heard clanking footsteps as a constable marched O'Connell in chains down the corridor to be delivered to Fox-Selwyn and Montmorency in the adjacent cell.

The sound of the door slamming and the key turning set off a string of memories for Montmorency: recollections of loneliness, bullying, misery, and cold.

Montmorency was sitting behind a square table in the middle of the room, facing the door. Beside him was a chair for Fox-Selwyn, but he was standing, ready to address the prisoner. They had a plan of attack. To begin with, Montmorency would stay quiet, and Fox-Selwyn would ask the questions.

"Mr. O'Connell," said Fox-Selwyn, seriously. "Sit down." He motioned to a small wobbly stool, specially chosen to make O'Connell feel uncomfortable and look insignificant opposite Fox-Selwyn's giant frame. "We are here to ask you some very important questions. Will you please state your full name and address."

O'Connell mumbled his details with his head bowed. Fox-Selwyn listened for a rattle of keys: the prearranged sign that the neighbors could hear everyone in the cell. It came. The Commissioner had another signal ready, too. If Montmorency and Fox-Selwyn heard a burst of violent coughing they were to stop at once. The cough would tell them that they had gone too far, by either probing too hard or promising too much. As the Home Secretary put it, "One cough and the deal is off."

O'Connell sat slumped, dejected, not at all the defiant, energetic man Montmorency remembered. When he finally looked up at Fox-Selwyn and Montmorency he recognized the two men from the Pagoda at Kew.

"So you were coppers!" he said. "Clever. I knew you plainclothes men dressed down. Never knew you dressed up."

"Never mind that," said Fox-Selwyn. "You know why we're here. Tell us about the bomb at Waterloo."

"Nothing to do with me."

"Really?" said Fox-Selwyn. "Mr. O'Connell, we think it was. Indeed we know it was."

"How? How do you know?"

"I'm asking the questions, Mr. O'Connell," said Fox-Selwyn, with a superior air. "But since you ask, I might as well tell you. You were seen."

It was the first of many lies Fox-Selwyn used to undermine O'Connell's confidence. In the next room, the Commissioner and his men squirmed. They would at least have attempted to stick to the facts. But they were beginning to see why the Home Secretary had brought outsiders in to do this job, and were glad they wouldn't be taking the blame if it all went wrong.

Fox-Selwyn continued: "You see, we know all about Waterloo. What we're really interested in is King's Cross. Two people died at King's Cross. An unnamed vagrant, and a Mrs. Molly Mead. A charming lady. A mother. Murdered. I put it to you that you planted the King's Cross bomb, too."

"It wasn't me."

"Well, excuse me if I don't believe you, but why should I? I know you're a liar. You said you didn't bomb Waterloo."

"Because I didn't!"

"But you were seen," said Fox-Selwyn, repeating his own lie. "We know you did it."

"But I never did King's Cross."

"So you admit you bombed Waterloo, but not King's Cross?"

"Yes . . . No . . ." stuttered O'Connell. "You've got me confused."

"Then tell the truth and it will be simpler for you. You bombed Waterloo Station?"

O'Connell was silent, staring at the table, thinking. Fox-Selwyn asked again.

"You bombed Waterloo?" Fox-Selwyn raised his voice. "You bombed Waterloo, didn't you?"

"Yes, all right. I did," said O'Connell, giving in. "But not King's Cross. That was someone who looked like me."

Fox-Selwyn and Montmorency had prepared themselves for this moment. The moment when O'Connell admitted the crime they believed he'd done. As planned, they hardly reacted at all, though the admission was the key to the rest of their scheme. In the next cell, the Home Secretary was squeezing his knees together with glee, and pressing his glass to the wall to hear more. Fox-Selwyn continued, picking up on O'Connell's last few words.

"Someone who looked like you," he sneered. "How convenient. Someone you know?"

O'Connell was silent again.

"Do you know who did it, Mr. O'Connell?" repeated Fox-Selwyn. "Mr. O'Connell, do you know who murdered Molly Mead? Speak, man. You must have an answer. Yes or no?"

"He didn't mean to kill anyone!" O'Connell shouted. "It wasn't meant to go off till after hours."

"Who didn't mean to kill, Mr. O'Connell?" said Fox-Selwyn. There was another pause, then O'Connell whispered his reply.

"My brother."

"And where is this brother of yours?"

O'Connell looked at the floor. "I don't know."

"Oh, how very convenient!" Fox-Selwyn was pacing around the room now. "Is that the best you can do for a story? You're not the murderer, you know who did it, but you don't know where he is. Do you seriously expect me to believe that?"

Fox-Selwyn put his point with such force that he almost convinced himself that O'Connell was lying, even though, of course, he knew that it was true. What little evidence they had suggested three things: that O'Connell wasn't the King's Cross bomber, almost certainly knew who was, and was as mystified as anyone as to what had happened to him.

It was time for Montmorency to speak. "Mr. O'Connell," he said softly. "My colleague here seems convinced you killed Molly Mead and that tramp at King's Cross. Why should I believe that you didn't?"

O'Connell was silent again, but he had sunk down, leaning his head on his handcuffed fists. Montmorency let him think for a while. Then he asked again. "Mr. O'Connell. Is there any reason why we shouldn't charge you with murder?"

In the next cell, the Commissioner could think of a good one: a complete lack of evidence. But O'Connell didn't know that.

Montmorency persisted. "Why should we believe that the King's Cross bomb had nothing to do with you?"

O'Connell looked at Montmorency and finally said something: "Because I tried to stop him!" It was an answer neither Montmorency nor Fox-Selwyn had expected, but Montmorency continued calmly.

"Tell us more, Mr. O'Connell, and tell us the truth."

They had no reason to disbelieve the story O'Connell came out with. It fitted the few facts they knew. O'Connell said he had an older brother, Patrick, whose wife had died in childbirth. They had come over to London from Ireland a few years before. Both worked at Kew. Patrick's little daughter, Mary, was ill. A doctor had offered treatment, but it would be costly. Patrick had appealed for help, putting out the word amongst the Irish community in London. Eventually he'd been offered money by a group of Fenians, in exchange for planting two bombs: one at King's Cross, the other at Waterloo. The first had gone off, but Patrick had disappeared. O'Connell had been left with the child, but was denied the money until his brother's task had been completed. He'd searched for Patrick, but could track him only as far as the lodgings he'd taken on the first night. He'd come to accept that Patrick had probably been killed in that blast. But he still needed the money for the doctor, so he had planted the Waterloo bomb himself. He'd gone again for the money, but the plotters still wouldn't pay him, only his brother. He had to persuade them that Patrick was dead. The only person who had any information about him was the girl from the lodging house. She could confirm that Patrick had disappeared.

So that's why he was after Vi, thought Montmorency. *That's why he was so desperate to catch her.*

"I had to find her," said O'Connell, unaware that Montmorency knew all too well that this part of his story was true. "I nearly caught her, but she disappeared. Disappeared into thin air. So I never got the money. But it's worse than that. It turns out that Patrick never needed the cash; that he need never to have gotten involved with those people in the first place. Someone told me about a hospital where you don't have to pay. That's where Mary is now. That's where they arrested me."

In the next cell, the Home Secretary was convinced, and assumed the interrogation was over. He even felt quite sorry for the man. So he was taken aback when Fox-Selwyn lashed out at O'Connell again.

"O'Connell! If you expect us to believe all that you must be out of your mind." He went on, stretching the truth to breaking point: "You've told us enough to convict you. You can expect to hang for the murder of Molly Mead. I'll call for them to take you back to your cell."

That was the prearranged signal for Montmorency to come forward with the deal. He pretended that the idea had just come to him.

"One moment, sir!" he said to Fox-Selwyn. "There might be a way of avoiding the murder charge."

"And why would we want to do that?" barked Fox-Selwyn.

"If Mr. O'Connell were prepared to help us, sir. If he were prepared to give us information about the people who hired his brother. Perhaps it might be possible to offer him something in return."

O'Connell took the bait, and willingly offered to help them. In the next cell the Home Secretary was squealing with joy, imagining how pleased the Prime Minister would be to hear of this result. The Commissioner was aghast with relief and amazement. He didn't need to cough and cancel the deal. Somehow, without any real evidence to support it, he had a confession to the Waterloo bomb, and no need to deal with the King's Cross case at all. The two detectives from the Irish Branch were excited, too. Perhaps O'Connell could finally get them on the trail of the London Fenians, and they could capture the ringleaders at last. Sitting on their bench with their ears against their glasses, and the glasses pressed to the wall, the four eavesdroppers all felt like winners. In the next cell, O'Connell believed he had talked his way out of a death sentence, and Montmorency and Fox-Selwyn thought they had pulled off a great victory against the odds, saving Vi from the witness box in the process.

But Montmorency had been wrong to say that there would be no losers. As planned, the public and the press continued to believe that the King's Cross explosion had been caused by a gas leak. They wanted someone to pay for the sloppy workmanship that had cost a life. The directors of the Gas Company, still doing their duty to "national security" by maintaining the fiction about the blast, looked for someone to blame. The poor man who had (faultlessly) welded that section of pipe was dismissed from his job. He was dead by his own hand within a year.

CHAPTER 43

AUTHORITY

Doctor Farcett's journey to Tarimond was long, slow, and cold. By the time he got to Glasgow he had worked himself up into a state about the need to arrest Father Michael and Maggie Goudie as soon as possible. He was surprised to find that at Glasgow police headquarters they took a different view. When he arrived, late in the evening, the officer on the desk kept him waiting while he dealt with an old woman who had lost a parrot. Farcett's attempts to intervene simply made the policeman angry, and less inclined to hear what this excitable visitor from London had to say.

"I must speak to someone in authority," insisted Farcett, perhaps a little louder than he intended.

"Aye, sir," said the sergeant. "At this hour, I am that man. My superiors have all gone home, and they would not thank me for calling them away. Now if you'll wait your turn, sir, I'll be with you when I have finished with this young lady."

The woman was flattered by his description of her,

and came over all coquettish, slowing down the parrot transaction considerably. Farcett shuffled in his seat, sighing expressively, and doing his own case no good at all.

Eventually the sergeant saw the lady out, and invited Farcett to approach his desk.

"Now, sir. Tell me, what is all this about?"

"It's an emergency. On Tarimond," said Farcett, breathlessly.

"I see," said the sergeant, with mock gravity. "Well, we don't get one of those every day." He pointed to the map on the wall behind him. "Let's see now. Tarimond is about as far from here as we go, without actually arriving in America. And there's an emergency there. Now what exactly do you want me to do about it, Mr. . . . ?"

"Farcett. Doctor Robert Farcett." He had the presence of mind to stress the word "Doctor." It sometimes helped instill a little respect.

The sergeant did become a bit less facetious. "All right then, Doctor Farcett. Perhaps you'd better give me the details." He turned to a new page in his notebook, and slowly refilled his inkwell.

Farcett tried to tell the story of the dead babies,

Father Michael, and Maggie Goudie. The policeman made some notes, but it was clear he doubted either Farcett's judgment or his sanity.

"So your evidence for these allegations, Doctor Farcett, is what exactly?"

"Well, I've analyzed all the statistics, and Doctor Donald Dougall, who is a specialist in children's medicine, has concluded that the only explanation of the symptoms is deliberate poisoning."

"And this Doctor Dougall. Where is he? Can't he bring his findings here?"

"He's in London," said Farcett, rather weakly.

"London. I see. Well, that's a great help. . . ."

"But he's sending you his full report. He's of the view that action needs to be taken immediately."

"Against whom, exactly?"

"Father Michael and Maggie Goudie. It has to be them. Or one of them. They're the only people with the opportunity and the expertise."

The sergeant tried to be patient, but was in no mood to act: "Well, we'll see," he said emolliently. "Why don't we just wait for this report and see what it actually says?"

As the policeman grew calmer, Doctor Farcett became more agitated: "But that could take days.

Those people have to be stopped now. I can't wait here. I've got to go to Tarimond!"

The sergeant closed his notebook. "Well, it's a free country. You do as you please. But we can't do anything without evidence. I'll make a few inquiries about this Father Michael of yours. You say he was a Glasgow man?"

"Yes, until ten years ago, and Maggie Goudie was a nurse at one of the hospitals."

"Well, we'll see what we can find. But don't let yourself get overexcited, sir. It's a hard life on the islands, and babies die all the time. That doesn't mean they're all murdered."

Doctor Farcett made one last attempt to press his case, but he could see that this policeman was not going to give way. Nothing would be done until inquiries had been made, and Dougall's report had been received. But Farcett couldn't wait that long. He had to check on Jimmy MacLean and Morag's unborn brother or sister. For his own peace of mind he had to leave for Tarimond straightaway.

In the winter weather, boats were scarce and the sea was rough. The inns Farcett stayed at along the way were uncomfortable. It was three days before he was in sight of the island, and all that time he pictured Jimmy MacLean wasting away at the hands of Father Michael. He imagined the priest visiting Jimmy's father, pretending to bring solace, but taking the chance to slip his poison into the child's milk. As the boy sickened, Father Michael would preach sermons lashing the islanders for their wickedness and exhorting them to come to him more and more often to atone for their sins. Farcett tried to imagine Maggie Goudie doing the same evil things. He couldn't. He didn't want to believe that she was as guilty as the priest. At most, he could see her swept along by Father Michael's charisma, and turning a blind eye to his deeds or covering up for them. But he knew he would have to confront her, and that the scene could be painful for them both.

At last he was in that final, leaky, rowing boat, setting off for Tarimond's rocky beach. In the distance he could see the gray stone church on the headland, and the cluster of graves overlooking the sea. As he drew closer he could hear the church bell, too: a solemn rhythmic tolling, calling the islanders to prayer. Farcett tied up the boat, and climbed up towards the graveyard. The little bell had a weak, tinny clang. Between each note came a wheezing squeak as the bell swung back, ready for the next pull of the rope. It wasn't Sunday. The people of Tarimond must be marking a special occasion. When he reached the top of the cliff he realized with horror what it was. There was a pile of freshly dug earth alongside the grave of Jimmy MacLean's mother, Jeannie, who had died giving birth to him. It was a funeral. Could it be that Farcett had arrived just too late?

The bell stopped and the harmonium started up inside. The first hymn was under way. Doctor Farcett quietly entered the church. A few heads turned to check on the latecomer, and gradually the volume of the singing dropped as people told one another of his arrival. Father Michael had his back to the congregation, facing the altar with his arms outstretched. Alongside him was a coffin. Farcett thought it looked rather large for a child. He stared at the priest's back, loathing him. As the singing died away and fell into surprised chatter, Father Michael turned to see what had caused the change of mood.

"Praise the Lord!" he cried, beaming a smile at Farcett. "The Lord has sent the good doctor back to us! Doctor Farcett, we are here to bury our oldest resident, Elspeth MacLeod. Elspeth died yesterday, peacefully, in her sleep. Join us, Doctor, to send her back into the care of the Lord!"

Farcett wanted to shout out to everyone about the sins of Father Michael, of how he had stolen a generation away from Tarimond. But the warmth of the greeting, the smiles of the islanders, and the sight of the MacLeod family, there to say farewell to their beloved granny, stopped him. He stood through the service in agony, exchanging polite nods with familiar faces. Morag's mother was there, heavily pregnant, a reminder of why Father Michael must be stopped. Farcett scoured the pews for a sight of Maggie Goudie. And there she was, tucked away in the corner, smiling back at him. At her side was John MacLean. And in a basket at his feet, asleep but plump and healthy, was his baby, Jimmy, Tarimond's symbol of hope.

This wasn't the arrival Farcett had imagined. This was no place to confront Father Michael or Maggie. He was caught up in the press of islanders, and the ritual of the funeral rite. At the graveside, he watched as Jimmy, wide-awake now, waved and gurgled in his father's arms. Tears of relief ran down Farcett's cheeks. "Come now, Doctor," said Father Michael. "Elspeth was an old lady and she'd had a good life. She's at peace now, away from the pains of old age. There's no need for tears."

"I'm not crying for her," replied Farcett, doing his best to sound civil. "It's just . . ." He didn't know what to say. "I'm just . . . I'm just very, very tired."

"Come back to your old room then," said the priest.

"Aye," said Maggie. "It's wonderful to have you back, but I can see you're exhausted. Go away to your bed, and we'll talk in the morning."

John MacLean passed over little Jimmy for him to hold. The tears came again as Farcett hugged the precious bundle to his chest.

"Come on now, man," said Father Michael, putting a friendly arm around the doctor's shoulders. "You're done in!"

And Farcett went with him. The moment had gone. He could not make a scene. He was trapped in the home of a man he believed to be the incarnation of evil. Yet he did as he was told. He went to bed.

CHAPTER 44

>>

VENGEANCE

Farcett lay awake worrying for more than an hour, but then his exhaustion took hold. When he woke, it was the middle of the night. The whole island was asleep and the house was quiet. He dressed and let himself out into the dark, then sat on the headland till dawn, wondering what he would say in the morning if anyone asked him why he had come back. He rehearsed the two encounters he was dreading. He decided he would confront Father Michael first, and then go to see Maggie Goudie. But his plan was upset. There was a rustling noise in the reeds.

"Robert?" It was Maggie Goudie's gentle voice. She was standing behind him, carrying a basket. "I brought some eggs for your breakfast," she said. "I couldn't sleep all night. I knew you must have come back because you had some news of the investigation. I had to come to ask you. Do the experts know why the babies have died?"

Farcett looked at her. The concern on her face didn't look like the guilty anxiety of a killer afraid of being unmasked. Everything about her spoke of nurturing, life, and love. He tried to tell himself not to be fooled, but even so he spoke gently.

"Yes, Maggie, the experts do know. And Maggie, it's bad news. Very grave news indeed. Maggie, this will be hard for you to hear, but there is no other explanation. I showed our notes to one of the greatest authorities in London, someone I respect and trust absolutely. And he is in no doubt, Maggie: The babies were murdered. All of them."

"But who would do such a thing?" gasped Maggie.

Farcett stood, silent, looking out to sea. Then he turned to face her, wondering if she could ever kill.

"Robert, tell me. Do you know who did it? And how?"

He still couldn't bring himself to accuse her, but he could tell her the method. "Poison," he said. "A slow-acting poison. Something no one here could possibly have detected."

"But who would poison a baby?" she asked in disbelief. "And who could get to every child . . ." She broke off, understanding from the look on his face that she was under suspicion.

"You think I did it, don't you? Robert, how could you think it was me?"

"Not you alone, no," he stuttered.

"What! You think we have a gang of criminals here, and that I'm their ringleader! Oh, Robert. Think. You know me. I could not hurt a child!"

"But he could."

"He? Who is 'he'? We are peaceful farming folk. Where is this murderer?"

"Over there, asleep in his bed," said Farcett, nodding towards the priest's house. "Later on he'll eat a breakfast of eggs, bacon, and porridge supplied by the farmers whose babies he killed!"

"Father Michael? I don't believe it. I won't believe it. I've known Father Michael for years. I brought him here. . . ." She realized what she was saying. "And that's why you suspect me, isn't it?"

"One of the reasons. You two are the only ones with the opportunity to do it. You both visit every newborn, you both have time alone with them. I must admit that he has the more obvious motive."

"Which is?"

"Control. Dominance of these people through fear. We've both seen how he does it. You've seen him in church."

"Yes, but I've seen him in private, too, and so have

you," Maggie insisted. "He's a good man. He helped me fight to keep those babies alive."

"That's just it, Maggie. He was always there. And with each death he bound the whole island closer to him and to his church. Think about it, Maggie. What do the people of Tarimond know of this man? Why did he come here?"

"He came because I asked him to!" said Maggie, crying now. "He was my friend!"

Farcett recalled the image of the two of them together on that very cliff. "Your friend, yes. Just a friend?"

"What do you mean by that? Are you suggesting that I am involved with him?" and suddenly kind, peaceful Maggie lashed out at Farcett with a slap that left his cheek stinging.

He was ashamed. "Maggie, I don't know what to think. I don't want to believe that you are a poisoner, but if it wasn't you, it must have been Father Michael. The police on the mainland are checking on him now. I believe they will be here soon to take him away."

"So why have you come back? Why not just leave it to the police?"

"Because of Jimmy. I wanted to make sure that Jimmy was safe."

"And he is. Father Michael can't be poisoning him."

"Exactly. He knows there's an investigation under way. He wouldn't dare. Don't you see? Jimmy's very survival points to Father Michael's guilt."

"I hope you're wrong," said Maggie. Her face was alive with shock. "Oh, Robert, how I hope you are wrong!"

"But it seems the police think I'm right," said Farcett, pointing out to sea.

Across the bay, a large boat was coming towards them. Two uniformed men were rowing and two more holding lanterns to show the way.

"They'll be taking me, too, won't they?" she said. "Robert, I swear that whether Father Michael is guilty or not, I have done nothing to harm anyone."

He looked at her. He believed her.

"Go home, Maggie. I will talk to the police. It is in their hands now, and they know that you can't get away."

"No. I will face them," said Maggie, bravely. "I know I am innocent." And she and Farcett ran down to the shore to guide the boat in.

"I'm Doctor Farcett," he said as the first policeman climbed from the boat. "I take it you have received Doctor Dougall's report."

The officer shook Farcett's hand, and pulled him

over to one side. "We have, sir, and our investigations have revealed some disturbing facts about Father Michael. We have come to take him away."

"And Maggie Goudie?" said Farcett, calling her over. "This is Maggie. She insists the deaths are nothing to do with her. I must tell you, I thought she was involved. But officer, believe me, I am far from sure now."

"We found no evidence concerning the lady, sir," said the policeman, as Farcett shut his eyes and moaned with relief. "We have come for Father Michael, sir. Is he at home?"

Farcett led them to the priest's house. Father Michael was in the kitchen whistling happily as he made a pot of tea. The policemen went in without knocking. Standing outside, Farcett and Maggie heard first a cry of surprised welcome, then words of confusion, then a shout of denial. Other islanders had seen the boat approaching across the water, and had come to see what was going on. It was light now. Eventually Father Michael emerged, unbound, but with policemen on either side. He stopped to speak to the growing crowd. In the wind, his robes were flapping and his uncombed hair flew back away from his face. He looked once more like the terrifying figure Farcett had seen on his first day on the island.

"My friends!" cried the priest. "I beg you, do not believe what is said about me. These men say that I have killed your babies. They are taking me to the mainland, where I will clear my name. Pray for me, please. I am going, but I will be back, I promise."

Most of the islanders had caught only a few of his words. They asked one another what he had said. In moments suspicion grew into fact, and the news spread that Father Michael had killed a generation of Tarimond's children.

A policeman turned to Doctor Farcett. "You'd better come with us, sir. They will be wanting to interview you in Glasgow."

Farcett collected his bag from the priest's house, and pushed his way through the crowd of people who were gathering there, demanding more information. The policeman urged him on. As he walked, Farcett tried to explain, and the islanders passed on snatches of what he said. The word "poison" was all around him.

Down on the beach, he paused to say good-bye to Maggie.

"I forgive you, Robert," shouted Father Michael from inside the police boat. "You are wrong, Robert. You are wrong." The vehemence of the priest's protestations of innocence cut into Farcett's heart.

"What have I done?" he said, as he embraced Maggie for the last time.

"If you are right, Robert, you have done the right thing," said Maggie, her face red with tears. "We wanted to find out why our babies died, and you have. You are taking away the cause. You are saving lives. God knows I blame myself for this. I brought Father Michael here. I begged him to come. May God forgive me!"

"No, Maggie," said Farcett, kissing her forehead. "You have nothing to reproach yourself for. You are not to blame. Forgive me for the harsh things I said to you. I will write to you, Maggie. Please, write to me, too."

Word was spreading across the island about what was happening. People were running from all directions towards the beach. They grabbed at Farcett's coat as the policemen pulled him on board their boat. Before it had cast off, the bewilderment of the crowd had turned to a seething rage. A rock was thrown and grazed Father Michael's head. He dropped to his knees in frantic prayer. The policemen quickened the pace of their rowing to get clear of the mob, but before they reached the next island they could see flames licking across the roof of the priest's house. The bereaved islanders of Tarimond had started to take their revenge.

CHAPTER 45

FAREWELL, CONTESSA

Montmorency and Fox-Selwyn were busy throughout Farcett's absence, not just with developments in the O'Connell case, but also coping with Vi and her mother. Vi had adapted perfectly to life at the Marimion, playing the part of daughter and maid brilliantly, and winning the hearts of the hotel staff without speaking a single word of English. The servants couldn't understand what she saw in Scarper, who seemed to take her out most days, but they made a handsome couple. Violetta and Montmorency did, too. With the Bag Man out of the way, there was no real need to keep Vi and her mother at the hotel, but the men didn't have the heart to return them to the damp of Covent Garden, particularly as Mrs. Evans was far from well.

Her health had been poor to start with, and had only gotten worse with the rich diet at the Marimion. There was one advantage to her decline: Her raving became whimpering, and then silence as she slept away her days. It was just as well. The doctor wasn't there to give her any medicine. When he returned after ten days of traveling, Farcett confirmed that there was no hope, and she slipped away painlessly in the night within a week. As she had died at the Marimion, it seemed appropriate that she should be buried in style. Fox-Selwyn paid for a carriage with plumed horses, and the small party of mourners (Violetta, Montmorency, Fox-Selwyn, and Farcett) attended a brief but dignified service at St. James's Piccadilly, followed by a burial in one of London's more fashionable cemeteries. Vi moved in with Fox-Selwyn until she could settle her future, and Montmorency returned to his little room at Bargles.

It was there, the night after the funeral, that the conversation in Eats Major turned to Father Michael's forthcoming trial. Doctor Farcett was being kept up to date with developments by the Glasgow police, and passed on the details to his friends.

"Has the old villain told them what the poison is yet?" asked Montmorency.

"No," said Farcett. "He's still insisting on his innocence. For a man who's listened to thousands of confessions, he seems to be remarkably reluctant about making one!"

"Unless he didn't do it, of course," said Fox-Selwyn, casually. "The evidence in your case seems almost as thin as it was in ours! Don't forget, if we hadn't got that confession from O'Connell, they'd have had to let him go."

"It would be appalling if Father Michael got away with it," said Farcett.

"And it would be appalling if there turned out to be another explanation," said Montmorency.

"Look," argued Farcett. "You know Maggie Goudie, can you honestly bring yourself to believe she did it?"

"Not at all," said Montmorency. "And you know I always thought there was something creepy about that priest. Even if he did rescue us from Morag's parents' bed!"

Fox-Selwyn waved to the waiter. "Sam, more gravy over here!" he shouted, and the conversation turned to the slapstick scene of that first night on Tarimond. After dinner, Doctor Farcett and Montmorency ended up acting out the whole thing on the tiny bench in "Plotters," with Fox-Selwyn watching from the doorway. At midnight they went away to their separate beds aching with laughter.

CHAPTER 46

WHY JIMMY?

That night, Farcett woke with a start at three o'clock. He had not been sleeping well recently. He had never settled down after the drama on Tarimond. There had been nightmares, and recurrent images of Father Michael's tortured face as the policemen took him away. Now Montmorency's question over dinner came back into his mind. What if there was another explanation for the deaths? Fox-Selwyn was right. Strictly speaking, there was very little concrete evidence against the priest. True, since his arrest several islanders had come forward with stories of strange behavior on his part. Some recalled odd looks and sinister words. Others said he had taken too close an interest in Maggie and her school. But it was odd that none of this had been reported or even gossiped about before. The Glasgow police had heard stories, too. They were serious enough to send them after him on Tarimond. But what did they really amount to? Some of Father Michael's old parishioners hadn't liked him. It was rumored that he drank. Some nurses complained that he was always hanging around the hospital, and especially 'the maternity wing, cuddling the babies and chatting with the staff. Had he been collecting poisons when their backs were turned? Or was he simply an eccentric clergyman trying his best to do his job?

Farcett did what he always did when he was troubled by thoughts of Tarimond. He reached into the drawer of his bedside table and took out his bar of Maggie's precious soap. Just the scent of it transported him back there, and brought comforting memories of her calm efficiency and of the happy days when the two of them had done so much to improve the islanders' lives. But for all his occasional sentimentality, Farcett had a scientific mind, and the story of the Tarimond poison worried that part of his brain that fed on cold, hard facts. It was a faculty that had been clouded by his jealous rage against Father Michael, and now it was clamoring to be allowed to ask questions he had suppressed before. What if the poisoning had a natural cause? Surely the key would lie in a study of little Jimmy's case. Was there anything different about him that might explain his survival in an environment where every other child had died? Was the only reason for his health the murderer's fear of being caught while Farcett and Montmorency were on the island? Or could it be that some natural agent, which had poisoned every other child, was missing when Jimmy was born?

Farcett traced Jimmy's progress, going right back to those first moments when Maggie had lifted him out into the world. He strained to re-create the exact sequence of events, squeezing Maggie Goudie's soap as he struggled to picture the scene of Jimmy's birth in the tiny cottage.

Maggie had taken the baby through to his father. Farcett remembered that. After that, she had never left poor Jeannie's side. Not until after she'd died. Even then she had stayed to clean Jeannie up and to lay her out, washing her, perfuming her with that special soap. . . .

The soap! Could that be it? But it was made from local oils, herbs, and flowers. How could it be anything other than innocent? All the mothers used it, and none of them grew sick.

But hadn't Donald Dougall said that tiny babies could succumb to toxins to which older people didn't react at all? Maggie Goudie gave the soap to all her mothers. She washed the newborn babies with it. Oh, how he had praised her for all the hygiene! But Jimmy

MacLean had not been washed in Maggie's soap. Jimmy MacLean had been washed by Doctor Farcett with kitchen soap, in the kitchen sink. The other Tarimond babies had been fed by their mothers, suckled on breasts cleansed with Maggie's special soap. Jimmy MacLean had drunk goat's milk from a jug sterilized with boiling water. He had been cuddled to sleep by his father, so crazed by grief and wracked with work that he hardly washed at all. And he had been cosseted by Doctor Farcett himself, who washed constantly, but with the harsh carbolic that gave him an aroma as distinctive in its way as Maggie's herbs, oil, and flowers. That was how Jimmy was different. That was why Jimmy had survived. He had not been exposed to Maggie Goudie's soap.

Farcett stared down at the soap, its pale oily base dotted with fragments of leaves and petals. What if it harbored some microbe or chemical that was too much for the babies' tiny bodies to stand? He wrapped the bar in a clean handkerchief and slipped it into the pocket of his jacket, which was hanging over the back of a chair.

Throughout his investigation into the Tarimond deaths, Farcett had imagined the moment when the mystery would be solved. He had even let his old, ambitious self take over from time to time, projecting images of public adulation at his great scientific feat. In his mind's eye he could see awards, applause, and the renewed respect of his colleagues in recognition of a great achievement in the field of public health. Even when he suppressed the idea of fame and professional glory, he saw himself quietly, personally satisfied by a job well done. Surely the saving of future lives on Tarimond could only bring him joy? And yet, here, alone in his bedroom, he felt a visceral sadness. He knew he would have to have the soap tested, and that any poisonous agent in it might be dead, or too tiny to detect. But somewhere in his heart, he also knew that his theory was right, and that his dear friend Maggie Goudie had unwittingly been responsible for untold grief.

He looked at the clock. It was half past four. He would have to wait nearly five hours before he could take the soap to the laboratory for analysis. Doctor Dougall was expecting to be a prime witness for the prosecution in Father Michael's trial. Now, if Farcett's theory proved correct, he might become the mainstay of the defense.

As Doctor Farcett finally fell asleep that night, far away on Tarimond Morag's mother was tossing and turning in her bed. The baby was kicking inside her and she couldn't get comfortable. Her husband had long ago left their little closet to sleep on a mattress on the floor. She ran her hands over her huge stomach. It wouldn't be long now.

CHAPTER 47

≫

THE LAST RACE NORTH

Donald Dougall was exasperated by Farcett's insistence on analyzing the soap, but he accepted that it had to be done. He had told his colleagues that it would be exciting to have Farcett working at Great Ormond Street. He had used the word in the professional sense, talking up the surgical skills of a gifted doctor. He hadn't expected policemen, murder inquiries, and sudden disappearances north of the border. Now Farcett wanted to go away again. He knew that Morag's mother would be in labor soon, and he had to stop Maggie Goudie from using the soap, just in case. He wouldn't wait for the results of the analysis. He wanted to set off straightaway. After seeing Dougall, Farcett visited Lord George Fox-Selwyn to tell him his plans.

"Do you think you could possibly take Vi with you, too?" said Fox-Selwyn. "Chivers doesn't complain, but I think she's driving him crackers."

"She could be useful," admitted Farcett. "She could wait on the mainland for Dougall to send his results.

Then she could bring them over. Come to think of it, Montmorency might want to go back again, too. I'd better ask him."

"Oh, dash it. Why don't we all go?" said Fox-Selwyn. "I want to see this Tarimond place of yours, and there'll be no fun here with you all away. I wonder if Cook could rustle up some toffee for the journey."

Cook did them proud. There were cold meats, salad, a huge pork pie, fruit, little cakes, and of course a slab of toffee. Vi was overwhelmed by the size and beauty of the frosty countryside as it flew past the train windows. Montmorency was glad to be overpainting the horrible memories of his previous trip to Scotland. At the last minute, Fox-Selwyn lost his nerve about crossing to the spartan accommodations on Tarimond, and offered to be the one who stayed behind in Glasgow, waiting for Dougall's letter. In between fine dinners, and trips to galleries and shows, he visited Father Michael in prison and told him what was happening. Unlike Montmorency, he found the old priest's combination of earthly frailty and deep spirituality engaging. Even before Doctor Dougall's report arrived, he sensed that Father Michael was probably innocent. The priest gave daily thanks to God for his new friend.

Farcett, Montmorency, and Vi found a boatman to

take them all the way to Tarimond. They could see the skeletal remains of Father Michael's house long before they reached land, and Farcett knew that the first thing he must do when they arrived was find Maggie Goudie, apologize to her for what he had done and said, and explain the new theory: even though it was potentially devastating for her. Montmorency took Vi to Morag's house, where the family was full of hope. Morag's mother was due to give birth at any time. She believed that Father Michael's arrest gave this baby a chance at life, and so the visitors didn't tell her the latest news. Montmorency helped in the barn, while Morag got to know Vi over the washing.

At first, Vi seemed a fearsomely glamorous figure to Morag, but her easy manner and probing questions soon loosened the islander's tongue.

"They're a funny bunch, these men, aren't they?" said Vi. "Always dashing about solving other people's problems."

"Aye, but they've had a few problems of their own, you know. Mr. Montmorency was not too well when I first met him."

"Really?" said Vi, adding with a saucy wink, "What was wrong with him, then? He's always seemed pretty healthy to me!"

Morag realized she might have let out a secret, and changed the subject. "Oh, nothing that Doctor Farcett couldn't deal with. Did you know him in London, too?"

"He came and went at our hotel. Looked after my mum something lovely — till she died, of course, but that weren't his fault. I never thought his heart was in London, though. Always thought it was up here, if you know what I mean."

"You mean Maggie Goudie, don't you? We all thought he was a bit sweet on her. I wondered if he'd stay and marry her. She'd be a fine catch. Plenty have tried. She broke my uncle Harvey's heart years ago. They were walking out together for a good while, and he wanted to take her with him when he got his job at Glendarvie, but she wouldn't go. That evil priest persuaded her to stay. Said she was needed here to care for the people. Harvey never forgave him, even though it was probably for the best. She can't have loved him if she wouldn't follow him. Harvey told me such stories about Father Michael. Maggie had talked about him when they were courting. She told him all sorts of things that he did in Glasgow. Harvey said he once helped a sick old lady to die. That's a sin, you know. He'll go to hell for it. And now we know he was killing the babies. He was so fearsome. We all knew there was something wrong with him, but he had us all scared."

Vi had been warned not to talk about Father Michael. So she picked up the reference to Glendarvie.

"You worked at Glendarvie, didn't you? I've heard Lord Fox-Selwyn talk about you."

"Yes, I worked for his brother and his wife. Just for a wee while. It's a very grand place. I lived well there. But I'll tell you something. I'd rather be free here than in service there. You rich people may have hot water pipes and coffeepots, but we have the sky and freedom, and I'd rather work hard here for myself than run around after some fancy lady!"

"Rich!" said Vi. "Oh, Morag, if only you knew. Where I live there's poverty and dirt like you've never seen." And Vi described her old Covent Garden home. "I'm telling you, Morag. What you've got here is luxury."

Morag's mother staggered to the door of the cottage, holding her belly.

"Run and get Maggie Goudie, Morag," she called. "I think my time has come."

Vi took her inside and waited for Maggie and the doctor. They arrived just in time to see a little girl safely into the world. Morag's mother called her Violet, after the kind and funny woman who held her hand during the worst of the labor, and made her such a lovely cup of tea after the birth. Violet and her mother smelled of carbolic, not herbs and roses, but the baby showed every sign of surviving to become a playmate for little Jimmy.

CHAPTER 48

»

THE RESULTS

Two days later, Montmorency was chopping wood on the clifftop when he spotted a rowboat on its way to the beach. A fat man was lounging on the seat at the back, weighing down the stern so far that the oarsman had to struggle to keep contact with the water. Montmorency recognized his old friend at once, and called out to Vi, who was collecting the biggest splinters to use as kindling on the fire.

"It's Lord George Fox-Selwyn," he shouted. "Arriving in his usual style!" He waved a greeting.

Fox-Selwyn saw the familiar shape, and waved back, attempting to stand in the boat and rocking it dangerously from side to side. It seemed inevitable that the craft would turn over or fill with the lapping water and sink, but no. It recovered from each lurch, as the huge man struggled to get upright and the boatman pulled at his coat, imploring him to sit down and keep still. Eventually he did, and the boat wobbled one last time, depositing Fox-Selwyn into the waves just as it reached the shore. Montmorency ran down to rescue his friend, whose first steps on Tarimond were to be so like his own: wet and dripping. Like Montmorency, he was to spend the night of his arrival watching his fine clothes drying over Morag's mother's fire.

"Get the papers from my pocket," Fox-Selwyn cried from beneath a mountain of rough blankets. "Dougall's sent the test results."

Montmorency pulled out the sodden clump, and started peeling the pages apart. The ink had run. They were almost illegible. Just a few words could be seen. They included "bacteria," "toxins," "microbes," and "animal."

"It's a good thing I read it all before I came," said Fox-Selwyn. "It seems Robert was right. The soap was full of bugs. Living in the oil, apparently. None strong enough to affect an adult, but too much for a tiny baby. Once they were infected they just couldn't fight it. They probably tried. That's why they survived as long as they did. But the poor souls were doomed right from the start."

Doctor Farcett arrived and took his turn at deciphering the report. "Animal toxins!" he said. "How could they get there? The soap is made from vegetable oil and plants."

"But have you seen where Maggie keeps the ingredients?" said Montmorency, thinking back to the line of little balloons hanging from a pole across her kitchen ceiling. "The oil is stored in pouches made from the stomachs of seabirds. The soap is in sheep's stomachs to stop it from drying out. Perhaps that's the answer."

"Well, whatever it is," said Fox-Selwyn, flapping his damp undershirt in front of the fire, "congratulations, Robert. You were right."

But Farcett wasn't smiling. "Right? Right in the end perhaps, but look at the damage I did on the way. Think of Father Michael. Did you see his house, George? That burnt-out shell up on the cliff."

"Yes, I did," said Fox-Selwyn.

"Well, that's my fault. I jumped to conclusions and had him hounded from his home and dragged off to prison. How can you say I was right?"

Fox-Selwyn looked serious. "Robert, you were no more in the wrong than Montmorency and I were when we decided the Bag Man had bombed Waterloo. We had no real evidence beyond a few unconnected facts and our own instincts. But we pursued him because we thought it was the right thing to do. And we got him to confess."

Montmorency thought of O'Connell, starting his long sentence in a London prison, unaware of how he had been tricked into admitting his guilt. The man thought he was lucky not to hang. He didn't know how unlucky he was to be in prison at all. He may have committed the crime, but his confession had been tricked out of him.

"We were fortunate, that's all," said Montmorency. "It turned out that we were right, and now the Home Secretary thinks we're marvelous. You did your best, too. You were mistaken, but had you been correct you might have saved a great many lives."

Farcett was unimpressed. "Instead I've ruined a good man," he muttered.

Fox-Selwyn was alarmed at the drop in the mood of his friends. "Come on," he said. "Think of the good news. No more babies will die." He squeezed Farcett's shoulder. "And Father Michael will survive. The police have let him go. He wanted to come here with me, but I persuaded him to wait until the islanders knew the truth. After all that has happened, it might even be best for him to look for another parish, and for Tarimond to have a different priest. But he has forgiven you, Farcett. He knows you meant well."

Doctor Farcett was still in the depths of despair.

"And now we have to tell Maggie what the report says," he mumbled.

"No you don't," said a familiar voice. Maggie Goudie was standing in the doorway. She had just arrived, but had heard enough to know that Doctor Dougall had confirmed Farcett's suspicions, and she had been the unwitting cause of all the deaths. "Can I see the report?"

Montmorency handed her the soggy paperwork. She took her turn trying to make out what it said.

"Toxins of animal origin," she read aloud. "How can that be? My soap is made from plant oil, leaves, and petals."

Montmorency interrupted her. "Which you store in the stomachs of birds and animals."

Maggie sank to her knees as she realized how the toxin had bred and thrived in her own kitchen. "God forgive me!" she cried.

"He will, dear." The soft voice of Morag's mother calmed her. "Maggie, I have lost five children, but I know you didn't mean them to die."

The men were humbled by the quiet dignity of what she said.

"Let's hope the rest of the islanders take the same view," whispered Montmorency to Fox-Selwyn. He didn't want to frighten Maggie, but he feared another outbreak of mass rage and violence, like the scene when the police had come for Father Michael.

"I must tell the people what has happened," said Doctor Farcett, who had been sitting, staring into the fire. "Montmorency. Ring the church bell, and get everyone together."

And they made their way to the headland, leaving Maggie behind them, in Fox-Selwyn's care.

CHAPTER 49

≫

THE MEETING

The church was dark and dirty. It had been neglected since Father Michael's departure. Strange words and symbols had been chalked on one wall, illegible, but somehow conveying contempt and pain. Doctor Farcett lit some candles and stood before the altar as the bemused islanders came to see why the bell was ringing. He scanned the familiar faces, and when it seemed to him that everyone was there he raised his hand to quiet them, and bravely spoke.

"My friends. I have come here to ask for your forgiveness. I have made a terrible mistake, which has cost this community dear. Because of me you lost your priest. And I can see, just by looking at the state of this building, that some of you have lost your faith. I have come to tell you that I was wrong. It has been proved beyond doubt that Father Michael was in no way to blame for the deaths of your children."

There was a silence as the islanders took in the news, then the inevitable question from someone at the back. "So who did it?" Another voice asked, "Was it Maggie Goudie?" Somehow word had gotten around that she was under suspicion. "Did the witch poison the babies?"

The mood began to turn sour as faces looked around, seeking Maggie. A hubbub of allegations passed through the gathering. Farcett recognized the growing surge of hate. He feared he might lose control of the meeting and raised his hand again. "No! Stop!" he shouted. Montmorency pulled once more on the bell rope to shock the crowd into silence, and Farcett continued, "Remember what happened last time you lashed out with blame! Maggie Goudie is a good woman. I have seen the way she cares for you, and it matches anything I have seen anywhere. She could never have known what was killing the children. Let me explain."

Farcett carefully set out the facts about the septic agents that had done so much harm. He reminded everyone how Maggie's practice of storing things in animal skin was nothing unusual on Tarimond. He held up a sac of one of Maggie's soothing oils, and rubbed it into his own skin. "See," he said, "for a grown man, or even a crawling child, this oil is harmless." He sniffed it. "It's even rather beneficial. You've all used it to treat your aches and pains. And haven't you felt better for it?" There were a few nods of assent. "Your bodies have no trouble fighting off the tiny germs that come not from the oil, but from the place where it is stored. Are you going to attack the woman who made it simply because she didn't know? Did any of you know? I didn't, and I have years of expensive medical training. I ask you to forgive Maggie Goudie her mistake, just as I ask you to forgive mine!"

And as the people thought back to the morning they lost Father Michael, their shame overcame their rage and they listened on as Farcett answered questions about how tiny unseen organisms had beaten their babies in their fight for life. John MacLean came to his aid. He carried baby Jimmy forward.

"This is my son. He lives. Maggie Goudie cared for him, and he has survived."

Morag's mother held up little Violet. "I trust Maggie with my new baby, too. Even though five before her are dead. She didn't mean to kill them."

Montmorency added his voice. "I am an outsider, but I have seen Maggie Goudie at work. She has brought you health and education. Comfort her now, as she shares your grief."

Farcett pointed out individuals in the crowd. "Hamish. Remember how Maggie bound your broken arm?" The farmer held it out to show that it was strong again. "Janet, when your mother had that fever, who bathed her forehead?"

"It was Maggie."

"And did she give her treatments to bring the temperature down?"

"Aye, she did, and they worked. Didn't they, Mam?" An old lady by her side nodded assent.

Soon people were offering unsolicited praise for Maggie. "She taught me to read," said a young man.

"And me to write," added another.

Even Vi joined in. "I'm from London," she said. "I've seen real murderers and vicious villains. That woman Maggie is no killer. She's a heroine. You should be proud of her!"

Farcett spoke again. "Maggie saw what happened to Father Michael. She is frightened. Let's go to her now and show her she has nothing to fear!"

There was a murmur of assent, and the islanders filed out and off to the cottage where Maggie was waiting, nervously, with Fox-Selwyn. He saw them coming, and placed himself between her and the door, fearing a lynch mob, offering Maggie a broom in case she needed to fight off attackers. But the crowd stopped and silently drew into a circle outside the house, where they broke into spontaneous applause. Fox-Selwyn went out to meet them, leading Maggie, who was weeping tears of gratitude and regret. After hugs, kisses, and handshakes, the islanders eventually left, and the Londoners settled, exhausted, with bowls of soup in Morag's mother's kitchen. They all slept on the floor that night. Even Morag's parents wouldn't have tried to squeeze the mighty form of Lord George Fox-Selwyn into their little closet-bed.

CHAPTER 50

A FUTURE FOR TARIMOND

The visitors stayed for a week, boarded by families all over Tarimond. To everyone's surprise, Lord George Fox-Selwyn adored the island. He loved the rugged majesty of the scenery, though he fancied viewing it from something more comfortable than Morag's mother's cottage. On the last day he organized a party on the beach, to say thank you to everyone who had given him and his friends hospitality. Montmorency built a bonfire, and organized the roasting of a pig. Vi baked cakes under Morag's supervision. It was the first joyous occasion on Tarimond for a very long time.

Silhouetted against a breathtaking sunset, Fox-Selwyn clapped his hands above his head to silence the music and the dancing. "My friends," he shouted. "I have an announcement to make. As you know, we are leaving tomorrow. But we will be back."

There was a mixture of cheers and good-natured groans. "In fact, *I* may be back rather often. When I get to the mainland I intend to hire an architect to design me a simple summer home here."

"I'll do it for you cheaper!" came a voice from the back.

"Thank you, sir," said Fox-Selwyn, "but this may be quite a big job. You see, while he's at it, I'm going to ask him to throw in an infirmary, a school, and a new house for a priest. I think you all deserve a little something in return for being invaded by us Londoners! Now drink up. Come on, ladies, this is your last chance for a dance with Montmorency!"

There were cheers and laughs as the fun started up again. Hard against the cliff, three stony-faced old women, sitting on a hairy blanket, were already complaining sourly about the building works. Out at the water's edge, Maggie Goudie, Farcett, Fox-Selwyn, and Montmorency were discussing designs and sites. A slightly tipsy Vi sidled up to them.

"Excuse me, George," she said to Fox-Selwyn. "I mean, excuse me, my lord, but might you be wanting a housekeeper for this house of yours?"

"Well, I hadn't really thought it through, Vi," said Fox-Selwyn. "But now that you mention it, I suppose I will."

"Well, I would like to apply for the position," she said, with mock formality, adding, "I could keep it warm for you when you're not there."

"What a nice thought, Vi," said Fox-Selwyn. "We can talk about it when we're back in London."

Vi's face fell. "Well, you see, George . . . I mean, 'sir' . . . I wasn't actually thinking of going back to London."

Montmorency butted in. "Are you suggesting, Vi," he teased sarcastically, "that life on Tarimond is preferable to life in your little house in Covent Garden?"

"Anywhere's better than that, Montmorency," said Fox-Selwyn. "You got out of it fast enough!"

"But where will you stay until the house is built?" asked Doctor Farcett. "It's bound to take a while, and you might get bored waiting."

"Oh, I'll have plenty to do," said Vi. "And I was wondering if Maggie here would take me in. I could give her a hand in return."

Maggie looked startled, but before she could speak, Vi explained her real reason for staying.

"You see, I think I'll be needing a little help from Maggie in a few months' time."

It took a while for the full meaning of her words to sink in. First Montmorency, then Doctor Farcett, and then Lord George Fox-Selwyn realized what she meant.

There was to be another baby on Tarimond. The new generation had begun.

DATE DUE

WITHDRAWN

0001195722

FIC
UPDALE

Updale, Eleanor.

Montmorency on the rocks : doctor, aristocrat, murderer?

456757 01440 65383A 007